COUNTING DOWN

A NOVEL

LILAH BOONE

COUNTING DOWN

MONA & BLACKBIRD BOOKS

Cover design and artwork by Lisa Barbero.
www.lisabarbero.com

ISBN 061567304X
ISBN-13 978-0615673042

10 9 8 7 6 5 4 3 2 1

To B, who gave me the courage to believe.

PROLOGUE

Whitestone Village, Bronze Age Europe, 1587 BCE

Something was coming and Callum knew it wouldn't be much longer before whatever it was arrived. It was his job to know what lay ahead, to prophesize and foretell the future of his people.

From an early age the natural world showed him patterns that other eyes overlooked. He saw the future in the stars, in the movement of the moon, and the rhythm of the sun. For this reason the priests of the tribe had taken him into their service as a young boy. For many years they trained him to harness his gifts and by the time manhood was upon him, Callum of Whitestone was the Keeper of Time.

Still, nature remained at times aloof, keeping her secrets just out of sight. Callum spent his time studying the patterns, interpreting the starlight, and deciphering the old paintings in the caves and barrows. Yet still he wasn't sure exactly what change was coming or how to prepare for it.

He stood, staring into the night and opening up his mind to the visions that often came. But nothing spoke to him. Even the trees, with their subtle wisdom, were not whispering to him tonight. With a frustrated sigh he tightened the cloak around his shoulders and began the short walk home. His family would be waiting for him, refusing to sleep until he returned. The children would want stories and his wife would want his arms around her in the night.

Callum's thoughts were on his wife as his feet stepped across the sod covered ground, picturing her face alight with a smile as he entered their home. She would have a hot cup of tea in her hand, made from the herbs that grew around their home. She would welcome him with a kiss, and his worries would wash away like sand from the shore.

He had known Aislynn since they were infants. They were born on the same day in the same village. Together they had run in the fields of wildflowers, up over the hills until they reached the stone laden coast where the ocean broke and misted upon the land.

Before Callum was fifteen years old the priests had discovered him. On one early autumn day they had taken him onto the small island sanctuary to pursue the years of study required to join their ranks. There were rituals to memorize, mysteries to contemplate, and gods to honor. Callum had not wanted to leave. Not because he would miss his mother and his brothers, but because he would miss the little girl who was his best friend.

Three years passed before Callum was brought back to the village to attend his first midsummer rights as an adult. He remembered the anticipation of seeing her again, of knowing she would be among the women who stood around the fires searching to take a mate under the summer moon.

He had feared she would not recognize him, that she would choose someone else in the village who had caught her eye while he was away. It had been near torture for him to consider such an idea. Even as a child he had known she was the one he wanted to be with forever.

On that warm summer night he took his place with the priests, lighting the sacred fires and reciting the words he had worked to commit to memory for years. As he stood in the center of the circle, he could feel her presence, knew she was watching him.

The celebrations began as the full moon rose over the fields. Song permeated the night and the sound of drumming echoed the ancient rhythm of the Earth and her people. Callum's heart matched that rhythm, his eyes scanning the ring of people around the blazing fire. Faces lit up with the warm glow of embers and the passion of the season.

He examined each woman, watched her move in time to the drummers. Would he know her face? he thought. Would she have the same light in her eyes he remembered from their days as children; the light that had followed him to the Priests Cove and haunted his every breath.

Several couples headed off into the night to lie in the tall grasses along the edge of the ritual field. Where was she? Had she forgotten about him? Had she fallen in love with someone else? Suddenly a presence was behind him, a hand reaching forward to take his. With a polite rejection waiting on his tongue, he began to turn. And then the fingers laced through his, locking together like they were made from the same flesh.

Aislynn stood before him, taking the breath from his lungs, the words from his lips. She said nothing and when he finally opened his mouth to speak she surprised him with a kiss.

Back in the present, Callum stepped into the warmth of his home. Ten years had passed since that kiss and still he anticipated each one that followed with eagerness.

She met him at the door, his infant son on her hip, waiting as he removed his cloak before handing him his cup. Her kiss was sweet, comfortable, yet held a tone of the night ahead.

His twin daughters came running, latching onto his legs like two very large burdock seeds. He laughed, bent down to them. "Shouldn't you two be sleeping?"

They giggled in unison, Esree answering him with his own smile shining on her face. "Papa you know we cannot sleep without one of your stories."

He scooped them up, one in each arm. They were getting far too big to carry, but Callum wasn't ready for them to grow up. He would carry them as long as he was able. "What story would you like tonight then?"

Together they answered him. "The one about the swans, Papa. Tell us the long necked swan story."

He smiled, set them down on the bed they shared. "The Tale of the Swan again?" His face held feigned shock which quickly turned to a chuckle. "Alright then. Settle in my little blossoms."

He began the story, glancing beside him at Aislynn swaying the baby to sleep in her arms. She touched his shoulder, smoothed his hair and ran a tickling thumb over the back of his neck.

With the children asleep and in their beds, Callum stoked the fire and sipped from the cup in his hands.

"Your brothers are going hunting tomorrow," Aislynn said. "Were you planning on going with them?"

He kept his eyes on the dancing fire. "I had considered it, but there is more work to do. I was planning on going to the caves again."

"The prophecies are not going anywhere, Love. They are already ancient and will only be a little more so if you wait one day." She touched his shoulder. "You should go, enjoy yourself. I know how you miss them."

His hand met hers, caressed her knuckles. "Perhaps you're right. We could use meat this winter."

He pressed her palms to his lips, caught the scent of the bread she had been baking all day. He smiled to himself and turned back to the fire. "You've been baking."

"Hmm. We needed bread."

He chuckled to himself at the annoyed tone in her voice. She hated to bake. In fact, she hated cooking all together. His wife would rather be smelting metal by the fire, working and shaping cast strips into jewelry.

Callum had made her wooden molds and bartered with the metal smiths in the village to make sure she had the right tools. Once a month they made a trip to the next village to trade her work for woven cloth, skins, pottery, and other necessities.

He looked down to admire the works in progress she kept on the stones in front of the hearth. "I like this one," he said raising a bracelet set with sea worn stones into the light.

He didn't have to look at her to know she was smiling. "I thought you would," she said. "It was made for you."

She took his wrist, fashioned the cool metal cuff around his forearm and laced the leather straps that would hold it in place. Her eyes appraised the piece, scanning over it with scrutiny. "It should be thicker."

Callum squeezed her hand. "It's perfect. You craft lovely things."

She smiled then, cupped his face, and laid a kiss to his cheek. "We should sleep."

"Sleep comes later," he whispered and tenderly brushed his lips against hers.

He felt her mouth curve into a smile against his. "Much later."

CHAPTER ONE

Wednesday, December 12th 2012, 11:22pm

"Come on Abby. You mean the world to me, Baby. I know we can work this out."

Abigail Connelly looked down at the lacy, obnoxiously purple and extremely well padded bra between her fingers. Unceremoniously, she tossed it on to the second hand coffee table that stood between her and her live-in boyfriend, Alex Peterson.

She felt surprisingly calm and maybe even a little numb. A kind of bland indifference settled over her chest. She wasn't going to scream or yell and she certainly was not going to cry.

"No I don't think so." Her face was blank. "We're done. It's never going to work between us."

Alex opened his mouth in what could only have been described as an act of incredulous amazement. "You can't really be serious? Baby, please. This thing between me and..."

"Miss Lilac Miracle Bra?"

"Yeah. Shit. I mean no. Whatever. It didn't mean anything to me, Baby. I swear. It was just a mistake. Honestly, it didn't mean a thing."

"It never does." She crossed her arms over her chest. "You cheated on me Alex. After only one year you couldn't keep it in your damn pants. Did you really think I would just say it was no big deal, give you a second chance, and leap into your waiting arms like nothing happened?"

Alex moved around the table to Abby. His eyes were pleading and, to Abby's surprise, completely sincere.

It was Abby's curse to notice such things like unspoken sincerity. She was ever observant, always watching. Even when she didn't want to see, she took in everything.

"I love you Abby." With somber eyes he reached out one hand to touch her arm. "I want to be with you and only you. Nothing else matters."

Abby took a moment to breathe, pretending to look at the clock on the wall behind her. Suddenly she realized she just didn't care. She didn't feel anything at all. There wasn't a hint of tears, no real anger brewing inside her. Had she known this would happen all along? Been expecting it and preparing for the past year?

She looked at Alex and saw the real pain, heavily tinted by guilt, shining back through his expression.

"I realize you believe that's true," she said in a calm, quiet voice. "But our relationship is over. I'm sorry. It's really just that simple."

Alex's arms fell to his sides, his shoulders heaving a little as he plopped back onto the couch. He leaned his frame forward, grabbed the half empty beer on the table to drain the last of it in one long sip.

His hands ran through his hair, loosening up the stiff gel that coated each strand. "I'm sorry."

Abby almost shrugged but caught herself. She was actually relieved that the Alex Peterson chapter of her life was over. Of course she was hurt. At least she convinced herself she should be. He had cheated, betrayed her in the worst way. And that should be painful. Right?

It wasn't that Abby didn't care for Alex but she knew it wasn't in the way she was supposed to. They had been saying I love you like some people say hello and goodbye. There was no feeling behind the words. She said them because he said them, because she was expected to say them. And it just wasn't enough anymore.

The height of their relationship had come and gone; faded like beauty and youth and all that other clichéd stuff old poets write about. Now they were nothing more than one of Shakespeare's sonnets; nice, somewhat memorable, yet ultimately not a life altering experience.

Alex was always busy at his gallery and Abby was constantly painting or working on commissioned illustrations. They lived in New York and they were both immersed in the rich and complicated art scene of the city. They had little time for each other. Worse, neither of them went out of their way to make time.

Abby would probably never be able to deny that she was attracted to Alex in a completely physical way. For a split second she thought about going to bed with him once more for old time's sake. But Alex was too emotional and guilt ridden and Abby didn't have much emotion for him at all. It wouldn't be fair to lead him on or toy with him that way. Plus, having sex with him would be like saying what he'd done was okay. And it wasn't. If nothing else, she had to hold on to some shred of dignity.

"I know you feel bad about the whole thing. I get that. I really do. But the more I think about it, our problems go beyond you sleeping with whoever has the matching purple panties to go with that bra."

Alex looked up in mild surprise. "They do? Wait I thought we were pretty happy together."

She sucked in her breath and exhaled heavily. "We had lots of um… fun which was admittedly pretty great. But that's about all we had. And I want more than that. No, I need more than that. Sex is great, but it's like only having chocolate fudge on your sundae when you like whipped cream and cherries too. Oh, and strawberry sauce. Lots of strawberry sauce."

Alex seemed to be taking her words in before he spoke, most likely trying to dissect her obscure analogy. "Okay, but we can work on that other stuff. We can spend more time together, go on dates again, and all that romantic crap." He smiled in his usual seductive manner. "We've already got the hots for each other Baby. If all that's missing is flowers and champagne I can do that."

"Oh Alex." She turned sympathetic eyes in his direction. "I don't think contrived ideas of romance are going to fix this." She didn't want this anymore; no longer wanted to pretend their relationship was enough to be fulfilling for either of them. "I think we should just accept that we're not going to work and get on with our individual lives."

"I'm not sure I can do that right now Abbs. I can't just walk away from this, from you and our life together."

"What life together?" Abby's words were calm. "We barely spend time in the same room and when we do it's just for a quick tumble. If you wanted to work on this you should've done something a long time ago. We both should have. Besides, you don't even see me Alex. You're too busy staring at yourself."

His eyebrows rose. "Well it was more than just sex for me and I'm not ready to give up on us."

"After the seriously bad choice you made, it's not really up to you anymore."

Minutes went by with neither of them speaking. Alex was visibly upset. Abby could tell by his set jaw and determined expression that he wasn't going to let their relationship end that easily. He was a stubborn man who hated being told he couldn't have something. Or maybe he really cared. One way or the other she wasn't going to give in to him. She had principles and so help her, she wasn't going to succumb to his charm or his tempting advances. They were done. Over. Period. She would remain diligent...steadfast... or whatever.

"Where will I go?" Alex walked to the fridge, pulled out another beer. "This is where I live. All my stuff is here."

Abby thought for a moment and tucked her short blonde hair behind her ears. Alex had no family in the area or even many real friends. Least of all any that would let him crash on their loveseats and take up time in front of their bathroom mirrors. Alex was notoriously vain and needed more time getting ready in the morning than a bride on her wedding day.

"I really hadn't thought of that," she said. "What about staying at your new girlfriend's place?"

"She's not my girlfriend. I barely even know her."

"Oh, that's just great." Abby clenched her eyes shut and sighed.

He ignored her. "Besides, I think she lives outside the city with her parents."

"I hope she was at least legal. Did you check her ID?"

Again he ignored her, resumed his place on the couch. Looking up, he flashed his best little boy eyes at her. "I can't be homeless Abbs. I mean, I could sleep at the gallery, but where would I shower and stuff? I couldn't make it as a cardboard box guy who smells like cheese and wears stained clothes. I'm not going to sell much art from the walls working the hobo look. And with Christmas just around the corner..."

Damn him, Abby thought. She couldn't turn him out on the streets. Though part of her really, really wanted to. In fact she imagined she'd get some sort of pleasure out of knowing he was camped out on the concrete-like couch of his gallery office with no TV and no beer stocked fridge. She sighed and closed her eyes for a second.

Abby let out a heavy, frustrated breath. "Fine, you can stay here until you find a place. But you sleep on the couch Alexander Peterson. Got it?"

"Yes Ma'am." He looked up with a wide grin. "It's a nice couch. I always liked it. Very cozy, you know." He patted the sofa like it was his favorite pet, kicked his feet up and clicked the remote to turn on the TV.

"Yeah, this won't be awkward at all," Abby mumbled. "Are you still going to sell my work at the gallery?"

"Of course, Baby. You know you're my favorite artist." Abby held back the urge to roll her eyes.

"Great. I appreciate it. Oh, and one more thing."

"Yeah, what is it Gorgeous?"

"No more pet names. No more Baby, Sweetie, Honeyass, or whatever weird combination of bizarre sentiments you feel like using this week. We're not a couple so we don't do terms of endearment. Okay?"

"Yeah, okay." His eyes were wounded as he took another sip of his beer. "I understand."

"Great. I'm going to bed then. See you in the morning Roomie." She emphasized the last word on purpose, hoping to get it through his head that they shared an apartment now and nothing more.

Once in her room the determination Abby had felt in the living room started to fade fast. The bed looked too big and cold to sleep in alone. She hated sleeping by herself with no one to throw an arm over in the middle of the night. And how would she dose off without hearing Alex's rhythmic breathing and subtle nose whistling?

She walked into the connected bathroom to brush her teeth and take her anti-depressants like she did every night. She opened the medicine cabinet, screwed the cap from the orange bottle and took a pill from top. With the little white capsule sitting in her palm she began to wonder. Why wasn't she more upset? She had lived with Alex for over a year, had even thought she might be able to love him at one point. Why wasn't she crying in agony and reaching for the nearest pint of chocolate ice cream?

Had she ever really cared for him the way she was supposed to, the way he wanted her to? No, Abby had let Alex into her life because he could make her feel something, if only for a time. She realized then that since she had started taking the pills five years before, she hadn't felt anything really, no true emotion. Her life had become little more than one big apathetic blur.

The only upside had been her work. She was able to paint without being governed by her moods or emotions. And surprisingly people liked to buy art that was dead and unfeeling. In the last three years alone she had sold enough to make a nice life for herself and for the most part she had been happy. At least, that's what she thought it could be called.

Life should have meaning, she thought. She wanted to know what it was like to feel again, to really experience the gamut of human emotion. There was more to life than a career and decent sex. She wanted to laugh sincerely and cry at the end of sappy movies. She wanted to know what it was like to love someone and really love them; love them so hard that you couldn't imagine life without them.

With a mix of determination and uncertainty, Abby walked to the toilet and dumped every last pill into the water. As the little capsules swirled around the porcelain and finally disappeared, she let out a sigh. Her therapist was going to be pissed.

CHAPTER TWO

Thursday, December 13th 2012, 7:52am

Abby did a lot of dreaming and usually knew how to recognize a dream from reality. But she rarely had nightmares or dreams of a real serious nature. Typically her nocturnal adventures were made of talking kittens and sexy movie actors. Which was why she was so surprised to find herself in the whirlwind of chaos that filled her sleeping mind.

People ran all around her, circling like frenzied, panic stricken sharks. Towers of fire sprung up from the ground like geysers out of the pits of hell. The earth shook beneath her feet. Piercing screams invaded her mind. She pressed her hands to her ears to block out the horrifying sound.

As she looked up on top of a high, grass covered hill she saw a fair skinned man dressed from the waist down in leather breeches. Pieces of metal jewelry wrapped around his neck and wrists. Tattoos stood out on the pale skin of his upper arms, moved over his shoulders and spiraled onto his neck. With a wooden staff in one hand, he raised his arms above his head, and looked straight into her. His eyes glowed like liquid jade as he opened his mouth to speak. Over the sound of the entropy around her, Abby heard his melodic voice ring out clearly as though he were standing right beside her.

"The Destroyer comes. The end is near. We must prepare for the arrival of the Ancient One. The Destroyer of Worlds approaches! Prepare yourselves!"

His tone turned into a chant as if he were reciting a song he knew all too well. His arms rose up higher towards the turbulent sky. Light glinted off the stones that hung from his staff and clouds swirled angrily above him.

"When blood drops upon the Earth, the Destroyer will appear, and mountains will open up and belch forth fire and ashes. Trees will be destroyed and all living things engulfed. Land will be swallowed up by the waters, and seas will boil."

Behind the man a storm raged, but it was a storm like no other Abby had ever seen. The sky was red and glowing as if the sun itself had begun to surround the planet. The heat was overwhelming and Abby suddenly realized that the people who were once running around her in terror had begun to collapse at her feet. She was gripped with the sudden urge to save them all but didn't know how. She had no idea what was killing them or how to stop it. A sense of hopelessness overcame her making her knees feel soft under her weight.

She ran, stumbling over fallen stones, to the children and cradled their limp bodies. Blood stained their angelic faces and Abby let out a grief stricken wail. Tears sprung to her eyes before she could stop them while a petrified scream escaped her lips. Then all at once the world went black.

* * *

When Abby awoke the night had gone. Rays of sun streamed in through the window and right into her olive eyes. It took only a second for her to realize she was not alone in her bed. It took another second for her to remember that was no longer the norm.

Alex's familiar arms wrapped around her waist and she could feel his early morning arousal pressing against the curve of her backside. She quickly pushed his heavy arms off of her and slid to the edge of the bed. She turned fiery eyes on his sleeping face before smacking his cheek just hard enough to sting. Alex's eyes flew open immediately.

"Jesus Abby. What's gotten into you?" He covered his face with his hand, his jaw hanging in shock.

"Are you serious? Really? Are you just tuning in to this broadcast? Yesterday I find out that you slept with another woman, which by the way is a pretty huge deal. So we split up. Was I the only one who was clear on that? We broke up Alex! Over. Done. Finished." She paused for effect and continued. "Then I very kindly agree to let you stay on the couch, my couch, so you don't have to be turned out on your ass. And yet this morning I somehow manage to wake up being greeted by your... little friend."

Alex flashed those eyes at her again. "Come on Baby. The couch was stiff and lumpy. The TV was supposed to keep me company but the cable went out. So I got lonely and I missed you."

Alex smiled all too sexily and inched a little closer. Abby knew very well that he was completely naked under her green gingham, low thread count sheets. She leapt out of bed with the agility of a gymnast before he could get too close.

"Oh no you don't. Come on Alex. I thought we had a deal. If you can't stick to it you should pack up your things and move into the gallery. I don't care if there's no shower and no TV. I don't care if the whole place starts to stink from you and the buyers start running away. I can sell my work somewhere else. I sleep in the bed alone." She took a second to catch her breath. "And stop calling me Baby."

Abby saw the look on Alex's face and suddenly realized she was standing in front of him in nothing but a pair of red thong panties.

She instinctively brought her hands up to cover her breasts.

"Hot." He mouthed the word with a mischievous look in his eye before breaking into a laugh.

"Damn it," Abby said under her breath then spun on her heels to run into the bathroom. She slammed the door behind her with a theatrical bang.

"If you don't get the hell out of my room I am coming out there to beat the ever living shit out of you with the heaviest object I can find." Her voice was sharp and serious as she yelled through the door while simultaneously scanning for the nearest projectile.

"Okay okay. I'm going back to my exile on the sofa. Don't get those unbelievably sexy candle apple red panties in too tight of a bunch."

"What an asshole," she mumbled then shouted through the door. "Shut up Alex!"

Abby heard his muffled chuckle, listening as he shuffled around and pulled on his jeans. She could hear his belt buckle jangle loosely, clanging against his zipper as he walked through the bedroom door and shut it behind him.

Abby leaned against the bathroom door and sighed. She seemed to be doing that a lot lately. Apparently Alex wasn't going to make this easy on either of them. But she refused to give in to him and his stupid sexy grin. She didn't love him and was done with empty sex. Forever.

As a sign of her dedication to avoid the tempting man currently camped out in her living room, she made a silent vow to start wearing her ugliest baggy sweat suit to bed.

CHAPTER THREE

Sunday, December 16th 2012, 2:14 pm

Days passed and Abby was beginning to think she couldn't take any more. After experiencing the same extreme apocalyptic dreams night after night, and dealing with the enticement of her sexed up quasi ex-boyfriend being around twenty-four-seven, she was simply on the verge of breaking into pieces.

She cursed herself every day for dumping her pills, but in the next second reminded herself that she was feeling things again and she was grateful for that. She was finally Abby again, un-medicated, slightly miserable, Abby. She told herself the misery was just part of being a person who could feel the full spectrum of human emotion and it would be worth it in the end.

Some space and some time to think would make all the difference. There never seemed to be enough time in the day to get things done and she couldn't remember the last time she sat down to watch TV or read a book. She was always moving, always running.

And always making art. She was completely obsessed with painting and drawing all sorts of images from the dreams. Each one was different and the more she worked the more detailed the paintings got, revealing new parts of a story she couldn't yet begin to understand. Every time she completed a painting she recorded her work by taking high resolution pictures of each canvas. Something other worldly or out of the scope of her everyday life was telling her that those paintings would serve as some kind of documentation or diary. She was sure they would be necessary eventually. She just had no idea how she knew that.

The real kicker - the real icing on Abby's proverbial, three tiered crazy cake - was that when she wasn't painting or dreaming about the end of days, she was hording food and water. She crammed it all into the back of her old Jeep along with anything else she thought could be used as survival supplies.

Abby was totally stumped as to why she was acting so nutty. In fact, she was starting to worry about herself. She drank way too much at night with the empty hope that she just might be drunk enough to skip out on one of those horror movies her subconscious mind kept playing on a loop. Life had gone from apathy to one big consistent act of fear for Abby. She was always afraid, always thinking about her own self preservation.

She could tell Alex was starting to get concerned because he was dropping comments about the paintings and saying things like "That's nice Abbs. You trying to relive the glory days of art school or something?"

That was Alex's polite way of saying he didn't like what she was doing; that he thought it had been done before and looked like non-visionary student work. Alex hated bad art the way a rich woman in Beverly Hills hated no-name clothes. At least she could be grateful he didn't say it belonged on the wall of a motel room.

She could admit that the dream paintings were not her usual style. They were more realistic than she usually liked to work, but that didn't matter. In this case she was not painting for art's sake. She was painting to create a record of what she was seeing and experiencing during the night because it was important. Abby thought maybe they were the most important pieces she had ever painted in her whole life.

As for the hording and nightly binge drinking: Alex had asked a few questions but otherwise he seemed to be ignoring it as part of some weird artist behavior. After all, artists were quirky and weren't to be taken seriously regarding anything other than their work. Odd shifts in mood and routine were not to be paid attention to. It was all part of the delicate process of making art. At least that was Alex's theory. It was easier for Abby to just play along, keep her head down, and carry on.

The whole thing was pretty crazy to Abby on some level where she remembered what it was to be normal. But something inside of her was being driven. She was constantly filled with a sense of purpose; that something significant was going to happen all too soon. Abby was sure her life was about to get pretty scary. Scratch that. Downright terrifying. And she was going to have to fight through a bunch of obstacles to survive whatever was coming her way.

The painting Abby was working on at the moment was a close up of the man on the hill. He was tall and carried a long stick with feathers, bones, stones, and other talismans hanging from it. From what Abby had read in books and seen on TV, she recognized him as a holy man, a priest from some ancient time.

She dipped her brush into a deep shade of red acrylic and moved it over the canvas with deliberate strokes. With the short brush clenched between her teeth she stepped back to examine her work. Her blonde hair was pulled up at the nape of her neck, her long bangs and other stray tendrils falling towards her face. She pushed a wayward strand from out of her eye and nudged the tortoise shell reading glasses up on the bridge of her nose before adding another stroke of blood red.

"Hey Abby!" Alex called from the living room. "You need to come have a look at this."

Abby continued her painting without looking up. "Can't right now. Too busy. Painting."

"Come on Abbs, you can work on that bizarre series later. This is really important."

She threw her brush in the water can with a huff then wiped her paint spattered hands on the old white button down she used for a smock. When she walked into the living room Alex was propped on the edge of the couch staring open mouthed at the flat screen.

"Have you seen this?" Alex pointed to the fuzzy, flickering screen with the remote. "Damn, I wish the picture would clear up. Every now and then you can see something though. And the audio is coming in fine."

Abby glanced at the screen not expecting to see anything relevant, when suddenly her heart rocketed into her throat. One paint stained hand covered her mouth in shock as she listened to the middle aged female news anchor speak.

"Iron rich, red rain is falling in the south of France and earthquakes, ranging from minor to catastrophic, have been reported all over the world. Scientists are theorizing volcanoes may also soon start erupting across the globe. This seismic activity proposes the real and severe threat of tsunamis. National governments are assuring all citizens that the reports are most certainly exaggerated and they are encouraging everyone to stay in their homes and remain calm."

"It's crazy right." Alex turned in the sofa to look at her. "I know natural disasters are more common these days, but this is like... biblical. I keep waiting for the plague of locusts to swarm through Manhattan."

"Oh my god," Abby whispered. "We're too close to the ocean. There's no safe place to hide. We can't stay here. We have to go. We have to go now!"

"What? Go where? What are you talking about? You heard the lady. She said to stay in our homes. Wait, is this about the compulsive hording you've been doing lately?"

Abby removed her glasses, closed her eyes, and recited the words she had come to know by heart over the last four days.

"When blood drops upon the Earth, the Destroyer will appear, and mountains will open up and belch forth fire and ashes. Trees will be destroyed and all living things engulfed. Land will be swallowed up by the waters, and seas will boil."

"What the hell was that?" The look on Alex's face was one of complete horror. "You're really starting to freak me out."

"I don't know. I've been having dreams and every night I hear those words. That's what the paintings have been about. They're the images I see every night." She pulled on her ear anxiously. "I have no idea how I know it, but I just know this is really bad. I think it's like end of the world type stuff or something. We have to find shelter somewhere else because... well because I'm pretty sure New York is about to be swallowed up by the sea."

"Jesus Christ! What? Are you serious?" He jumped up from his place on the couch and began to pace nervously. "This is nuts. It doesn't make any sense." He continued to pace, cracked his knuckles out of habit. "There's no way you could possible know that."

"I know. Believe me, I think it's crazy too. But what's the worst that happens if we leave? We go on a trip, the apocalypse doesn't come, and we go back to our lives. But if I'm right, and I hope I'm not, then we stay here and die."

After a momentary anxiety attack he faced her. "Seriously this is bat shit crazy, Baby. Sorry." He took a deep breath. "But on the slim chance that I have not been living with a total whack job for the past year, I'm going to believe you. Basically because it's better than biting the big one in a giant, deadly, and what I can only imagine could be classified as horrific, tidal wave. So yeah, a vacation might be nice. Let's get out of Dodge."

"Good. I know a place where we will be safe. Get packed up. I have a call to make. Oh, and pack light. Nothing that's not completely necessary. We're leaving here in exactly one hour."

CHAPTER FOUR

Sunday, December 16th 2012, 4:24pm

"So why does your uncle have a bomb shelter in his back yard?" Alex sat in the passenger seat of Abby's Jeep as they drove down Interstate 78 towards Pennsylvania.

"It's in his front yard. Well an acre or so to the side of the house really. And it's there because the guy who owned the farm before him was sort of the paranoid type. He lived there during the whole Cuban Missile Crisis thing and got wrapped up in the crazy fear propaganda. Kind of sad when you think about how much he must've shelled out to have it built and then Armageddon never showed up."

"Yeah well if you're right, it looks like it might be here now. So I for one am unendingly grateful to that guy for being a loony tunes Kansas militia man."

Abby chuckled. "Yeah, good point. When Jimmy moved into the place fifteen years ago Mom and I both thought the farm was going to be a massive burden to him. That didn't stop us from living there with him though. Eventually we both grew to love it too. And now I guess that old farm is turning out to be something of a godsend."

"Hey, do you think the crazy man left some big guns and stuff in the bunker? Maybe a grenade or two?"

"What would we need guns and grenades for? You planning on starting a one man army?"

"I don't know. I guess in case things get to looking like a riot and we have to shoot off looters and stuff. Or, in the slim case that computers are taking over the world, we have some way to defend ourselves."

She gave him a sideways smile. "You watch too many movies."

Alex pretended to pout for a second and then grinned. "Well, it would've been cool to at least get to blow something up. You know, kind of a bad ass bonus to having to live through a real world judgment day."

They sat in companionable silence for a few minutes, listening to the static laced broadcast on the radio. The roads were crowded but they were moving at a steady pace. Snow was starting to fall on the blacktop though it wasn't sticking just yet. Abby turned up the heat a notch as a shiver passed over her skin and wished she hadn't quit smoking. Her nerves were so frayed at the edges that some nicotine would really hit the spot.

"So, what do you think is going to happen to us Abbs?"

Abby took in a deep breath. "I don't know. It might have been my idea to take this trip, but I really don't understand any of this. I have no idea why I got picked to have weird dreams about the end of the world or what exactly is happening to me. But I guess it's a good thing. I mean, we can't be sure what's going to come to pass but if something bad does go down, at least we got the heads up and have time to get somewhere safe."

"Yeah, thanks to you and some other guy who was afraid of Commies and nuclear fallout we might get to live to see the aftermath. I guess paranoia pays off sometimes."

Abby huffed out a laugh. Alex might be a pain in the ass most of the time, but it was nice to have him with her. She couldn't imagine having to make a twenty hour trip to Kansas all alone, especially if the world decided to cave in on itself and turn to molten lava along the way.

Very quickly the snow began sticking to the pavement and coming down much harder than the light dusting it had been before. Abby slipped the Jeep into four wheel drive and gripped the wheel tightly with both hands at ten and two. She was grateful there was still some daylight and hoped that the storm might let up before nightfall when it would be much harder to see the road.

Abby turned down the radio and looked out the window to the sky. "Didn't that news anchor say something about strange and severe shifts in weather?"

"Um yeah I think so. She said that the weather might be out of whack for a while. Something about the sun having spots, flares, and storms or whatever. I guess that sort of thing directly affects the planet's climate." He shrugged. "But what do I know?"

"Okay, well I think this storm might be a problem. I'm not sure if this is possible, but I feel something weird."

"What do you mean? Weird how?"

Abby glanced at him with worried eyes. "I think this is what a tingling Spidey-sense feels like."

"What? You think something is about to happen?"

"Yeah, and it's not good. I don't know what though. Could be the storm. Could be whatever big thing is coming."

"Oh that's just great." Alex shifted uneasy in his seat. "You know it might not be a bad idea for you to keep some things to yourself. If I'm going to be taken out in your Jeep during a blizzard I'm not sure I want to know about it. I think it would be much nicer to just chit chat, listen to some tunes on the radio, basically just enjoy the ride. And then blam! Dead. No worries, no anticipation. Just done."

"I'll keep that in mind for next time."

They rode for a while without talking much. The snow continued to fall as they moved into the mountains of Pennsylvania. By all accounts it was a nice drive. The mountains were majestic, as mountains tend to be, and the scenery was beautiful. Maybe thirty minutes or so went by before they both drew in their breath in horrified unison.

Alex was the first to react. "Are you seeing this? What the hell? Oh my god. Shit! Do you see that?"

"I see it." Her eyes darted around, taking in the situation. "Um... you should hold on to something."

Abby dropped the Jeep out of four wheel drive so she could accelerate faster and pushed the gas pedal to the floor. Ahead of them, about a hundred feet down the road, huge boulders were bounding their way to falling straight onto the traffic below.

"What are you doing?" Alex grabbed the handle above his seat with both hands. "You can't outrun them."

"Maybe not, but that's the plan. Just close your eyes and pray really hard."

Abby noticed suddenly that the earth was shaking beneath the tires of the vehicle. They were in the middle of an earthquake, which probably hit pretty high on the Richter scale, and was obviously resulting in a legitimate land slide.

She sped down the interstate, weaving in and out along the way and jumping onto the narrow shoulder when necessary. She felt the tires sliding along the snow coated asphalt and fought to keep the back end of the Jeep from fish tailing. Unassuming drivers honked their horns and gave them annoyed looks or flashed middle fingers. Alex tried furiously to point out the boulders falling from the sky, but none of them took the hint. They just kept driving, all the while cursing the crazy blonde in the Jeep.

Smaller rocks pelted the blacktop and shattered to send a hard shower of pebbles onto the roof and windows of the vehicle. Abby held her breath and continued driving, hoping a big piece of stone wouldn't send the windshield crashing in.

All around them they started to hear the sound of crunching metal. Drivers violently jerked the wheels of their cars in attempts to miss the onslaught of earth falling, only to collide into each other with loud, deadly thuds.

Without warning a huge chunk of mountain fell to the right of the Jeep, landing inches from Alex's door with a thundering sound. It missed them barely, but managed to take out two other cars before it stopped moving.

"Holy shit! That thing almost killed us." Alex fought to catch his breath. "Oh god. I think I'm going to throw up."

"Not in here you don't. Just keep it together. There's no time for panic right now and I am not riding to Kansas with vomit scented upholstery."

"I always loved you Abby. I'm sorry for everything. If you make it out tell my parents that I wish I had been a better son."

"Are you giving me your last words? Seriously Alex, you are the single most dramatic man I have ever met."

She swerved onto the grassy median and drove as fast as she could. She glanced down and saw the speedometer read over ninety miles per hour. Out of thin air another car swung in front of her with a hard jerk before the driver hit the brakes and came to a dead stop. Abby squeezed her eyes shut and shifted the wheel with a silent prayer. She heard the distinct sound of metal scraping metal but there was no crash to follow.

They had nearly slammed head on into a white BMW. Instead of becoming human test dummies, they had just grazed the other car leaving a fresh white racing stripe along the green paint job of the Jeep. Abby took a calming breath and pulled back onto the interstate carefully.

As they made it back onto clear roads both of them sat in amazed silence. Then all at once they broke into hysterical laughter. The knowledge of being alive overcame them both as they gripped each other's hands and breathed in deep sighs of relief. The road before them had cleared. There were no boulders and traffic had become lighter.

With the momentarily laughter over, Alex turned back to look at the chaos they had just escaped and saw what Abby could only glimpse from the rear view mirror. Vehicles of all types were tipped over, tangled together, on fire and smoking, or crushed beneath boulders. The site was absolutely terrible and incredible all at the same time – the sort of thing most people only saw in movies.

"Shouldn't we do something?" Abby looked back through her mirrors.

"I don't think there's anything we can do." Alex's tone was quiet. "I'm sure they will get an ambulance crew up here as soon as possible to save who they can. And if we go back and there's another tremor, we could just be joining the casualties."

Abby nodded and did her best to blink back tears. "Yeah, I guess you're right."

While Abby was happy to be alive, the knowledge that people must have been killed in the land slide weighed on her like one of those deadly boulders sat on her chest. A certain amount of survivor's guilt settled in and rested on her shoulders.

They were still and silent for a few moments, almost as if they were individually saying prayers for each lost soul.

"I still can't believe that happened." Alex's grin removed the stillness and lightened the mood. "And I can't believe you did that. Man, if I'd known you could drive like that I would've pushed you into stock cars instead of art shows."

Abby gave a little smile, sadness still clinging to her expression. "Yeah, I'm not sure how I did it. It happened so fast. I just reacted."

"Well bravo girl. We're still in one piece." Alex laid his hand on hers and gave it a light squeeze.

"Yeah we are. Let's just hope that's the most exciting thing that happens on this trip. We've got like nineteen hours to go still and I'm pretty sure I've got to pee already."

"Um, not me. I think I did my share of peeing back there when it was raining rocks."

Abby looked at him with a disgusted sideways glance and he chuckled wholeheartedly.

"I'm kidding." He pointed to his pants. "See. Nice and dry."

Abby laughed and slapped his shoulder lightly. It was good to know she and Alex could be friends after all. This was a new dimension of their relationship and she was grateful to know that he could take her from tears to laughter in a matter of a few seconds.

* * *

Approximately nineteen hours later they were driving down the main street of Clover Lake, Kansas. The modest town was predominantly populated with construction workers, school teachers and their families. When the farmers, shop owners, and everyone else were added in, the overall population only hit somewhere around fourteen-hundred. It was a quiet and quaint town and Abby had always felt pulled to its simple charms.

The center of town was surprisingly empty considering it was lunch time on a Monday afternoon. Apparently the residents of Clover Lake had skipped the news and decided not to loot or riot just yet.

The Connelly farm was only minutes outside of town, nestled comfortably on one hundred and eighty-two acres of open land, forested hills, and planted fields. They would be reaching their final destination in a matter of minutes.

For the most part, their journey had been uneventful, though they had witnessed some unusual things along the way. And Alex, in his typical sarcastic style, had a comment for each of them.

In West Virginia there was a whacky looking street preacher standing on the highway, in the middle of a construction site, wearing an orange hard hat and a sandwich sign around his neck proclaiming that the end was near. He held his hands high enough in the air for everyone to see and stared up into the sky expecting to be beamed up at any minute. They had driven past him with the windows down specifically to hear his fire and brimstone proclamations.

"Hey, what do you know? The Devil is going to ride in on a many headed sea monster and take away all the sinners to Hell," Alex had exclaimed. "Is that in one of your paintings Abbs?"

In Indiana they saw a line of nuns, black and white habits and all, walking down the freeway with their rosaries in hand. About a dozen or so of them marched in time together with their heads down, apparently deep in contemplative prayer.

Alex had chuckled. "Now there's something you don't see every day. Do you think it will get me sent to Hell if I think one of them is hot?"

What followed was an in depth discussion on where in the world those nuns were going and what the earlier street preacher had really been talking about. This then led them to an argument about faith, religion, sin, morals, and everything in between.

Illinois had not disappointed either. From what they could see on Interstate 70, looters were running amok in the streets and several fires were blazing through the smaller towns. When they tuned into the area news station, Abby and Alex found out that a series of spontaneous tornadoes had run through the state on a rampage. Apparently the locals were getting wise to the end of the world rumors and they weren't too happy.

As they cruised through Clover Lake Alex was at the wheel. Both of them were exhausted but that didn't stop them from doing some friendly bickering about art. It was by far one of the things they argued about the most.

"Oh please. You're such an art snob Alex. The reason there are any clichés to begin with is because they resonate with people. Everyone can recognize the theme and they relate to it. Just because something's been done before doesn't mean it's no longer relevant."

"Yeah, but it's all old hat. You know? No one wants to see the same regurgitated crap time and time again. There can be original takes on clichés?"

"Oh, I totally agree with you on that point. The problem is, people aren't as kind to the new ideas. I swear if I have to see one more Van Gogh on the wall of a doctor's office waiting room I'm going to lose my lunch right on the linoleum. And you know I love Van Gogh."

Abby usually talked with fervor, gesturing with her hands a lot. At the moment, due to driving straight through half the country, she was too worn out to move much. Her seat was tipped back slightly as she reclined sleepily.

Abby continued, "And what's with all the Klimt posters pasted to the walls of every college student's dorm room."

"Well come on now. It's not just any Klimt they use for wallpaper. It's The Kiss specifically." Alex put up one index finger emphatically.

"Absolutely. It's like no one even realizes he did anything other than that one piece in his whole entire career. I'd like to pull them all aside and introduce them to something new but it won't do any good. Because, back to my original point, everyone wants what's familiar. The cliché."

"Okay, I get it. But you have to admit Monet's Water Lilies are still seriously over manufactured pieces of shit. They are freaking everywhere. And I mean everywhere. I can't get the brakes on my car replaced without seeing one version or another of those things on the dealership wall." Alex faked a tiny shudder. "I swear they're haunting me."

Abby let out a tired laugh. How was it they could talk as friends now that they were no longer having sex? Why hadn't she noticed that he was witty and clever and always kept her on her toes? When did Alex become the kind of guy she could sit and talk with over coffee all night?

He was the same person he had always been. It was Abby who had changed and suddenly she was beginning to feel something for him, something new that was more real than she had know with Alex before. Or maybe she was just tired and extremely stressed out. She let her mind wander from feelings to more lustful things.

"I know that look," Alex said, breaking Abby's train of dirty thoughts.

Abby quickly threw her gaze out the window. "Shut up Alex."

"I'm not saying a word." There was a hint of laughter in his voice. "I am no words guy over here. Just taking a leisurely drive through rural Kansas."

He waited a minute before continuing. "Um, where am I supposed to be going again?"

"Oh right." Abby snapped out of what was going on in her head and looked down to examine the handwritten directions in her lap. "You're going to turn up here at that stop sign.

And then the house is about a mile down on the left."

"Got it. I guess we're about to get to our new home then. At least for a while anyway."

"Yeah. Home sweet bomb shelter."

CHAPTER FIVE

Monday, December 17th 2012, 12:02pm

The all weather radials on the Jeep crushed loose rock as Alex and Abby pulled into the driveway of James Connelly's farmhouse. From what Abby could see the house hadn't changed since she had been there last. After five years the yellow paint still looked fresh and new. Standing on the front porch, painted white to match the shutters of the house, was her Uncle Jimmy.

Some southern rock blared from inside the house as he walked down the steps rubbing his hands on a grease stained rag. True to his obsession with a certain 1980's TV show, he was working on restoring a 1969 Dodge Charger to mint condition. It sat in disrepair to the side of the double wide driveway with its hood popped up.

Jim was the brother of Abby's late mother and was only eleven years her senior. He had never been married and had no children. His family consisted of his faithful old hound dogs, Bo and Daisy, or the Dukes as he sometimes called them, and the various animals that lived on the farm.

He was on the taller side with dark blonde hair and a finely chiseled face behind deep-set eyes. Walking towards them in his brown flannel shirt and old jeans, Abby thought he certainly looked the part of a Kansas farmer.

"Hey Jimmy." Abby smiled as she got out of the Jeep then reached out to offer up a hug. Due to the lack of serious age difference it had always felt a little odd to Abby to call him Uncle Jim. Her mother had always called him Jimmy and it was a name that stuck.

"Hey Kiddo. You finally made it back to Kansas. How was the trip?"

The two hound dogs came running, plowing into Abby. She laughed, knelt down to greet them with affectionate rubs and pats. "Hey guys. I missed you too."

She looked up at her uncle again. "The trip was long. Very long. We didn't even stop to sit down and eat a proper meal. Dollar menu drive thru all the way." Abby shifted her glance to Alex, nodded in his direction. "This is my... um friend, Alex."

Alex and Jim said their hellos, shook hands, and sized each other up. Her uncle was the only real father figure Abby had ever known, so she assumed it was natural for him to be a bit wary of any man she brought home. Part of her even liked knowing he was protective of her. It made her feel special and maybe even a little precious.

"Thanks for letting us come out here. We really appreciate it." Alex took a look around. "This is a great place." His eyes appraised the land around him, sweeping past the fields and the outbuildings.

"Thanks, though it's not like I had a choice." Jim raised an eyebrow. "When my only niece calls me up and starts talking about the end of the world, I tend to listen."

"Right, about that," Abby began. "Is the shelter all set? I'm not sure yet when we're going to need it, but I guess it should be ready to go as soon as possible."

"Well, straight to business I see," Jim said. "To be honest I haven't been down there yet. I had some other things to take care of around the farm. Damn horses are coming down with something. Plus I needed to get the new starter installed on the General." He patted the front end of the car like it was one of his dogs. "I told my business partner about our um... situation and he said he would take a look down there, make sure the cobwebs were cleared."

Abby looked towards where she knew the bomb shelter was buried beneath feet of soil. "Oh, that's right. You have a partner now? I remember you mentioning something about that."

"Yup, Kyle Windstone. He started here about five years back as a farm hand, just after your mother passed and you decided to try city life. He was my best worker, I trusted him, and he had some old family money that he wanted to invest." Jim turned back to the engine of the General and wiped off a spot of oil. "Since we had gotten to be good friends I let him buy half the property from me a couple years ago. He built his own place just over there past the corn."

Abby followed her uncle's hand to see a blue house that looked very much like his own, except newer and possibly even a little bigger. She noticed now that the one driveway extended all the way up to Kyle's house where his cherry red pick-up truck was parked to the side of the porch.

"Oh, and I see you added some windmills too and are those solar panels?"

"Yeah. Those were all Kyle's idea. We don't have electric bills anymore. He's got the wind turbines and solar power running the whole farm."

"Wow, that's great Jimmy. Kyle sounds very resourceful. I'm glad you've had some help around this enormous place and we can use all the help we can get right now."

"Yeah back to that," Jim began. "Are you going to fill me in a little more at some point? I'm still not sure what you're thinking is going to happen. I mean, I've seen the news and stuff, but I don't know if we're really looking at an apocalypse situation. Looks more like some bizarre weather. It will probably pass. And life has been pretty normal around here so far."

"I'll explain everything over dinner. First, let's get these bags in the house, maybe get the two of us weary travelers a shower, and some time to get settled in. Then we'll cook up something to eat and have a nice long chat. Sound good?"

Jim absently toyed with a cable under the hood of the General. "Works for me. I've got herb marinated pork roast sitting in the fridge."

Alex's eyes lit up. "Oh god. Food that's not a cheeseburger served up by a pimply high school kid. I love this guy already."

Abby went to the back of the Jeep to open the hatch and grab her bags. "My room still there, Jimmy?"

"Um... actually I sort of turned it into an office. But your mom's old room still has a bed in it."

Alex joined Abby at the rear of the vehicle, began pulling bags from the hatch back. "I guess I'll take the couch then."

Abby nodded and pretended not to notice the tone hiding in his words.

Hours later the three of them enjoyed a nice meal of Jim's pork, fresh cooked carrots, garden salad, and chunky, non-instant mashed potatoes. All the vegetables had been grown on the farm and the meal was nothing short of perfect.

Throughout dinner they discussed the situation at hand and what they could do to save themselves from what Abby was sure was the certain death of mankind. She knew her uncle wasn't exactly sold on his niece suddenly being a devastation predicting fortune teller, but that didn't stop her from relaying to him everything she knew about the dreams or the feeling of impending doom that had warned her of the landslide in Pennsylvania. She pulled out her green laptop and showed off the pictures of the paintings in wide screen, hoping that he would begin to understand the severity of the situation.

Jim scooped himself up a second helping of potatoes. "This is all a little farfetched, Abby. I mean what's this Destroyer supposed to be anyway? It sounds like a bad sci-fi flick."

Alex spoke up. "I thought the same thing at first. But after the stuff we saw and lived through on our way out here, I'm starting to come around pretty quick."

Abby washed down her food with a sip of diet coke before speaking. "Look, whether I'm right about everything or not, how does it hurt us? At the very least we spend some time in a bunker waiting out possible destruction that never comes." She shrugged. "Maybe it's better to be safe than sorry."

* * *

A short time later as Abby stood on the porch having an after dinner cup of tea, she wondered if she could be wrong about everything. Actually, she hoped she was wrong.

She didn't care about looking like a fruit loop. They could lock her up in an asylum and throw a straight jacket on her for the rest of her life if it meant the world wasn't going to change beyond recognition.

Her uncle's plastic Christmas tree stood in the window. Its colorful lights mingled with the white fairy lights strung from the porch as they twinkled back and forth in the light breeze. It seemed unusually warm for the holiday season. She remembered it being colder when she was younger. There was a certain chill in the air that made Abby wrap her sweater tighter to her, but it didn't feel like winter at all. The Dukes seemed to agree as they slept lazily on the porch floor.

From the corner of her eye Abby saw a man moving through the yard and crossing to the barn. She assumed it was Jimmy's business partner, Kyle, but he didn't look like your average mid-west farmer. She wasn't sure if it was the light from the strings of electric Christmas cheer hanging above her head or a weird trick of the moonlight, but the man now entering the traditional big red barn was literally glowing. It wasn't like he was glowing in the dark, but a subtle shine emanated from within him.

Abby waited without taking her eyes off of the barn until the man came wandering out again carrying three cases of bottled water in his arms. It was then that he saw her. He stopped dead in his black suede work boots before casually walking up to the porch.

They stared at each other for a few timeless minutes, Kyle at the bottom of the porch stairs looking up at Abby with a curious expression. He set the water down on a step and moved towards her with a hint of wonder in his eyes. The dogs lifted their heads and simultaneously wagged their tails against the porch floor.

"You must be Abby." His tone was soft and echoed the awe written on his face.

Abby was caught off guard, still trying to figure out how he could be glowing if she wasn't hallucinating. She searched her brain for the right words. "And you're Kyle."

They reached out their hands, Kyle's covered in a work glove, for an uncomfortable first shake. They continued to stare silently into each other's eyes like they were both looking for answers to life's greatest questions.

There was something about this man that went beyond his weird internal light bulb. Abby felt like she knew him somehow. His features looked familiar to her, like a painting she had created with her own hands. Each line and crease was something she knew by heart. Even his voice; with what few words she had heard, was something she somehow remembered. Its timbre was as well known to her as a song she had loved since childhood.

Kyle took a few slow steps up the stairs and stood beside her at the porch railing. "This is going to sound strange…"

"You're glowing." She blurted out the words without thought and prepared herself for accusations of lunacy.

Kyle looked stunned. After a second or two of thought a realization struck his features and he grinned widely. Eventually that smile changed to a quiet laughter.

"What's so funny?" Abby folded an arm around her middle, resting her tea cup on her hip. She pulled on her ear with her free hand and twisted the lobe slightly between her thumb and forefinger. "I know you may have heard some rumors that I'm a tad bit shy of sane, but until now I haven't been seeing anything weird like this. Well not while I'm awake anyway."

Kyle looked over at her with a smirk in his eyes. "You're glowing too." He spoke slowly, again throwing that grin her way.

Abby was completely thrown. Now it was her turn to hear something that would normally not make sense in a rational world. But the world was getting less and less rational all the time and a lot of things didn't make sense to Abby lately.

She looked at her hands and examined them thoroughly, bending her fingers and flipping her palms up and down. She didn't feel like she was glowing. But what did glowing feel like exactly? Aside from the silver rings on her fingers, there was nothing shiny about her.

Abby chuckled nervously and gazed up at Kyle. She took in his features with an artist's eye, noting details in an almost clinical way and filing them away in her mind.

He was almost a foot taller than she was and he looked long and lean even under his jacket. By the lack of line in his face and the texture of his skin she assumed he was about the same age.

She would've used a shade or two darker than sienna or maybe even raw umber to paint his hair. It was longer on the top and sat on his head in natural disarray, trailing down to short sideburns.

His wide set eyes, topped by prominent brows, were a shade of green that almost matched her own. She mixed colors in her head, planning out the formula for his olive irises. They were darkly rimmed by his lashes and she could see little flecks of gold that caught the light.

His face was angular, his jaw sharp and shadowed by a day's growth. She noted the shallow dimple in his chin and left cheek that became more obvious when he smiled. She imagined accentuating his cheekbones with white highlights.

Kyle Windstone was paintable, she decided. And attractive. In fact, after examining him for a length of time she felt like a million little butterflies were waging a war in the pit of her stomach. But there had been many men who Abby found attractive. What made this one so different? She couldn't put her finger on it, but something about him made her feel strangely pleasant. Like standing on the porch with him was exactly where she was supposed to be.

Abby pushed those feelings down, mentally chided herself for letting her head get away from her. What she really wanted explained at that moment was why they were both self illuminating like deep sea creatures.

Well, she also wanted to find out where she knew him from. He hadn't been at the farm when last she lived there and she was sure they had never met before anywhere else. She would remember a face like that. Yet, somehow she actually felt like she did remember him. Though it didn't seem possible, Abby was sure she knew the stranger standing in front of her like she knew her own phone number. The familiarity wasn't a conscious thing. It was just there.

Kyle's voice brought her back to the present. "Have we met before?"

Abby eyes widened a little as Kyle echoed her thoughts. "I don't think so. Maybe you've seen the pictures Jimmy keeps on the mantle."

"I think it's more than that. I seem to remember you in a really intense and weird way that I'm having a hard time explaining."

"I think I know the feeling, but we've never met." She shifted her mug of tea into her other hand. "I'm really confused to be honest. There's been way too much of the strange and unusual going on for me lately. You and the human light show will just be added to a growing list of things covered in crazy-sauce."

Kyle grinned, gestured for the two of them to sit on the swing suspended from the ceiling of the porch. After they were comfortable Kyle started talking again.

"Considering we both appear to be glowing, I'm guessing that everything I'm about to say is going to sound like a rerun." Kyle took a breath and turned in the bench to face her. "Lately I've been having dreams about the end of the world."

When Abby said nothing he continued. "After the dreams started I began storing water, food, and all kinds of miscellaneous survival type stuff in the barn, my shed, and just about every empty space I could find. I don't know why, but I knew I had to do it. That lives, mine included, depended on it. I even had that old bomb shelter upgraded while Jim was away in Topeka."

Kyle took a breath and blew it out as though he had been waiting his whole life to get that secret off his chest. "This is all old news to you right? It happened to you too?"

Abby nodded. She felt a kind of elation at knowing there was someone she could share her unusual world with, someone who could understand and not look at her as though she had three heads every time she opened her mouth. "I started having the dreams last week and I've been in hyper survival mode ever since. I even painted the dreams in extreme detail. I probably filled at least fifteen large scale canvases."

"Paintings huh?" He thought for a moment, continuing only when Abby leaned in expectantly. "That's interesting because I wrote them down, told the story from the dreams in the best way I knew how. I felt like I had to keep a record of what I saw. And you're a painter by profession right?"

"Yeah, I paint, illustrate, and all that.." She shrugged, took a sip of her tea. "It usually pays the bills."

"Huh, that sort of makes sense then." He paused for a breath. "I'm a writer when I'm not working the farm. Well, I've only been published a few times in small magazines, but I was an English major in college and I've been writing stories and poetry all my life."

Before they could talk any further on the subject Alex came running out the front door and slid to a stop on the porch, startling Abby, Kyle, and the sleeping hound dogs in the process.

"It's happened." He was out of breath with a frantic, wide eyed looked on his unusually pale face. "It happened just like you said it would Abby. I can't believe it's all gone."

Abby jumped out of her skin and stood up from the swing. "What Alex? What happened?"

"The City." He brought his hands up to grip his head, obviously struggling with the news he was about to deliver. "New York just got swallowed up by a tidal wave."

"Oh my god." Abby gasped and covered her mouth in horror. She had been praying that her vision was just a delusion and now the reality of it struck her hard in the chest, taking her breath away.

"It's been wiped from the map. California was hit too. They think Hollywood has been sunk under the sea like Atlantis. Your uncle is still watching the news, trying to learn what he can. I am pretty sure he doesn't think you're nuts anymore."

Abby nearly collapsed on her feet. She heard Kyle move behind her, but Alex was the first one to catch her. She wanted to sob against his chest, but couldn't seem to find the tears. She simply closed her eyes, leaned against him, and let his arms give her strength. All of their friends, everyone they saw on a daily basis, were gone. There was nothing left.

"If it weren't for you we'd still be there." Alex rubbed her back absently as he held her. "We wouldn't have made it out. Not if you hadn't saved us."

Kyle stood awkwardly behind them, cleared his throat politely to get their attention. Abby turned away from Alex, broke free of his embrace to look at Kyle. The gentle glow she saw radiating from the center of his body filled her with a sense of hope. Some of her convictions returned to her and she straightened until she was standing tall.

"Um... Alex this is Kyle Windstone, Jimmy's business partner."

"Hi," Kyle said with a quick wave. "Good to meet you."

Alex eyed the other man. "Yeah, you too."

"Glad you're here to lend a hand." Kyle expression turned somber. "We've got some serious work to do if we're going to live through what happens next."

Abby felt her stomach flip at his words and she suddenly realized that the two of them had a lot more to talk about. Kyle Windstone was like her; whatever that meant. If she read his look correctly, the time to start fighting for their survival was closer than she had imagined.

CHAPTER SIX

Tuesday, December 18th 2012, 6:31am

Kyle had been out of bed and working since five in the morning. He spent an hour tending to the horses and feeding the chickens before moving on to the task of hauling more water into the shelter.

The December weather was oddly warmer than usual and he was already sweating through his tee shirt as he transported the cases three at a time. If he had known the sun would be so hot he would've worn something lighter than black. He wiped perspiration from his brow and felt it soaking into his dark hair.

He knew the sun looked different, but he was no expert. It seemed brighter or bigger somehow, but it was hard to tell since he really couldn't look up for any length of time to study it without threatening his retinas.

Kyle's mind raced with end of the world concerns as he navigated the narrow steps of the hatch.

He was pretty sure they would be underground for a while and wanted everyone to be as comfortable as possible. Clean sheets and fresh smelling towels would be a nice thing to have. Any luxury at all would help preserve their long term sanity and hopefully stave off bouts of claustrophobia.

He was still trying to figure out how to maintain access to radio and TV broadcasts while they were below the surface, but he couldn't be sure there would be stations to pick up once it all started anyway.

Then there were the dogs Jim loved so much. Kyle fully expected they would be coming into the shelter with them and he hated to think that all of the humans would have to live in a space that smelled like dog waste for an indefinite amount of time.

Kyle was feeling overwhelmed when his thoughts unexpectedly turned to Abby. He felt a distinct wave of emotions that were anything but common to him and he found himself imagining things that he should never be thinking about his best friend's niece. But those wayward thoughts didn't frighten him as much as the fact that he simply wanted to be near her, take in her smile and talk with her. He could be content with that and it freaked him out immeasurably.

It's not that he was cold hearted or void of romantic notions. Actually, his nature was just the opposite which was part of the problem. He had allowed himself to care one too many times and only gotten burned. He had learned to keep his heart neatly tucked away and out of sight. The fact that the mere sight of Abby Connelly had been able to awaken something in him he thought was long gone – that he believed he'd killed and buried – was both intriguing and terrifying.

Sure, there had been girlfriends in the past. He was no amateur at the dating game. But for the past few years or so he had done little more than carry out one brief and meaningless relationship after the other and only when the opportunities presented themselves. There hadn't been anyone who could actually stir his heart in a very long time and love wasn't something he consciously sought after. In fact, he usually tried to keep it as far away as possible.

He couldn't put his finger on a reason besides the obvious, but Abby was different. It was pointless to deny that he was intensely attracted to her, even though he didn't understand why. She wasn't at all his type. She was more petite than he usually went for, standing just over five feet. And she wouldn't be considered extraordinarily beautiful by most standards. Simply put, she was physically average.

But his connection with Abby went beyond anything tangible. In the first place, she was whatever he was; whatever weird type of being glowed from the inside out. Plus they both had the dreams and inside information about the things that were coming. Albeit, Kyle's dreams had been going on for a lot longer than Abby's.

While she confided that she had only been dreaming for the past week, he had been having the same series of recurring nightmares for close to a year and a half. There hadn't been time to tell her the night before. Besides, he figured after the news she'd just heard, what she really needed was some rest and not more talk about Armageddon.

The whole glowing thing had left him more than a little confused. He understood that they both had personal light sources because of who or what they were, but he didn't see the purpose to it. Not yet. Maybe it was so they could recognize each other or maybe even so they could identify others like them. He didn't know, but he was sure there had to be a reason for it.

As he came up from the shelter he heard the sounds of people stirring within Jim's house. Everyone was up and he realized suddenly that he was looking forward to seeing Abby again. He felt a wave of anticipation radiate from his middle and he gulped audibly.

"Morning Windstone," Jim called as he crossed the yard and approached the entrance to the bunker.

Kyle turned from the stack of water he had slowly been moving into the shelter. "Hey, what's up? How are things going this morning?"

"As good as can be expected I guess. I think they're still pretty shaken up about what happened on the coasts last night. We all are."

Kyle looked down at his hands, removed his gloves. "Yeah, it's pretty unbelievable." Jim looked Kyle in the eye suspiciously. There was a short pause as the two men stood in the lawn.

"You knew it would happen." Jim's tone was flat.

Kyle looked away briefly, smacked his gloves against one hand before facing the other man. "Yeah I knew."

"When were you planning on telling me about this? I could've been helping you all this time." The older man sighed. "Abby says you've been storing water and food like she has, that you two have been having the same bizarre nightmares. Why didn't you say something?"

"Would you have believed me? Seriously Jim, think about what you're asking. You probably would've let me go through the motions of hording and storing, maybe even humored me a little by helping with some of the heavy lifting, then just written it all off as the crazy delusions of a madman."

"Okay, I'm not saying you're wrong. I probably would've thought you were losing it. But Man, I've been your closest friend for at least four years now. We live two acres apart and share this land like brothers." Jim put his hand on Kyle's shoulder. "In the future, if there is a future anyway, at least give me the benefit of the doubt."

"Yeah okay. You got a deal." Kyle gave his friend a weak grin.

"Okay good. Now, what's with this glowing skin thing or whatever it is and when did you upgrade the bomb shelter? I can't believe I didn't notice something like that."

Kyle glanced towards the Yellow House. "Wow, your niece has been talking a lot already this morning." He purposely didn't use her name.

"Actually she just got up. I guess she told that Alex kid last night and he mentioned it to me this morning over coffee."

Kyle raised an eyebrow. "Interesting breakfast conversation. What's going on with the two of them anyway?"

"He cheated and they split up less than a week ago. Abby doesn't have many friends, so I guess she's sort of hanging on to him."

Kyle nodded, pushed his sunglasses up on his nose. "So they're not together then?"

"Not anymore. Anyway, are you going to answer my questions?"

Kyle blinked and tried to clear the little blonde from his mind. "Um... I have no idea what the glow is all about. Apparently Abby and I are the only ones who see it. When she looks at me she sees it and when I look at her I see the same."

Jim took a step back, cocked his head to consider the information. "Wow man. This just keeps getting weirder by the minute. It's got to mean something."

"Yeah, I just haven't figured that detail out yet. As for the shelter, remember when you went to Topeka for a week to visit that girl you were dating?"

Surprise came over Jim's face. "Really? You said the town came by to work on a pipe and tore up the lawn. Who do you get to upgrade an old bomb shelter anyway?"

"Twenty-first Century Bomb Shelters dot com." Kyle smirked. "As I said, I was trying to hide the crazy going on in my head."

Jim sighed heavily. Kyle realized his friend was a simple guy who liked a simple life. All this doomsday stuff, with weird dreams and shining people, was probably a little much for him to take.

Both of the men turned their heads as the sound of voices came up from the country road that crossed through the farm. They walked up to the front of the house together to watch a trail of families, marching like a caravan minus the horses and wagons. It was like something most people only witnessed on the nightly news. They were refugees migrating from their homeland.

"Where could they be going? And where are their cars?" Jim kept his voice low.

Kyle shook his head, eyed the scene solemnly. "Something must have pushed them from their homes. Maybe they ran out of gas. Or maybe there was so much traffic on the highway they decided to hoof it off the main roads."

Kyle was gripped by a sudden urge to save them. His eyes fell on the women carrying babies and toddlers in their arms and his heart clenched into a knot. Someone had to help them. They would never make it alone.

As Kyle weighed the situation he saw Jim from the corner of his eye, staring at him knowingly. Kyle flinched, his body wanting to go to the travelers on the road and offer them safety.

"Don't Kyle." Jim gripped a hold of his friend's arm. "We can't save them all without killing ourselves in the process."

Kyle looked over at him, feeling the outrage scream through his chest. He slumped down to lean on the bumper of Abby's Jeep and tried to hold himself together. The faces of those children haunted him. They had no idea what was coming and no way to survive it. He rested his head in his hands, feeling his strength slip away.

"Damn it," Kyle finally said, his frustration getting the best of him.

Jim joined Kyle against the Jeep, stared off into the odd sky. "I know you feel like this is all on you man, but it's not. You might be a human night light, but I'm your right hand and I will help in any way you need me to. You're not alone in this."

"Thanks. I appreciate that." He stood straight and ran one hand through his hair. Kyle was on the verge of saying something inspirational to his friend, but figured it would only sound forced.

He was saved from that awkwardness as Abby came out the front door. Thankfully she hadn't heard the people walking and they were far enough down the road now to be over a hill and out of sight.

"Hey guys. What's on the agenda for today?" Abby greeted them with a smile that didn't register in her eyes as she plodded down the front steps.

Seeing Abby immediately improved Kyle's mood. Her glow was faded in the sun, but it didn't stop her from making everything seem brighter. She wore an old pair of paint splattered blue jeans, brown boots with even more paint on them, and a clean, light blue tee shirt with some sort of artsy screen print on it.

Her hair was shining and freshly blow dried, fluttering around her face to brush against her cheeks. He momentarily wished he could run his hands through that hair.

Her appearance didn't really matter to him, which only added to his freaked out state of mind. Yes, he thought she looked adorable in her old paint stained clothes, but she could've been wearing an old lady muumuu for all he cared. It was the smile in her eyes that sent a sense of warmth over him and made him momentarily forget about the danger that loomed over his head.

Kyle found his voice and started giving out a few orders. "Okay. Let's get all the stuff Abby brought into the bunker and organized. Then we have to spend some time checking out the place to make sure it's going to hold up. I'm sure none of us want to be stuck under a few feet of earth without clean air." Kyle stopped to look around for a second. "Where's that Alex guy?"

"Right here." Alex busted through the front door. "Sorry, I was just watching the news. I'm ready to get to work."

Kyle looked him over. His hair was coated in some kind of gel, his clothes were freshly pressed and far too fancy to work in, and the cologne he wore was so strong it masked the smell of horse manure coming from the barn.

Kyle's face was expressionless. "Right. Good. There's a lot to be done."

* * *

The four of them worked throughout the morning, not taking a break until lunch time mercifully rolled around. By the time the sun was high in the sky they had given every inch of the bunker a once over, checking all the systems and making sure there would be tools available for repairs in case anything broke down.

They moved the last of the large stores of water that Kyle had been keeping in the barn, of which there must've been hundreds of gallons that all needed to find a home inside the modest shelter. He had even included packages of drink mix to add flavor when they got bored with plain water. Either he had a lot of money or a lot of time to prepare. Abby decided maybe it was a bit of both.

They packed canned goods, dry foods, boxes of MRE's that Kyle had purchased at a local army surplus, toiletries, medical supplies, and other necessities into the storage spaces inside their soon to be underground home.

"I need to get some food in me." Abby stopped stacking cans as her stomach groaned. "I'm so hungry I'm about to start eating our emergency rations. Spaghetti and meatballs with a shelf life of fifty years is starting to look like a banquet."

Kyle smiled in her direction and the small gesture made her heart beat a notch faster. "I think we could all use a little break."

Food in hand, the group went out onto the porch to eat their various types of sandwiches. There was no real discussion, only the distinct sound of crunching and chewing. Jim passed around a bag of potato chips, everyone taking a handful to accompany their modest meals.

As Abby took a bite of her peanut butter and jelly she noticed that she was being watched. Through dark sunglasses her eyes landed on Kyle only to see him quickly avert his gaze.

He didn't glow as much in the daylight, she noticed, letting her stare trail up his forearm and over his sleeve. Or perhaps it just wasn't as obvious. Instead his body gave off a faint shimmer of light that simply looked like the sun was hitting his skin even as he sat in the shade of the porch.

She took another bite, continuing to gawk at him. Her eyes wandered to his neck, to the tendons that ran under the skin below his Adam's apple. He was the opposite of bulky, his frame long and lean. She decided this guy didn't carry a gym membership in his wallet but working on the farm probably more than filled his quota of exercise.

He turned to look at her then. Their eyes met in a quick instant making Abby jump slightly. For a long moment they held the stare, neither of them feeling the need to look away. Abby stopped chewing and Kyle simply looked into her like he was now the painter and her portrait was his next project.

Abruptly Alex coughed a little too loudly, breaking the peace of their lunch and the spell between Abby and Kyle. Abby knew that her ex-boyfriend was irritated by what he'd seen moving between her and someone he saw as his competition. Obviously, he wasn't really trying to hide it. It was his not so discrete way of letting her know that he was still planning on making another go at their relationship. Abby knew there was no hope of that now.

There was a connection between her and Kyle that Abby couldn't deny. She didn't know yet if it went beyond sharing dreams and iridescent skin, but she knew that she wanted to find out. She wanted to get to know Kyle inside and out; find out what his passions were, learn about what and who he loved. She wanted to know him with a certain desperation that she wasn't used to feeling. She wondered if this was what being off her meds was like. Was this what everyone else felt like all the time?

After lunch the four of them worked into the night. It was well past prime time before they stopped for a late supper.

During this meal they all spoke to each other, but none of them wanted to ponder any more ways to survive disaster. Instead they talked about mundane things; little things that normal people talked about at normal meals.

There was discussion of Abby's work, where she had recently been showing and who her latest clients were. The everyday workings of Alex's gallery came up as well. None of them mentioned that all of that was now lost and buried beneath miles of ocean. For the moment they preferred to pretend all was right in the world.

Kyle and Jim told stories about the farm, about birthing foals and dealing with a recently deceased blind rooster who never stopped crowing. They all laughed when Kyle insinuated Jim had sent one of his dogs after it late one summer night, saying Jim had draped the poor bird in a raw meat necklace to entice the lazy hounds.

Abby let out an uncharacteristic giggle. "Oh, that's so awful. Please tell me that didn't really happen."

Kyle set his napkin on the table with a shake of his head and a smile. "No, of course not. Honestly, we loved that bird. Jim especially. I assure you poor blind Gary was a very old chicken who died naturally and peacefully."

For all intents and purposes they were four people getting to know each other or catching up as was the case of Abby and her uncle. The only real negative tension in the room came from Alex. Occasionally he would shoot a look to Abby when she talked or laughed with Kyle or glower at Kyle over a fork full of food. Abby did her best to ignore her former lover and enjoyed the lightness of the evening.

When the meal was over no one moved to clear the table or do the dishes. Leftovers went to the dogs and Jim pulled beers for each of them from the fridge. Beers led to tequila shots and before any of them realized it they were all a little tipsy and enjoying what seemed to be an endless amount of friendly conversation.

The men talked about cars and other stereotypically male things while Abby listened and interjected where she could. She tried to be polite but honestly had no knowledge of engine blocks or trade deadlines.

There was a silent agreement between the group to not turn on the television or even think about what the future may hold. They had created a temporary world where they could merely take pleasure in what it was to simply be human and remember what they were working so hard to preserve in the first place.

With midnight rolling by, Jim stood up to stretch his legs and announced that he was going to bed.

Alex was very drunk and was nearly falling asleep at the table, with his head rested firmly in his hand. "That sounds like a great idea." He slurred a bit on his words before turning to Abby. "You ready Babe?"

There was a moment of uncomfortable silence. Everyone seemed to be waiting on Abby for a response. Alex had forgotten himself and the status of their relationship within a puddle of beer and tequila.

"Actually, I was thinking since you've been stuck on a couch for a week that maybe I should stay in Kyle's spare room so you could have the extra bed here. As long as that's okay with you Kyle?"

Kyle sat up straighter and fidgeted with his beer bottle. "Yeah. I guess that makes good sense."

The look on Alex's face was at once blank and furious. "Oh. I see. I'm sure the two of you have a lot to talk about." He put up his hands to make air quotes. "Freakish radioactive skin conditions, prophetic nightmares. You've got a lot in common. I get it."

While Alex's words said that he understood, his tone was harsh and full of hurt. Abby wasn't sure how to handle the situation without escalating it even further. She had already made it clear that she and Alex were no longer a couple and she really did have a lot of things to discuss with Kyle. It wasn't a personal attack on Alex, but that was exactly how he was taking it.

"Okay... um I'll get my bags then. Be right back." Abby stood up to walk down the hallway with Alex suddenly on her heels.

He fairly crashed through the bedroom door behind her and closed it with a thud.

"What do you want Alex?" Her voice was laced with annoyance.

He positioned himself between her and the door, planting his feet on the carpeted floor. "I see the way you two look at each other. I'm not stupid Abby. You might as well just wear a tee shirt that says you want to screw that guy's brains out."

Abby turned on him with a huff. "You're drunk Alex. Why don't you just lie down and sleep it off?"

"Don't blow me off damn it! I thought we could make this work. I thought we were moving forward, finally having some fun together. What about us?"

"There is no us Alex." She softened her voice, feeling empathy for this man who was now her friend. "It's over now."

Alex opened his mouth to speak but Abby held up her hand and kept talking. "Look, I wouldn't have been able to make this trip without you. You are my friend and I'm grateful that we can have at least that. But that's were us ends."

Alex looked like he was going to scream. His face was red, his hands were shaky, and he was obviously not happy. He continued to stand between Abby and the door even when she had slung her bags over her shoulder and made a move to leave.

"Please get out of my way Alex." It wasn't so much as a request as it was a flat out command.

After a long moment he stepped aside with a dramatic sigh only to pound his fist into the top of the dresser beside the bed. Abby jumped at the sound but kept walking without turning around.

Jim peered down the hall as she left the bedroom. "Everything okay?"

"Yeah. Everything's fine. Alex is just a little upset right now. I'm sure he'll be feeling better in the morning."

"Want me to set him straight?" Jim took a step towards the hall.

"No, no. It's under control. But thanks Jimmy." Abby exchanged looks with Kyle. "I'll be waiting on the porch."

With Abby out the door Jim turned to Kyle. "Do me a favor and remember that she's my niece."

Kyle made a face. "I'm not going to take advantage of her, Jim. I think she just wants to talk, find out what I know. She needs to feel like she's not in this alone the same way I do." Kyle leaned in a little closer and lowered his voice a notch. "Plus she's a big girl, a grown up. I'm pretty sure she can handle herself."

Jim gave him a look that said even though Kyle was his best friend, he'd still kill him if he hurt his niece. She was the only family Jim had left in the world and he wouldn't stand for her being mistreated or used by anyone.

"I get the point Buddy." Kyle patted his friend's shoulder. "I'm your friend, remember? Now stop fussing like an old woman and get some sleep."

Kyle went out the door with Jim watching from the window as the two of them headed towards the Blue House.

"I don't see any glowing," Jim muttered to himself. "Everyone is losing their damn minds."

He looked down, clicked his tongue for the two old hounds at his feet to follow him up the stairs. "Come on guys. I think the three of us are the only sane people left on the entire planet."

Once undressed, he pulled back the covers and crawled into his big warm bed. The Duke dogs jumped up to join him, circling twice each before settling down at his feet. "And it's damn exhausting keeping up with crazy people." He yawned, clicked off the light, and quickly fell into a deep and dreamless sleep.

CHAPTER SEVEN

Wednesday, December 19th 2012, 12:38am

"Wow, great house." Abby dropped her two modest bags on the hard wood floors of Kyle's ample front foyer.

"Oh, thanks." He grinned. "It's home."

She noticed the black and white photography on the walls immediately. There were scenes from the farm; horses, the hen house, various close-ups of crops growing in the fields. They were simple yet perfect in their compositions, the grey scale tone lending a sophisticated feel to the images.

Abby gestured towards the framed pictures. "Yours?"

"Yeah." He looked up briefly. "It's sort of a hobby."

Abby smiled. "They're really good. I like them."

"Thanks." Kyle walked into the kitchen, flipped the light switch, and dropped his keys on an empty spot of counter amid piles of mail. Abby followed him, silently observing what she could see of his home.

"Thanks for letting me stay here. Alex was getting to be a little much, plus staying in my mother's old room was starting to haunt me."

"No problem. I understand that's got to be kind of tough."

The walls of the kitchen were papered in a surprising and delicate rose floral. The roses were a pale, muted pink against a creamy light yellow background. Tiny green leaves were sprinkled among the roses, accenting the sea green cupboards above raw, wood, butcher block counter tops.

"I love the kitchen," Abby said. "It's not what I expected for a man's house, but it's really beautiful."

Kyle shrugged. "I guess I'm a sucker for the traditional."

Abby smiled and watched as he shuffled through the paperwork on the counter and moved things around in an attempt to straighten up. How was it that his motions were so familiar to her? A sense of déjà vu washed over her as she realized his every action was something she recognized.

He mumbled something about no longer needing a cable bill before looking up again. "Oh, sorry. You probably want to get settled in. It's definitely been a long day. Let me show you where the spare room is." He took a step and gestured towards the stairs.

"Actually," Abby began. "I'm not really ready for bed just yet. I was thinking maybe we could sober up and have a little chat. I'm not sure we'll get many other chances to talk in private between Jim and Alex and whatever's coming our way."

"A chat about the end of the world it is then." Kyle nodded. "Okay. How about I put on some coffee?"

Before waiting for her answer he started readying the coffee maker then suddenly stopped in mid scoop. He closed the tin coffee canister and set it back in its place on the counter.

"You don't like coffee do you?" His question was hesitant and he seemed unsure of what he was saying.

"No." She sat down slowly at the old oak kitchen table and looked at him questioningly. "I usually drink tea if I want something hot."

Kyle looked at her blankly. "That's what I thought. Isn't that what you were drinking last night? Chamomile, right? I think I have some of that in one of these cupboards."

"That sounds great, but it will only make me sleepy. I think I need something with a bit more kick right now. My head's still a little fuzzy from one too many of Jimmy's shots."

"Right. Um... let me see what I've got." He popped open the fridge and bent down to look on the shelves. "How about some diet coke? You were drinking that earlier. That's your usual, right?"

"That's perfect." Abby smiled, relieved.

They sat down at the kitchen table with a touch of awkwardness hanging between them. How did one start a conversation about the apocalypse, Abby thought.

Kyle was the first to begin. "I have a confession to make."

Abby leaned in on her elbows and took a swig of her soda. There had been sexual tension looming since the moment they met and Abby fully expected that the flirting was finally about to begin in earnest.

"I'm all ears." She gave him a casual smile that she hoped was inviting and waited for him to continue.

"I'm not sure how to put this so I'm just going to come right out and say it. I think I know things about you that I couldn't possible know about a person I just met."

"That sounds rather bizarre." She laughed, a little uneasy. That wasn't at all what she had expected him to say. "What do you mean exactly?"

"I mean that I know you don't like coffee not because I noticed you drinking herbal tea last night. I know you don't like coffee because I just know you."

Abby took a minute to soak that in. Maybe it was her earlier alcohol consumption, but she couldn't seem to make sense of what he was trying to say.

Kyle continued, keeping his tone calm and even. "I know that you used to smoke cigarettes and sometimes still crave one. Like tonight while we were drinking you were wishing you had one. And I know you collect green things compulsively. Almost everything you own is some shade of green." His tone became even softer as he edged his fingers across the table, resting them just centimeters from her own. "And I know that you miss your mother so much that sometimes you sit alone in the dark listening to her favorite songs."

To say that Abby was taken aback was an understatement. She had known this man for just over twenty-four hours and didn't see how he could've garnished intimate details about her life, some of which she never spoke about. They had barely been able to talk to each other throughout the day while they worked, and what they talked about at dinner didn't have any relevance to what he was saying to her now.

"Did my uncle tell you this stuff? I mean finding out my favorite color is easy. Anyone who knows me even a little bit could tell you that." Abby was feeling a little incredulous and it was obvious in her tone.

"I know your toothbrush is green. So is the underwear you're wearing right now."

Abby's hand flew to the back of her pants to see if her underwear was showing. Before she could get over her shock he continued.

"Jim and I don't really talk about you. Not like that. Occasionally he will mention that you're doing well or showing your paintings at some fancy New York place, but not much more than that. These things... they just come to me randomly. I don't know how and I don't know why. But the moment I saw you it was like you were transmitting things to me. Wasn't it like that for you at all?"

"No. I mean, sort of. I felt like I definitely knew you from somewhere, but I didn't get details about your life or anything like that."

"What about since then? Has anything strange come to you? Any visions or random thoughts?"

Abby didn't want to tell him the things that popped into her head when she was around him. She couldn't tell him that he made her feel safe even when he was one hundred yards away from her. Or that simply knowing he existed gave her a sense of relief that could only be compared to coming back to the place she belonged after a very long time. She wasn't really ready to get that personal yet.

She wanted to be that close to him; wanted to be able to talk to him and casually touch his hand if the mood struck, but some part of her was too scared of being vulnerable. Instantly she sensed that he was scared too. Not of the disasters happening in the world or the big bad that was coming, but of her.

She turned in her chair to face him. "You're scared of me. Not physically. You don't think I'm going to cause you actual harm but.... it's something else. You're afraid of being close to me. You won't even touch me because you're so afraid."

She furrowed her brow, thinking back. It was true, she realized abruptly. He had been wearing his work gloves when they shook hands that first night and she recalled him giving her a wide berth more than once when they were working in the shelter together.

He stared at her in silence and she could almost hear his thoughts. It was as if he was silently asking her to tell him why he was afraid of being close to her. His face was expectant, bidding her to go on.

She continued with caution. "You're afraid because... because you freak out at the thought of getting too close to someone, of letting them know you." She raised an eyebrow. "Intimacy issues?"

He didn't acknowledge the comment but continued to listen.

"You have... feelings that you don't understand." She took a breath, clenched her eyes in concentration. "Wait, there's more. You think something will change... that you won't be the same and you won't be able to go back."

He reclined, stretched out his long frame and rested his hands across his chest.

"Okay that's good," he finally said. "Well done." His wary expression didn't match his words.

"I was right? Huh. That's a new one. I'm a little more confused than I was before though." She didn't question what she'd just learned about his feelings for her even though she desperately wanted to.

"Oh me too." Once again he shook off his serious expression and his mood lightened. "I have no idea what any of this means. All I know is that I feel something and that I know you as well as I've known anyone, maybe more so."

After a brief silence, both of them thinking but not speaking of the things they had just explored, they began talking about more business like matters.

Abby pulled her laptop from her bag and showed him the photos she had taken of her paintings. Kyle told her about having the dreams for the past year as compared to her week, and most of what he had learned from some research he had done on the internet. They compared notes, shared theories, and tried to agree on the conclusions.

Kyle told her about a planet or a sun, no one could really agree on what it really was. It had been discovered back in the early eighties sitting fifty billion miles away from Earth. By 1992 it was only seven billion miles away and closing. He told her that some people, mostly made up of fringe scientists and conspiracy theorists, believed that this celestial body might be responsible for global warming and all of the severe natural disasters the world had faced over the last decade.

"It's something to do with the way this thing reacts with our sun." Kyle swigged his soda before going on. "Some people think we live in a binary system, the Destroyer being the other sun in our solar system. And once every thirty-six hundred years it rolls around to cause a chain reaction that subsequently wreaks havoc here on Earth. To top that off, I ran across some tin-foil-hat theories about a black hole at the center of the galaxy and something about pole shifts that only happen once every two hundred thousand years or so. Those things combined can't be good. But, whatever the cause, it seems the results are going to be just plain catastrophic."

Abby wasn't anything close to an astronomer or a physicist, but parts of what he had said made sense. Something about the information was oddly comforting to her as well. It was nice to know what was happening could be explained with science; measured and understood as being real and tangible instead of the product of some unseen, supernatural phenomenon.

There was a lot of theory and opinion, but neither of them was sure of many facts. One of the few things they could both agree on as being concrete was that for some reason Kyle had more power, or whatever it could be called, than Abby did; most likely due to him having been using his abilities for much longer. He could see into the future further and with more regularity. He also seemed to feel their connection more strongly. But Kyle was quick to point out that they were both clearly in this together. For some reason they had both been chosen to have the knowledge to survive.

Abby leaned back in her chair. "I think I know why my dreams only started recently." She continued when Kyle looked over questioningly. "I have taken anti-depressants since right after I moved to New York. After we buried my mother." She paused in momentary memory. "The first night I had a dream was the first night I didn't take my pill."

Kyle showed interest. "Why did you stop taking them all of a sudden?"

"Well it was the same night I broke up with Alex and things were weird. I just wanted to feel like a real person, someone who had normal emotions. I didn't even cry over him."

"Maybe you didn't love him." Kyle eyed her, observing her reaction.

Abby allowed herself a moment to think about that. Of course it was something she had considered herself. Maybe her relationship with Alex had simply been convenient. He was someone to spend time with; to have some kind of pseudo-intimacy with.

"Honestly, if he hadn't cheated on me I was probably going to cut him loose soon anyway." She hesitated, looked down at her hands. "I'm not sure I've ever actually been in love with anyone. Everything I ever thought was real turned out to be something else."

"What did it turn out to be?"

"I don't know. But I never felt that special something, you know. I never felt really understood and cared for in some unconditional way." She laughed bitterly. "Even to me that sounds stupid. I don't even know what that would be like. If it's real or just something I imagined love should be when I was a fanciful teenager."

She took a swig of soda, echoed that bitter laugh. "Up until recently I just figured that my experiences were the way things were supposed to be. People came together, got physical, and that was it. I had grown to think that can't-live-without-you feeling was just a byproduct of fairy tales and paperback romances."

"I don't think so." Kyle's face was thoughtful. "Maybe you just need someone to come along and woo you the right way."

Abby smiled and tried not to blush. She took another sip from her coke can and let herself fantasize about the idea of being wooed the right way by Kyle.

They were becoming comfortable with each other very quickly. She had easily accepted that he simply knew her and she knew him. As odd as it was, regardless of how long or how little they had been aware of each other's existence, they were steadily beginning to act like old friends who had only perhaps been apart for a while.

Kyle got up to get them each another diet coke from the fridge. "I think whatever it is that's coming is going to get here at the stroke of midnight on the twenty first." Abby couldn't hide her shock. Of course she believed him but she had thought they would have more time to prepare and more time to figure out the answers to all of their questions.

"You're kidding?" She took the can from him and opened it. "That's extremely specific. Are you sure it's that exact time?"

"Yeah, pretty sure. That's what my gut is telling me plus it seems to be the date all the ancient prophecies point to. It's foretold by the Mayans, the Egyptians, the Cybil of Rome, Native Americans, the Bible, just to name a few." He took his seat again and turned to her with intense eyes. "It pops up everywhere when you look into the end of the world. I don't think we'll be above ground after that. Actually, I'm planning on having Jim and Alex pack up the dogs and get moved into that thing by Thursday afternoon. I don't want to take any chances."

"Okay. Well that shouldn't be too hard to explain I guess. They're already looking at both of us cross eyed since I mentioned the glowing thing."

Kyle picked up on her sarcasm and smiled. "We'll figure something out. If we have to we'll make up a story about falling asteroids or tell them some plot from a disaster movie. You should probably be the one to break the news though because you already have a good track record with that sort of thing. They'll believe you. Plus, you're prettier. I'll just look like a raving mad man screaming that the sky is falling."

She knew he was sort of teasing her and she returned his smile. "Sure, leave me with all the dirty work. Some friend you are."

"What? That's not a good deal?" His eyes widened in feigned disbelief. "I get to see the bad things and you get to break the news to your uncle and your clingy, hair gel obsessed ex boyfriend." He laughed at the reference to Alex. "You get to look crazy and I get to stay the sensible voice of reason. Fair, right?"

She laughed open mouthed and nearly touched his arm, sitting so close to her own on the top of the table that she could feel the heat coming off of his skin. She caught herself, remembering their early conversation and not wanting to push their newly found friendship to a place perhaps neither of them was ready for.

Kyle noticed her gesture and let his laughter ebb. Looking into her eyes he slowly inched his hand across the small section of table between them. Just as Abby thought she was going to feel the warmth of his hand he drew away slowly, exhaling a deep breath that hit the skin of her cheek.

The awkwardness lasted a mere second before Abby was speaking again. "So tell me about the things you write when you're not writing about disaster."

Kyle's face lightened and he took a second to sip on his soda. "Poetry mostly. Freeform, stream of consciousness type stuff that I usually go back and clean up later."

"That sounds nice. I'd like to read it sometime."

"I wouldn't categorize it as nice. Most of it lately is pretty dark, considering the circumstances of my life these days." He smiled but it didn't register in his eyes.

He brought his hand up to his chin, nonchalantly rubbed a thumb along his bottom lip in thought. Abby felt her pulse suddenly go to eleven and had to consciously keep her mouth from hanging open.

They met eyes again and Kyle leaned forward a little in his chair. "What about you?" he asked. "What do you usually paint when it's not the end of the world?"

Abby needed a minute to collect herself before responding. "Oh. I prefer figurative stuff. Mostly portraits, but I have an aversion to realism so it's not what people typically think of as portraiture. Well not really."

"I'd like to see it... your personal work. I have a feeling it's something I would like to hang on my walls."

Abby smiled. "Well the next time you're in New York you could come by the ga..." She stopped short. Most of her paintings were now sitting under the sea. There was no gallery to visit, no walls that held her canvases. "I mean I can show you my portfolio on my computer some day."

Kyle's face changed, his expression softening. His hand inched closer to hers again. Abby watched with anticipation as his fingers wrapped tightly around hers. She stopping breathing for an instant as his hand slipped into her smaller one. She closed her eyes, felt the calluses on his palms, the product of years of hard labor on the farm, and let out her breath in short gasps. All at once an overwhelming feeling swept through her like she was being drowned in a pool of raw, potent emotion.

Neither of them was prepared for the jolt of power that flew through them with that one little touch. It was like putting the last cable on a car battery to complete the circuit and jump it back to life.

Visions immediately started flowing between them until Abby found that she was standing back in that place of her dreams and staring up at the grassy hill. There she saw Kyle, dressed in the priest's clothes, his bare chest exposed under necklaces as he held aloft his sacred staff.

Their eyes met and Abby realized now that it had been Kyle's eyes she had been staring into every night since the dreams began. She all at once knew who he was and more importantly who she was. This was not some random vision. What she had been experiencing as a dream was in actuality a memory of another time, another place, another life.

The man she saw on the hill was more than just Kyle Windstone, her uncle's closest friend and business partner. He was more than the attractive Kansas farmer she had just met. The man she saw was intensely powerful and the chosen holy man of her people. Their people. He was her priest, her friend, and her lover. He was everything to her and when she looked at him she saw her past, her present, and her future all hidden within his flickering green eyes.

The priest opened his mouth and his voice rang out over the land:

When blood drops upon the Earth, the Destroyer will appear, and mountains will open up and belch forth fire and ashes. Trees will be destroyed and all living things engulfed. Land will be swallowed up by the waters, and seas will boil.

The Heavens will burn brightly and redly; there will be a copper hue over the face of the land, followed by a day of darkness. A new moon will appear and break up and fall.

The people will scatter in madness. They will hear the trumpet and battle cry of the Destroyer and will seek refuge within dens in the Earth. Terror will eat away their hearts, and their courage will flow from them like water from a broken pitcher. They will be eaten in the flames of wrath and consumed by the breath of the Destroyer.

In those days wisdom will be revealed; the few will be gathered for the stand; it is the hour of trial. The dauntless ones will survive; the stouthearted will not go down to destruction.

Suddenly she felt herself floating, scenes passing her on all sides. She moved back through time in a flash. She saw Kyle. No, that wasn't his name, she thought. And the sound suddenly surfaced on her tongue. "Callum."

She watched as if an outsider, witnessing the moments of contentment in their small home, hearing the sound of their children laughing. It was all so far away, faded as though she were looking through a pane of foggy glass.

He called her name, reached out to her in the night. "Aislynn." She knew his face, his voice, his touch. She had always known him.

When they returned to the present moment they were standing. Their hands were still joined and suddenly so were their lips. It wasn't a sweet, tender peck of a kiss. No, there was nothing polite or controlled about this kiss. It was hungry, piercing, and laced with desperation.

Kyle held Abby's face with one hand and trailed up her curves with the other, plastering her body to his like a second skin. When she let out a moan he quickly drew away and dropped to his knees. Pain contorted his features while he cradled his head in his hands. He was hurting but Abby had no idea why. There was no blood, no mark on him at all.

"Kyle! Oh god, are you okay?" Abby reached out to steady him, to comfort him, but he pulled away and put his hand up to stop her.

He looked up with watery eyes. "Please. Not yet. Please don't touch me again. Just give me a minute." His voice was strained, high in pitch as the pain pulsed in his words.

Abby sat back, resisting the urge to wrap him in her arms and care for him until the pain subsided. Her heart wrenched as she watched him suffer and her vision seemed to jump back in forth, flashing images of the past and the present in the same moment. As she looked down at him he was the priest in her vision one instant and Kyle Windstone the next until there was suddenly no separation between the two. She clenched her eyes closed, opened them again. When her sight fell again on the man before her she saw someone she already knew, someone she loved. Kyle and the man she remembered as Callum were one in the same.

At least a full five minutes passed before Kyle lifted his head and opened his eyes to meet Abby's. She couldn't read his expression through the remnants of pain.

"I'm sorry." He stood up, steadied himself on the edge of the table. "I'm okay now. That's how it happens to me sometimes. When the big visions come they leave a blinding pain in their wake."

"Is it gone now? Is there anything I can do to help you?" She fought the urge to reach out to him again. "I'm sorry Kyle. If I had known..."

"It's okay. Neither of us knew that was going to happen."

"Why didn't I get pain with the vision?"

He sat down, took a long sip of his soda, and leaned back in the chair with his eyes closed. After a few deep breaths he opened his eyes and looked at her without turning his head.

"I don't know. Look, I need some time to take everything in. To get some sleep, figure things out. I think it would be a good idea if we just turned in for the night." He was rigid, his face expressionless.

Abby tried to hide the feelings of rejection that stabbed into her gut like ten thousand pointy ninja stars. So many thoughts rushed through her mind at the same time, competing with each other for dominance.

Had she expected him to take her in his arms and tell her how long he'd waited for her? Regardless of their past life connection, they were still bound to the present.

"Okay. It's probably better that way." It took all her energy to speak evenly and fight to keep the hurt from showing on her face.

When Kyle didn't respond she moved towards the stairs. "I guess I'll find the guestroom on my own then."

Again he said nothing as she gathered both of her bags from the foyer and started up the stairs. On the second step she stopped to peer back into the kitchen.

"If you need help or anything, I don't mind." She said it just barely loud enough for him to hear. "I mean, if your head hurts or something."

"Thanks. I'll be fine." He stayed in his seat, his back turned to her. "Get some rest. I'll see you in the morning."

Abby continued up the stairs and found the spare room with the first door she opened. She tossed her bags on the floor, stripped off her jeans, and threw herself onto the floral bedspread with a mix of exhaustion and confusion. How was it that she felt like she missed him? That didn't make any sense. Her entire soul fairly ached for him and he was just downstairs. But he wasn't hers. Not in this life.

Memories invaded her, not the least of which was the memory of that kiss, and she felt the first of a well spring of hot tears come to her eyes. She wasn't sure if she was crying over Kyle Windstone or the man he used to be.

She convinced herself that the feelings she had for Kyle weren't hers. They belonged to someone else, a person from some other time, and she was only able to remember the intensity of them now because of the unexpected vision. Regardless, the pain she felt was real and she had never felt anything like it in her life.

Earlier she mentioned to Kyle that she'd never been in love before. She knew that was true now with complete certainty. Memories of real, amazing, and apparently undying love were now a part of her.

Abby didn't bother getting under the covers. Instead she lay there, curling her body into a ball and allowing the few silent tears to fall.

CHAPTER EIGHT

Whitestone Village, Midsummer, 1577 BCE

Aislynn was anxious, expectant, and far too sick of waiting. She had waited long enough for this day to come. Finally, after more than three years, he was coming home. The thought sent a flutter through her limbs, easing the anxiety that had made her slightly jumpy for most of the last month. As summer approached and the daylight grew, so too did the weight of Aislynn's anticipation. She hated waiting.

She was terrified in many ways. Would he still be the same boy who had tossed stones into the pond and taught her to watch the ripples, to listen to the sound the water made as it swallowed the stone? Would he be the same boy who had listened to trees, and communed with spirits only he could see? Would he still hold that mystery in his eyes and whisper nature's riddles to her under the moon?

Had the priests been able to change him so that she would no longer recognize his smile, the melody of his laughter? Had he forgotten the joy they had brought each other? Would he still want her? No, it didn't matter, she thought. She would make him want her again if she must. He was hers, always had been. She would never let him go without a fight.

It was Midsummer, the time when day and night were perfectly balanced and the sun and moon were equals in the sky. The priests were coming in from the cove to preside over the rites, to light the fires the way it had been done for generations.

Midsummer was a time to celebrate and a time to beckon the crops for a good harvest in the fall. It was a time of feasting and fertility. As such, it was a time when men and women came together in the night, to learn the secrets of each other's touch and promise themselves for the next year.

It was the women who made the choice, who took the men into the fields to lie under the stars. Of course the decision must be a mutual one. No man could be chosen by a woman he didn't want. Many a Midsummer had resulted in tears of rejection and the sorrow of unrequited love. Aislynn prayed she would not be added to those ranks.

The other maidens who would be attending the rites for the first time had been discussing their choices for weeks. Aislynn's friend, Deirna, was currently pondering the boys of the village, appraising each of them like livestock at the market.

"Lairim is of age this year as well," Deirna said. Her blue eyes glazed over slightly, reflecting the last moments of daylight from above. "And he has lovely arms. I think I could stand them around me for the next year." She laughed, tucked a stray hair behind her ear.

"Fine choice," Aislynn said, smiling politely. She glanced at Lairim for a moment. He was strong, stood proud on his young legs. But he was nothing compared to the man she was waiting for.

"Yes, and it's not as though we're saying forever. By next Midsummer I could choose another to take into my mother's home. Perhaps his brother, Ryell. He'll come of age next spring. But I think Lairim might make a good partner for now. Plus, he could give my mother the grandchild she wants."

Aislynn smiled. She wasn't thinking about babies and her mother had passed to the next world two summers before. Being an only child, and a daughter at that, the family home now belonged to her.

Aislynn had been the only daughter of an only daughter. There were no uncles, no father to help tend to her modest home. Her father had been a priest who had chosen to return to the cove after the Summer Rites and Aislynn's mother had taken other lovers over the years.

Such was the way things were done. But not for Aislynn. If her priest would not stay with her she would take no other lover. She would live alone in her thatched roof house waiting eagerly for each Midsummer to come around. Even if she began to starve or if the walls came crumbling down around her, she would touch no other man. But she prayed he wouldn't return to the cove. He was a man now and he had a choice. The priests could not decide for him anymore, could not sweep him away from her like they had before.

Aislynn and her priest had been born on the same day and had grown up together in the village. At the age of five he had brought her piles of daisies and sat with her by the pond to string them together the way their mothers had taught them. He told stories, even then, speaking of the land, the cycles of the moon, and the positions of the stars. Always he had known about the mysteries, as if he was born with the wisdom of the ages behind his young eyes.

At the age of nine he was spending more time with the other boys, learning to fight and hunt with his brothers. Aislynn had missed him, but still every so often a daisy would be waiting for her, tucked within the crack around her door, or sitting on the ledge outside her window. And when the other boys weren't looking, he would send her a smile. It was a smile he reserved only for her.

By the time adolescence was upon them their relationship changed again. His stolen glances became more frequent, more purposeful. They were miles away from the village, watching the sea crash upon the jagged rocks, when he kissed her for the first time. It was a pure kiss, full of hope and wonder.

Tentatively, and with great innocence, their lips had touched, introducing them both to feelings they had never known before. Even in that small instant there had been something between them, something untouchable and unexplainable. That was the moment Aislynn knew he would be her husband, and not just for a year but for eternity.

Days before their fifteenth birthday he was taken from her. The priests had come from the cove to celebrate the first harvest and seen something in the boy. Claiming that his purpose was a grand one, they ushered him off to their sanctuary to study the ancient ways of the land and the gods that lived within it. Three years had passed and Aislynn had missed him every day. He had been her best friend. Even when he was busy being a boy, he had never completely left her.

"Aislynn," Deirna said. "The sun is low. It's time to go."

Aislynn almost ran, but held herself back. Slowly she turned towards where she knew the circle of stone lay beyond. Goose flesh covered her arms, excitement slipping down into her toes.

Deirna locked her arm around Aislynn's, giggling to herself. "Are you nervous?"

"Only a little." She was nervous, but not because this was her last night as a maiden. She was nervous because she was afraid he would not accept her hand. Could there be another girl who would catch his eye?

Aislynn was not the most beautiful girl in the village. She knew that she was plain compared to some, but still her mother had always told her there was something special about her eyes. Her mother had said any man would want to know what lay within their mossy depths. Aislynn wasn't quite that confident. After all, mothers were always fond of their children's beauty.

As they approached the circle, Deirna's giggles only increased, but Aislynn was suddenly solemn. The priests were gathering in the center, preparing the ritual space with smoke and water from the sea. Immediately she saw him. His back was too her, one arm filled with a pitcher of ocean. She trembled unconsciously, tightening her arm around Deirna's.

"Is that Callum?" Deirna asked. "My, he's grown, hasn't he?" When Aislynn only continued to stare, Deirna patted her friend's hand. "Everyone knows he's yours Aislynn. You two have always been made for each other. Don't worry. You'll get no competition here. Besides, he's only ever had his sights on you. He will accept no other."

Aislynn trembled again. Gods, she hoped Deirna was right. She couldn't bare it if he chose another. She feared she would ruin the celebration with a fit of rage if he did.

The ritual began as the night caressed the land. Fires were lit and gods were honored. Aislynn didn't hear the prayers for her thoughts never left Callum.

She watched him move around the circle, saw that he now carried himself with the confidence of a man. Each step of his long legs was deliberate, practiced. She watched him, noted the thin beard that had grown in over his chin, the way his dark hair curled just behind his ears. He had grown tall, so much taller than she. The top half of him was bare with only the necklaces of a priest to fall upon his chest. His body had become stronger, lean with muscle.

The ritual ended, the drumming began, and Aislynn watched him still. His fire-lit eyes scanned the crowd around the circle, searching. He ran a hand through his hair, appeared to sigh with slight frustration.

The rhythm of the drums entered her, echoed through her body. Something stirred, broke open within her until she felt a rush of determination tighten her limbs, straighten her spine. Finally, she could wait no longer.

She approached him from behind, stood only inches from his back and took in the scent of the smoke on his skin. She brushed her fingers along his knuckles, tentatively touching him for the first time as a woman. He tightened, started to turn. Aislynn latched her hand into his, felt their fingers come together like two halves of single broken stone.

When he turned there were no words on his tongue, only a look of relief lighting his face. His eyes, so like her own, danced like the flames of the fire. They locked onto hers, soaked her in as though he were dying of thirst.

He opened his mouth to speak and Aislynn suddenly felt another stirring in her bones. His bottom lip trembled ever so slightly, and his words stuck in his throat. Before he could gain his composure she stood on her toes and reached for his face. With fierceness and passion she brought her mouth to his.

He kissed her back with his own longing, nearly sending her off her feet. His arms crushed her too him, one hand holding the side of her face as though to never let her go.

It took a combined effort to pull away so they could walk out of the circle and into the privacy of the night. Barefoot, they moved into a clearing, dropped to their knees and found each other's mouths again. The stars blinked above them and the moon watched over, giving them her brightest blessing.

As they lay together in the tall grasses, Aislynn was taken to a lovely place where she could remember only one word. "Callum."

CHAPTER NINE

Wednesday, December 19th 2012, 7:24am

Kyle stirred awake much later in the morning than he had wanted to. Having drank too much the night before on top of being given a migraine that would bring down an eight hundred pound gorilla, he had the hangover from hell.

As he lay in bed he knew a headache was the least of his current worries. Nothing a few ibuprofen wouldn't fix. But there would be no little yellow pill to stop the big bad apocalypse demon that was about to show up at his front door. And now Kyle Windstone, Kansas farmer, was suddenly supposed to be some kind of reincarnated magic man.

When he had touched Abby the night before he had known it would change them both in some way. Very specifically, he had known it would significantly change him and there would be no way to get back to the person he was before. Even though the vision they shared explained their connection, he still wasn't sure what to do with it. He also wasn't sure he was willing to face the feelings that came along with it.

Slowly he got out of bed and threw on the first pair of jeans he found on his bedroom floor. He stopped in front of the door to the spare room and listened for movement. After a few seconds of nothing but silence he pushed the door open a little and looked in on Abby's sleeping face.

Reincarnation wasn't a concept he really had a hard time believing in. The idea had always made sense to him. Everything was based on cycles. After all, when summer was over you could count on it coming back the very next year; same bat-time, same bat-channel. Nothing in the natural world ever seemed to come to an end. Why would the soul be any different?

As he watched her sleep he couldn't help but think about crawling into bed next to her, pulling her tight into his chest, and dreaming with her for a few more hours. The end of the world could wait.

With their first touch had come all the knowledge of another time, complete with all of the joy and sorrow that came with sharing a life together. He remembered all of the beauty they had experienced; the birth of their love, their children, and everything in between. The details were so stark that he felt as though it had been only yesterday. But he also remembered losing her, watching her die slowly after they had survived the Destroyer's initial onslaught. He hadn't been able to save her or their family.

The image came to him now from a well guarded section of his mind. He saw her lifeless in his arms, her face taking on the shadow of death. A sick wave passed through him and he involuntarily shuddered. She was his and he had never belonged to another. He knew that deep down, but he had no idea how to deal with it.

Thoughts raced like little stock cars around his head. He knew he wanted to be near her and that seeing her face gave him a simple sense of peace. Beyond that there was the physical pull. Those feelings he found easier to accept. Acting on the things he felt was a totally different matter all together. Though keeping that first kiss in a few hundred lifetimes out of his mind was not going to be easy.

Abby was a distraction. He needed to stay away from her as much as possible. There were more important things to worry about and he wouldn't allow himself to fail. Not again.

There was work that needed doing and watching Abby sleep was not only bordering on the edge of creepy, but it also wasn't getting anything done. He closed the door silently and headed downstairs to start his morning.

Kyle was standing in the kitchen pouring his first cup of coffee, still wearing only a pair of faded old jeans, when he heard Abby padding down the stairs. Shit, he thought. He had hoped to be showered and out the door before she woke up. He kept his back to her as she walked into the kitchen.

"Good morning."

He felt his heart wrench a little at the sound of her sleep softened voice. He clenched his eyes and resisted the urge to look at her. He could almost feel her eyes wandering up the bare flesh of his back, over his shoulders and arms where matching black tattooed bands wrapped around each of his biceps. His skin grew hot. I should've put on a damn shirt, he thought.

"Good morning." He walked to the table and set down his mug of hot coffee. "There's diet coke in the fridge."

"Thanks. Listen about last night..."

Kyle lifted a hand. "I'm fine now. Just a headache."

Abby frowned, spoke softly. "Oh. Okay."

He dared to look her in the eye for a fraction of a second. Big mistake. Confused rejection registered across her features making his brow crease in self loathing. He watched as she bit her lip and looked away.

Damn it, he cursed himself. Maybe he was playing it a little too cool. He didn't want to hurt her, but he worried that it might be inevitable. He couldn't allow her to think they were fated to be a couple because of what they had experienced the night before.

Kyle knew he needed to keep his head clear. He wouldn't allow himself to make mistakes this time. Being near Abby in a physical way would make it difficult enough for him to think straight. He needed to push her away emotionally as nicely as he could manage.

He sipped his coffee casually, kept his mug in front of his mouth as he spoke. "I'm going into town. There's a list of things that could still use doing. We're running short on time."

Abby just nodded her head slightly and let her eyes drift out the window to the odd reddish colored sky beyond. Kyle took another sip of his heavily creamed coffee, feeling the mild burn of the liquid on his tongue, and tried unsuccessfully not to look at her mouth or remember how it felt under his own. He didn't know what to say to her just then but he knew exactly what he wanted to say.

He wanted to tell her that he had been so taken with her on the night they met that he had felt compelled to scrawl out flowery stanzas of poetry, one after the other. He wanted to take her hand and tell her what he knew in his heart to be true – that they were connected and fate had indeed brought them together. But that's not what he said.

"There's a bathroom upstairs that's all yours. I'll shower down here." He knew it was a dismissal, but she smelled like a vanilla cake he desperately wanted to sink his teeth into.

Abby moved to walk up the stairs then stopped herself with her back turned to him. Kyle thanked multiple gods that he couldn't see the hurt in her eyes anymore.

"I dreamt of us last night, of who we used to be." Her voice was quiet yet clear and Kyle thought he may have even heard a touch of anger. "I know what I saw and I know who we are." She took another step away, stopped again. "Your name was Callum and I was the woman you loved." With that she continued up the stairs.

Kyle stood barefoot on the stone tiled kitchen floor, staring blankly at the coffee cup in his hand. Hearing his name – or what used to be his name – on her lips had left his heart thudding in his chest. He hadn't expected to hear it, but his soul remembered the sound.

He took a breath and set the mug down with a bang. He forced the fog from his mind, exhaled. There was no time for notions of past lives and soul mates. Before the Destroyer came calling, he had to make it in to town for some last minute provisions.

* * *

A little over a half an hour later Kyle was making his way through Clover Lake. What had once been a quaint Kansas town, complete with people walking their dogs and gathering about the local ice cream parlor, had become little more than a vacant lot. Kyle didn't see a soul as he scanned the streets for signs of life. A few of the shops were boarded up along Main Street and even the fire hall seemed closed for business.

He hadn't watched the news for days, maybe even weeks. He didn't need to. The visions in his head were enough for him to keep up on current events. He certainly didn't need to check out the widespread panic in high definition widescreen complete with stereo surround sound. It was obvious that by now everyone on Earth was pretty aware of what was going down. Even if they didn't know the details, the human race was famous for embracing a good apocalypse. Rumors alone would be enough to keep everyone cloistered in their homes and close to their loved ones.

With the shops boarded up or on lock down Kyle figured he was going to have to do some good old fashioned looting. He wasn't crazy about the idea, but he didn't really have a choice either. Besides, he didn't have a problem leaving money for what he took. Not that those pieces of paper were going to do anyone any good after today, but it would ease his conscience a little.

His first stop was the local grocery store. Surprisingly he found the doors unlocked and they slid open easily as he walked towards them. Though Clover Lake was a small town, the grocery store was a fairly large mom and pop production. The ceilings of the place were warehouse high and all but a few of the large overhead lights were off. This gave the place a creepy vibe that made Kyle feel slightly anxious as he let his eyes adjust to the dimness.

He looked around at the shelves to see most of them were empty or littered with random food items. He grabbed two reusable shopping bags from a rack and started shopping.

He found boxes of breakfast cereal down isle four, a few bags of oyster crackers on isle six, a ton of dry rice, cans of sweetened condensed milk, and tins of mandarin oranges on isle seven There was even a bunch of gorgeous, ripe yellow bananas misplaced in the dairy section. While he was there he grabbed the last package of butter and stashed it in his bag. Might come in handy, he thought. Plus it could be stored at room temperature for a little while without going bad.

He made a stop to pick up some toilet paper and found only tissues. Better than nothing, he figured. While he was at it he swiped up all the baby wipes he could find and fit them in his bags.

Kyle was rounding the corner of the frozen foods section when he heard something fall near the ice cream coolers and echo through the empty building. A tingle ran up and down his spine causing him to turn just in time to see a shotgun barrel pointing between his eyes.

"Jesus Christ," Kyle breathed, staring head on into the muzzle.

"That's my food you're stealin' son." The man behind the weapon was older and could only be described as grizzly.

Kyle didn't recognize him. He wasn't the owner of the grocery store, that much was for sure. The man in front of him looked to be in his mid-sixties. He was short with a full head of greasy, grey hair and an overgrown beard. Kyle knew the owner of the store, Mr. Hawkins well enough and this man didn't look a thing like him. He decided it was best not to point that fact out.

The gunman continued. "I've made my claim on this place and I don't take kindly to looters."

Oh shit, Kyle thought. This guy was staking claim to the grocery store like he'd just landed on the New World with a flag. The man was off his nut and Kyle imagined there would be no way to talk sense with someone like that. So he resorted to bribery instead.

"Oh, I'm not looting." Kyle kept his voice even and calm. "If you wouldn't mind taking the twelve gauge out of my face I could pay you for what I took."

The old man looked Kyle up and down, probably trying to access whether or not Kyle was a rich man. After a long moment the man finally lowered the rifle to the floor, leaning it against the row of coolers.

"Sounds fine." The old mad smiled, showing yellowing teeth. "And I'll take that jacket you're wearin' too."

"Okay that's good. Sounds like a fair trade to me." Kyle carefully set down his bags and pulled his wallet from his back pocket. He found two hundred dollars within the folds of black leather and handed it to the man. The older man inched closer and snatched the money from Kyle like the bills were a steak and he was a starving dog. But he wasn't fast enough.

Kyle took a hold of the man's upper arm and dragged him away from the gun easily, slamming his back into the wall with a thud. The old man's reflexes were no match for someone at least thirty years younger. Kyle looked down at his assailant with a disapproving glance before walking over to grab the rifle. He popped the barrel open, saw that it was loaded, and slammed it closed again.

"Sorry buddy, but I'm going to take your gun. You can have the money and this too." Kyle slipped his jacket off and tossed it. "But I'm not going to let you shoot someone in the face over a bottle of apple juice and a box of saltines." With that Kyle wandered out of the grocery store carrying a full bag in each hand and a loaded shotgun slung over his back.

"If this place has a basement, get in it and stay there!" Kyle yelled over his shoulder before stepping away to let the automatic doors close behind him.

Well that was interesting, he thought to himself. Just a few more stops and then back to the farm before lunch time. He was counting on the morning being productive for his three companions and trusted that all the preparations were complete. He was hoping the time they had left above ground would be mostly free of work. He had no intention of spending his last days of normalcy moving supplies into a bomb shelter.

CHAPTER TEN

Wednesday, December 19th 2012, 11:47am

Abby had been in a foul mood all morning, snapping one minute and silently pouting the next. Jim had noticed her unpredictable temperament and politely given her some space. Alex, on the other hand, was looking for a good fight.

"What's the matter Abbs?" Alex stacked boxes of MREs on the back bunks of the sleeping area as he taunted her. "New guy couldn't do it for you last night? Didn't he measure up, push all the right buttons?"

His grin was crude, making Abby want to punch him in the face until his perfect nose flattened out. Instead she simply unleashed some well deserved venom on him.

"Actually Alex, I'm just feeling a little worn out today." She tried to make her voice sound chipper. "New Guy, as you so cleverly called him, is a real champion in the sack."

Alex's grin faded. "You're so full of shit."

"Okay then. Just thought you'd be interested in hearing about the best time I've ever had in my entire life. It was amazing. I can barely function today. I'm not upset in the least. Just can't stop thinking about that huge..."

"Enough." Alex put up his hand. "I'm good. Don't need to hear another word."

"Fine." The forced glee left her voice. "Then get back to work and for the love of everything that is holy please shut your mouth. If you don't I'll let Jimmy wrap that roll of duct tape around your head and shut it for you."

Alex glanced behind him, through the open curtain and into the living area where Abby's uncle was inspecting the sink pipes. Jim tossed a roll of duct tape between his hands and raised an eyebrow. As Alex looked the older man in the eye, Jim twirled the silver tape around his fingers and nodded seriously.

"Great. Just my luck to get stuck in an underground chamber with a couple of crazy Connelly's. You Irish people should really learn to relax more. Drink some whiskey or eat a potato or something."

The loud sound of duct tape being pulled from the roll echoed through the bunker making Alex jump. "Okay okay. I'm done. I'll shut up."

But he wasn't done. Alex gestured to Abby to come with him to the far corner of the bunk area. He kept his voice low. "Seriously, just answer a few questions for me."

Abby sighed heavily. "I'm not going to go in to detail for you Alex. What I do is none of your business."

He gestured for her to be quiet. "Stop. I'm trying to be your friend here. Sorry I was an ass. I don't have to like that we're no longer a couple, but that doesn't mean I'm not going to worry about you. I'm just trying to understand what's going on between you and the farmer." His face held genuine concern. "Why are you so upset? Really?"

Abby felt the tension in her muscles relax a little and her shoulders fell. It was then that it all came out. Words gushed from her mouth like a raging river until she was close to tears.

"Wait a minute. Let me get this straight. You knew him in a past life? And you know this because you had a vision – a shared vision? With him?"

Abby nodded sadly. "We were together then and I was so... in love with him."

Alex looked at the wall in thought. "Huh. This all makes so much more sense now."

"What are you talking about?"

He almost laughed. "You've known each other for like a day but I never had a chance anyway. This thing between you and what's-his-face is apparently a whole lot bigger than I thought." His laughter came then. "I thought you were trying to get back at me by screwing around with him."

"No. I wouldn't do that." She stopped, considering the thought. "Well I might, but there's a lot more than physical attraction at work here."

"I should hope so." She glared and he continued. "Seriously Abbs. What's with those eyebrows? If we make it through to Christmas he's getting some tweezers in his stocking."

"Just because you don't go anywhere without hair product..."

"That's another thing. He should really do something about that hair. He just lets it lay there on top of his head..."

"Sheesh, you've been spending a whole lot of time looking at the guy. Do you want to date him?"

Alex scoffed. "I was just sizing up my competition, that's all."

"Well it's like you said. You never had a chance." She sighed. "I've never felt anything like this before in my life."

"He's your strawberry sauce." He continued when Abby sent him a questioning glance. "It's not a boy meets girl thing. It's a boy finds girl again after a really long time apart. Then boom. Love at first sight."

Abby looked at him, shock registering on her face. She had never heard Alex talk that way before and the sudden romantic standing before her was someone new.

Alex appeared almost serene. "Don't you see what this means? All that stuff is real. It's not just fairy tales and movies. It's actually a reality."

"Wait, I don't want to get ahead of myself. Yes, I feel something for him, something... well fierce, but that doesn't mean I'm planning on walking down the aisle any time soon. Past lives or not. The present is still the present."

"Yeah, but there's hope now." His voice softened. "Hope for everyone else and maybe even for guys like me."

Abby let his words sink in and felt a rush of realization. The hope Alex spoke of filled old voids inside of her, tucked its way into places she had never known were empty.

He touched her arm. "I won't get in the way anymore. I'm here for you." An impish smile crossed his lips. "Just don't lose my number in case it doesn't work out between you two."

She punched his shoulder companionably. "Very funny. By the way, when did we become girlfriends? You're the last person I would've thought I'd be talking about guys with."

He smiled. "Somewhere between a purple bra and the end of the world."

She returned his smile and the conversation ended as the sound of a car door slamming came from above ground. The three of them made their way to the surface to see Kyle walking towards the bunker.

At the sight of him Abby felt her stomach do a somersault and her hands began to tremble ever so slightly. She could barely stand to be near him, to look at him at all. It was like staring into the sun. How long could she stand it before she went blind or got burned? The better question was whether or not she was willing to risk it.

On one hand she was completely overcome with emotions that made her want to leap into his arms and go to bed with him. No, it was more than that, she reminded herself. It was more than attraction. On the other hand, she wanted to beat his ass for pretending like she didn't mean anything to him when she knew damn well that she did. She had seen that he cared for her, felt it in the vision. For a split second she considered trying to hunt down her prescription. She was feeling a touch bi-polar and numbness was starting to sound pretty good.

"Find some good stuff in town?" Jim called out as Kyle approached.

"Yeah, not bad. There were still some things left at the grocery store, though it was well guarded. I managed to get some goodies and walk away with a shot gun all for two hundred bucks."

Jim managed a smile. "Sounds like an interesting day. You'll have to tell me the details later."

Abby stood in place quietly examining her hands. The awkward silence was thick enough to touch. She could feel Kyle's eyes on her. And Alex's too.

Jim broke the silence. "Well we took care of the list and I can't think of much else that needs doing in the bunker."

"Okay that's great. I have a couple more projects to take care of today but you guys should grab some lunch and relax."

"Are you sure? If you need a hand or something I don't mind."

"No, really. I can handle it. Take some time to yourself. Watch a movie, play with Bo and Daisy or whatever makes you happy. I've got it under control."

* * *

After a sparse lunch of an apple and a glass of milk, Abby wandered into Kyle's living room. His books lined the shelves along the back wall, a mix of old literature, poetry, and modern paperbacks. As she checked the spines she realized she had read next to none of them. There were volumes by Joyce, Keats, Yeats, Kerouac, Poe; all alphabetized in perfect order.

She found The Poems of Oscar Wilde on the coffee table, absorbed a page, put it down again. She was too anxious to read. She was an artist and when artists needed a quick outlet they picked up the nearest drawing utensil. So she sat down on the porch of the Blue House with a diet coke and her trusty sketch book.

She could see the Yellow House from her spot on Kyle's porch and watched as her uncle ran around with the dogs in the yard, tossing a tennis ball in the grass for each of them. Alex was nowhere to be seen and was most likely sitting inside watching anything he could get to come in on the television and sucking down a cold beer.

Abby could also see Kyle, at least when he wasn't working inside the barn. She could hear the horses from where she was and the cluck of the chickens in their coop. Every now and again the sound of muffled hammering came from inside the barn. She had no idea what Kyle was doing in there but she was sure he had his reasons. Just like he had his reasons for avoiding her and for pretending like she didn't exist.

When she had walked into the kitchen that morning to see him shirtless and drinking coffee, she had hoped his attitude from the night before had only been because he was in pain. She had expected he would see that the two of their destinies were connected, that their souls were linked in a way that was bigger than them both. Was it so much to ask for him to acknowledge that? She wasn't asking for him to profess his undying love or anything. Their present situation was not the same. They were different people, but once upon a time they had been in love. He knew it and it drove her to the point of insane that he pretended he didn't.

Abby bit her lip in frustration and turned to her drawing with a huff. Her pencil moved furiously over the blank page, quickly sketching out the barn and the Yellow House beyond it and all the way to the road. She added in the unfinished General, her Jeep, Jimmy's truck, and Kyle's too. She looked up every few minutes to check the scene and get the details right.

She made an annoyed sound, tossed her pencil into the bushes, and stood. The drawing was crap and she was just too irritated to sit still. She needed to talk to Kyle.

When Abby entered the barn through the wide double doors she saw Kyle standing in front of the stall of a brown mare. The horse's head dipped down into his waiting hands as he patted the side of her face and stroked her black mane.

Abby studied him with eyes that were at once curious about the man he was yet acutely aware of the nature of his soul.

"Hi." She approached him, leaning up to rub the mare's ears. The horse turned from Kyle, sniffed at Abby's palm and lipped her outstretched fingers.

Kyle's face was blank though Abby could see something like struggle in his eyes. "Hi."

"I was hoping we could talk about what happened last night without you avoiding eye contact." He raised a thick eyebrow, glanced at her sideways before putting some distance between them and stepping to the next horse's stall.

She grinned slightly and tried to be casual. "So I guess this means you're still treating me like a leper?"

Kyle kept his attention on Bucky, an older gelding Abby's mother had always had a special fondness for. Abby remembered the horse well and smiled in memory as she waited for Kyle to say something. He pulled a piece of carrot from his jeans pocket and fed it to the horse. The simple action had Abby fighting to keep her steely composure.

Bucky nipped at the band of the thick black leather watch on Kyle's wrist but Kyle didn't seem to notice. He didn't bother to look at her when he finally spoke. "I don't know what you want me to say."

Abby took a few steps toward him, smiling at Bucky as the horse flashed her one big eye. "Say what's on your mind. It's easy. I do it all the time, often when I should be shutting up." She tried to laugh at herself, hoping to lighten his mood. "Why is it so hard for you to talk to me?"

He didn't answer, refused to look at her.

"Kyle please." She stepped closer. "Cal..."

His eyes locked onto hers, an angry fire burning within. "My name is Kyle Devon Windstone. I was born in 1983. I am a farmer. I will not be held to anything else." He ran a hand through his already messy hair, relaxed his jaw. "There's no time for this. We have things to do and we have to stay focused if we want to survive."

Abby planted her feet. "I'm not leaving until you talk to me."

He groaned quietly and turned pained eyes on her. "I can't talk to you. A big part of me wants to, but I'm not ready for this... whatever it is. I'm not comfortable giving myself away so easily, especially when I feel like none of this was a choice I made. Christ, we just met two days ago Abby. Whoever we are... were... it's too fast and it's not normal."

"I don't care what's normal. I know what I feel and I can't just turn it off like you can. I don't have a switch I can flip on and off."

"I'm not flipping a switch. I'm trying to be sensible. There are more important things to worry about."

"Sensible?" She laughed, threw her hands up in the air. "Since when does any of this make sense? Please Kyle, there's a reason we're both here and it's not just about the end of the world."

"I can't do this and worry about surviving at the same time. I can't be near you..."

"Why?" She took a step closer. "I don't understand why I'm so terrible. I'm sorry about the headache last night. I won't touch you again if that's what you're worried about."

He leaned his back against the stall, shoved his hands deep into his pockets. Bucky nudged his human friend's chin affectionately.

Locking eyes with her again, he continued. "I can't be near you because I lose my focus, get distracted."

"What does that mean? I don't understand."

He sighed, ran a hand through his hair again. "I get distracted not because I'm worried about another headache, but because I would live through it again just to kiss you one more time."

His words and intense gaze made her feel dizzy. She closed her eyes for a moment and exhaled deeply. She knew then that he felt the same things she did. But why was he fighting it?

With her eyes still closed a terrible thought entered her mind completely uninvited. A tingling sensation slithered over her skin. It was the same feeling she had experienced on the highway, just before huge boulders started tumbling down the mountain side and crushing cars. Her eyes flew open, snapping to Kyle with urgency.

"Everyone needs to get underground." Kyle said the words without anything from Abby.

They made it to the door when Abby stopped. "Kyle, the horses."

He stole a look at Bucky. "There's nothing we can do. We have to move."

She nodded, said a silent prayer for the horses and ran.

The two of them raced through the barn doors and up to the Yellow House. Abby's foot caught an uneven spot of ground sending her stumbling slightly from her feet. Kyle reached down and grabbed her upper arm to steady her, accidently brushing two fingers against the skin of her elbow.

Abby's breath came in sharply as information flashed through her head. "We don't have much time. We have to go now."

Kyle looked confused. Obviously he was not getting the same insight into the situation as Abby was. But there was no time to explain.

"Connelly!" Kyle yelled, waving his hands as they neared the house. "Let's go man. Into the shelter now."

Jim spread his arms out to his sides in question. "No time." Kyle was moving fast now, his long legs spanning two of Abby's steps. "Gather up the Dukes and head into the bunker as quick as you can."

Clouds started gathering overhead much quicker than anything Abby had ever seen before. "We have to move faster." She scanned the area. "Alex! Let's go!"

Her shout was directed towards the house from where Alex came running with a terrified look on his face. "Is it happening?"

Abby yelled up to where he stood on the porch. "Something's coming this way. We need to be in that bomb shelter before it gets here."

Alex didn't ask any questions, just started moving towards the hatch to get underground along with everyone else. He would be the last one she would have to worry about acting like a hero.

The four of them hovered over the shelter, opened the hatch, and started climbing down one at a time. Abby waved away the hands who tried to get her in first. She was not a fragile doll. It was her vision that was guiding them and she wouldn't be treated like a silly girl who needed to be looked after.

They were lowering Bo into the hatch when Jim yelled out. "Is Daisy up there with you?"

Kyle and Abby were still above ground and both of them began to search the farm with their eyes.

Kyle looked down the hatch at Jim. "We'll find her. Stay down there. No matter what happens."

Abby grabbed his shirt with a light yank. "Let's split up, cover more ground."

Kyle nodded and they were off, sprinting in different directions.

Abby went straight to the barn to search for the dog, running as fast as her legs would take her. The wind was picking up at a furious pace and the sky was now a strange mixture of red light and deep, black clouds.

As she came out through the barn doors empty handed the first tornado touched down behind her. She felt her feet come off the ground and the wind whipped her limbs around wildly. She was thrown hard against the panels of the barn and collapsed with a thud on the ground. The horses whinnied from within and she could hear their hooves hitting the ground in panic.

It took a moment to recover her breath. When she was back on her feet Abby suddenly found herself surrounded on all sides by twisters. There were two smaller funnels whipping in from the west, one from the east, another pair in the south, and a giant whirlwind heading towards her from the north. For a moment she was completely frozen, stuck within a mixture of awe and terror. Then everything went black and still.

* * *

Kyle found Daisy cowering beneath Jim's porch, panting and scared out of her little mind. "Come on Daisy girl." He was careful to use a gentle tone with her. "Everyone's waiting for you." He scooped her up into his arms tenderly and began hauling her towards the shelter.

He was lowering the dog down to a grateful Jim when he realized Abby wasn't in the shelter and a huge tornado had just touched down towards the north. Glancing around him he saw four more in the other directions moving in fast. A sick feeling tumbled through his body, making sweat instantly break out on his brow.

"Jim, is she down there with you?"

"No, she hasn't made it back yet. I thought you were together."

"Shit." Kyle moved his eyes along the land, searching for any sign of Abby. "Stay here. I'm going to find her."

Kyle just ran. Fear and desperation invaded him, slipping over his limbs and down into his gut. The thought of Abby being hurt or worse absolutely horrified him on a level he had never experienced before in his present life. She had to be okay. They deserved another chance. Damn it, Kyle wanted that chance.

He didn't think about where he was going, but headed straight to the area behind the barn. Something was guiding him and he knew exactly where to look.

When he found her she was knocked out cold, a piece of the corral fence wedged under her body. The wound on her head looked superficial but there was still enough blood to make him worry. He bent down and gathered up her small, limp frame easily into his arms. She stirred, lifted her head, and opened her eyes to look at him.

"It's okay. You were knocked out, but I've got you." He looked around, trying to plot out the best course to the shelter. Tornadoes still raged through the acres surrounding the farm and debris floated through the air at bullet like speeds. He pressed her head to his chest. "Try to keep your head down and against me."

Abby was obviously out of it. As Kyle carried her through the obstacle course of airborne fence posts and chunks of loose rock, she smiled almost drunkenly. He looked down at her and couldn't help but return the smile with one of his own.

"We're almost there." He raised his voice over the sound of the rapid winds. "You're going to be okay."

"I know." Her voice was quiet, barely audible over the sounds around them. But Kyle heard her clearly.

He felt the warm skin of her back under his arm where her shirt was pulled up and he felt her hands wrapped tightly around his neck. Even amid chaos and destruction there was still a kinetic spark that moved between them. But there were no uninvited visions and no stabbing headaches.

They made it to the shelter without further injury or incident. Kyle quickly hauled

Abby down the hatch before closing the door above him tight. Jim immediately carried his niece to one of the bunks in the back and laid her down gently.

Alex looked at Kyle almost accusingly. "Is she going to be okay? What good are your stupid visions if people still get hurt?"

Kyle grabbed Alex's shoulder and leaned in so their eyes were level. "Hey, she's fine. Just a bump on the head. She needs a couple hours of rest then she'll be on her feet again." His tone was calm. He couldn't fault the other man for caring.

Alex breathed a sigh of relief and went into the sleeping area to check on Abby. Kyle followed him but stood outside the curtained door.

He could hear Jim talking quietly as he cleaned the head wound with fresh water. "Oh, it's only a small cut. Nothing serious. She's fine."

Kyle peeked in and watched as Alex leaned over to observe Abby's wound for himself. He was so relieved that she was alright he thought he might actually break down. He needed a second to get himself together, to put on a strong front once again before facing the other men.

"Hey Abby, it's me Alex. Can you hear me?"

Abby's eyes flew open and she tried to sit up in the bed. Her head swung from side to side madly. "Where's Kyle?"

"Hush, lie back. You need your rest." Alex attempted to push her back down into the bed, but she fought him even in her wounded state.

"Where is he? Is he okay? Did he find the dog?" There was a touch of panic in her voice as she scanned the eyes of the men above her.

"I'm here." Kyle stepped through the curtain. "I'm alright and so is Daisy."

He saw the relief play over her face, watched the light within her brighten. He kept his eyes fixed on hers for a moment, hoping she might be able to sense how he felt. Kyle had a few answers now, understood some things better. He knew suddenly that together they were stronger. And there was no way that didn't mean something.

It was only by touching him that she was able to garnish more information about the tornadoes and warn everyone that they were coming so quickly. And he had felt her dread before she could speak it. When their eyes had met he sensed right away that something bad was about to happen.

They were connected for a reason and he wanted to carry out that purpose, no longer fighting what he inherently knew was meant to be. Yes it was fast. Yes he was scared. But none of that mattered when he looked into her eyes.

Jim touched his niece's shoulder gently. "Kyle carried you back to the shelter. Don't you remember, Kiddo?"

"It's kind of fuzzy right now, but it's clearing up a little. I think I was knocked out by a flying piece of wood or something." She paused, thinking back. "I remember being carried into the shelter but I wasn't sure if that was real or not."

"It was real." Kyle smiled at her then looked away to the other men. "I think we should wait it out for an hour or so then check to see if it's all clear. Tornadoes are short lived. Well usually anyway. Not sure what to expect right now. Hopefully we can get up top before nightfall. We still have to pack up our clothes and things before we're stuck in here."

Alex nodded emphatically. "Yeah, fresh underwear is a good thing. Plus I need my toothbrush, my gel, my cologne."

Jim looked up from the blood stained cloth in his hand. "I hate to break it to you Alex, but if I have to smell you bathed in that shitty cologne of yours for the next month or so in these tight quarters, I'm going to beat you silly with something blunt and heavy."

Abby laughed. "Seriously Alex. It's the apocalypse. No one's going to care if you smell like designer fragrances or not."

"Okay, point taken. No cologne. How about skin care stuff? You don't keep a face like this without a daily regime."

The other three rolled their eyes with a simultaneous groan.

"What? Everyone should moisturize."

CHAPTER ELEVEN

Wednesday, December 19th 2012, 5:15pm

Surprisingly, the tornadoes hadn't left too much damage in their wake. There were missing shingles, destroyed fences, an AWOL chicken or two, and a couple of holes in the roofs. Other than that, the farm was intact.

Kyle had always been fascinated by how that happened. A tornado could rip through a town destroying one home but leave the one beside it completely untouched. Maybe something or someone was smiling down and wanted to give them a break before all hell actually broke loose.

Kyle was grateful for that break and planned on taking advantage of it. It was his last night of life as he had always known it, before everything changed forever. He knew they would all be stuck in a bomb shelter for some time and he wanted everyone to enjoy these last normal moments doing whatever made them happy. Kyle was hoping to spend them with Abby. He was saying just that thing to Jim as they stood in the grass outside the Yellow House. Abby and Alex were packing up, readying whatever they would need to take with them into the shelter when the time came.

"Are you asking my permission to take my niece on a date?"

"Well, not really. I mean, yes I would like to spend some time with her in a date like way tonight, but I'm not really asking for permission. Just thought maybe you should know out of respect."

"Okay. Wait. Are you trying to tell me you're going to have end of the world sex with my sister's daughter?"

Kyle's eyes widened and he shifted on his feet uncomfortably. "Whoa, back that train up buddy. I'm not saying anything about sex. Of course, such things are often the product of two adults spending time together. Especially two people who are attracted to each other. So, I'm not ruling it out as a possibility."

Jim took a breath, looked at Kyle sideways for a long moment. "I can't really blame you I guess." His expression softened. "If I had it my way there would be a woman by my side too. It would make the whole end of days scenario so much more pleasant."

Kyle studied Jim's face. "So you're not upset?"

"No, I'm not upset. If it makes you two happy who am I to say? I'm more jealous than anything. Well, not of you with Abby. That's just weird. You know what I mean."

"Yeah I know what you mean, buddy. So, we're good then?"

Jim nodded. "Yup. All good. But what am I supposed to do with Mr. Hair-Care in there while you guys are doing the romance thing?" Jim gestured towards the house where Alex was probably packing his fancy shampoos and conditioners into his own personal, metro-sexual end of the world survival kit.

"Maybe you could cook up some of that pizza you've got stored in the freezer and watch old reruns all night. Or, to keep you both happy, why not settle him in with the first season of your show? Let him drink a bunch of your beer while you wax all meaningful about the intricate relationships and metaphorical struggles that come with being a Good Ole Boy. That should keep him entertained and you sane."

Jim raised his eyebrows, considering the suggestion. "Not a bad idea. Or I could force him to help me work on the General. Not that he would have any idea what to do. But at least he could hand me a wrench when I needed it."

"Now you're thinking." Kyle put his hand on his friend's shoulder. "Whatever it is you decide to do just make it worthwhile. We've got a limited amount of time left on the surface and everyone should be enjoying themselves whenever possible at this point."

Jim nodded. "Well, have fun on your date. Be a nice guy and treat her right. Because if you don't, I know where you hid that shotgun."

"No you don't." Kyle grinned. "Enjoy your pizza party."

"Yeah, can't wait." Jim sent him a sarcastic smirk before heading towards the Yellow house.

Kyle found Abby napping on his couch with the Poems of Oscar Wilde resting open on her chest. He could see white cords coming from her ears, connected to the green cell phone slash mp3 player that had slipped from her hand onto the cushions. Her mouth was open a bit and her reading glasses had fallen down on her nose an inch. For a moment he debated about whether or not to let her rest but shrugged that idea off quickly. She might have a concussion and there would be plenty of time to sleep below ground anyway.

He touched her ankle, gave her a little shake. "Hey Abby. You wanna wake up now? Get something to eat?"

She moaned a little and opened her eyes slowly, pulled the buds from her ears. "Do you have any aspirin?"

Her voice was soft from sleep and he could see she was groggy.

Kyle noted the wound on her head and saw that the swelling had gone down leaving only a small mark above her right eye. "Yeah, we'll get you some of that and some diet coke to go with it."

At that Abby brightened and sat up straight on the couch. "Sounds great. What's for dinner?"

"Well I thought I might cook. But I have to warn you. I can only prepare one thing that makes for a suitable dinner."

"Let me guess, spaghetti?" Abby smiled at him with raised eyebrows.

"That's a typical guy thing, isn't it?" He motioned with his head for her to come in to the kitchen.

Abby stood, pulled the glasses from her face and stretched her limbs a little before responding. "Pretty much. At least for a guy like you." She set her stuff on the coffee table and followed him.

"What's that mean? A guy like me?"

"Well you're not really the aspiring chef type, though I imagine you could cook anything you set your mind to. Mostly, I'd figure you for more of a burgers and hot dogs on the grill kind of guy. And I'd be willing to bet you make a mean pan of scrambled eggs with toast and bacon, but that's where the breakfast menu ends."

Kyle nodded then grinned slightly as he pulled out the one big pot he owned to begin filling it with water. "Am I that transparent?"

"I have a sense for these sorts of things." She tapped the bridge of her nose with her index finger. "But I know how to cook and I'd rather starve than do it. So who am I to talk?"

Kyle grinned to himself. Of course he already knew she despised cooking. That part of her hadn't changed in centuries.

She took a soda from the fridge and sat down at the table. "I've been meaning to talk to you about some things, while we have a second."

"Okay, but we need to make a deal first." Kyle put the pot on the stove and leaned against the counter. "We talk about apocalyptic sorts of things only until dinner is ready and then the topic's officially off limits."

"You've got it." Abby nodded then continued her thought. "I was thinking about the prophecy or whatever it is."

"Prophecy is probably pretty accurate."

"Okay, well the first passage has already come to pass, right? Blood rain, land swallowed by water, etcetera." He nodded and she went on. "And the last stanza just speaks of the aftermath of everything, so I think we should take a look at the second part."

"Right, well bright red burning heavens and copper hue over the Earth, check. The sky has been weird looking for a couple days now. That leaves a day of darkness and some kind of new moon appearing that will break up and fall."

"Right, and since the other parts of the prophecy have proved pretty literal, shouldn't we assume that tomorrow is our day of darkness and something looking like the moon will appear in the sky and fall to Earth?"

Kyle poured jarred tomato sauce into a pot. "Well could it be a new moon like as in the phase of the moon?"

"I don't think so. The moon is about half full right now so it must be something else. Something more ominous, I'm sure."

"So let's count on no sun tomorrow and possibly objects falling from the heavens." He leaned against the kitchen counter again and sipped on a beer.

There was silence between them for a time while Kyle prepared dinner and Abby simply watched him. He felt her eyes on him, silently enjoying the sensation as he worked.

With the cooking almost done she got up to set the table, put out bread and butter, and get fresh drinks for them both. She sat back down just in time for the spaghetti to come off the stove.

"So," she began. "Now that dinner is ready, and the end of the world is no longer a conversation choice, let's talk about us."

He looked up from pouring tomato sauce over pasta, cleared his throat before speaking. "Us?"

"Yeah, you've done a one-eighty since the attack of the killer tornadoes." They sat down to eat and Kyle looked at her questioningly before she went on. "I mean, last night and this morning things were weird between us and you seemed pretty intent on giving me the cold shoulder." She paused in twirling spaghetti around the twines of her fork. "I think something changed in the barn but I didn't expect spaghetti dinners just yet."

He buttered a piece of bread. "Yeah, well I guess you could say I figured a few details out and now I have a better understanding of everything."

"What exactly prompted this dramatic change in attitude?"

He took a second and a forkful of spaghetti to organize his thoughts. It was hard for him to talk about how he felt so he settled on something more tangible. "I didn't know about the tornadoes but you did. And I felt the doom vibe the moment our eyes met but not before." He turned thoughtful. "And when I brushed against your arm you got some kind of flash, didn't you? You suddenly had more information to work with."

"Something like that." She wiped sauce from her chin with a paper napkin. "It's like you and I complete some sort of circuit. We seem to always be connected mentally, emotionally, or whatever. But when we connect physically the power gets kicked up a notch."

Kyle squinted, processing the information. "I guess that makes some sense." He turned to his plate, avoiding her eyes as he continued. "So after that... uh event... I guess I came to the conclusion that I don't have to run from whatever this is between us, that I don't have to worry about being sidetracked from the main purpose or anything like that."

"Is that what you thought?" Abby almost choked on a laugh through a mouth full of pasta. "You must've gotten something completely different from that vision last night."

"I don't think so. I think we felt the same things." He grinned a little, mostly to himself. "Honestly, I wasn't sure what to do with it. Part of me thought it might be easier on both of us to stay distant. This thing between us is... intense, distracting. I thought maybe I could do my job better and keep you safer if we weren't friends or otherwise emotionally attached."

She laughed. "That's just silly boy logic."

He sent her a raised eyebrow.

"Sorry, but it's pretty dumb. Obviously we were meant to work together on this and, if past lives have relevance in the present, then we were obviously meant to be more than detached partners."

Kyle couldn't argue with that. "I guess we are more useful as a unit. I think that maybe us being... um... close to each other is sort of a necessity for survival."

She grinned with her mouth full, swallowed. "Is that your roundabout way of trying to get me into bed?"

He set his fork down and swallowed hard. "Oh. No. I mean, of course I think you're very attractive but I wasn't trying to imply anything by that. I just meant..."

Abby giggled. "It's okay. I know what you meant." He breathed a small sigh of relief and she went on. "You're right. We are more powerful together and I think there's a purpose behind that. I feel like if we aren't a team on this thing we risk more lives than just our own. We have a responsibility."

He agreed with a nod and stole a glance at the soft skin of her throat, imaging his lips trailing a line from there to her mouth. Distraction was certainly an appropriate word for Abby, he thought.

After dinner they cleared the dishes together and neither of them avoided brushing up against each other as they moved from the table to the sink and back. In fact, they made a point of it, creating a tight path in the ample kitchen that neither of them strayed from.

When the table was clear he turned to her with a playful smile. "We'll leave the dishes for tomorrow."

"What if there isn't a tomorrow?"

His smile widened and he shrugged. "I'm counting on it."

She returned his smile as he slowly raised a hand to press his palm to her cheek. He let his fingers slip along the soft skin behind her ear and under her hair. His eyes moved to her mouth while his thumb caressed her bottom lip. Her shuddering breath nearly sent him over the edge.

If he kissed her now, the way he wanted to, they wouldn't make it out of the house to the next part of his plan. He wanted to do this right, wanted Abby Connelly to know what it was like to be wooed for once in her life. He turned around towards the door and offered up his hand. She slipped her fingers into his, fitting perfectly together while they walked out into the night.

Abby looked down at where their hands met as Kyle led her towards the front side of the barn. She could see her own skin glowing, not just his anymore. She lifted her other hand and saw that it was also shining in the dim light.

"Kyle." She held her hand up in front of her, studied the white glow of it. "What's happening?"

He looked down at his own hands and shook his head inquisitively. "I don't know." He turned a bright smile on her. "But it's kind of cool."

Abby let out a laugh. "I guess if we're ever in a blackout we won't need to light any candles. And leaving the lights on is pretty much standard from now on."

Kyle laughed with her. "That might not be such a bad thing." He said the last with a flirty undertone that made her smile widen. An urge that was quickly becoming familiar stirred inside of him, forcing him to take a deep, suppressing breath.

In front of the barn Kyle had laid out a big blanket with paper plates, plastic forks, a store bought cheesecake, a six pack of beer, and a battery powered mp3 radio.

Abby eyed the picnic before her. "What's all this? Desert and drinks under the stars?"

"Exactly." He pulled out both of their music filled phones and set them on the blanket.

He had swiped Abby's from the coffee table when she wasn't looking. "First things first. We exchange phones and pick some favorite tunes for mood music."

He watched her face, saw the light around her brighten.

They thumbed through each other's phones, picking out songs and playfully teasing one another over their choice in music. After a few moments they settled on a playlist that had been labeled "chilled" on Abby's phone and started on their freshly thawed, premade cheesecake.

Music swirled around as they swallowed their last bites and Kyle opened beers for them. "I wanted to get some wine, but the grocery store was cleaned out."

"That's okay. I'm one of those girls who actually likes beer."

Of course Kyle already knew that, but he also knew wine was considered more romantic. His next surprise wouldn't really add a touch of romance either, but he knew Abby would appreciate it.

"Oh, I almost forgot. I have one more gift for us." Kyle pulled out a full pack of light cigarettes and waved them in front of Abby.

Abby let out a gasp that quickly turned into a laugh. "Where did you get those? They must be fifteen bucks a pack these days."

"Well I didn't exactly pay for them. I sort of found them when I was in town earlier. Thought you might enjoy the last smokes on

Earth." He packed the box against the back of his hand. "Besides, I'm a reformed smoker too and I guess you could say my will power is a little less than stellar since I started having visions about that which we are not speaking of tonight."

Abby's face was bright, almost astonished. Kyle soaked it in. He knew it was a silly thing for them to share, but civilization as they knew it was about to come crumbling down around them. If splitting a pack of cigarettes and a sixer of beer gave them some respite from the terror that was coming, it was more than worth it. Smoke 'em if you got 'em, Kyle thought, suddenly realizing these might be the last normal moments of his life.

"Oh my god. I had forgotten how good that was," Abby said as she took her first puff. "I feel like a teenager doing something bad though. But I think that's part of what I always liked about it."

"Rebelling against something are you?" Kyle looked at her sideways and let smoke waft out slowly from his mouth.

"You should know. You already know everything about me and I'm just scratching the surface of you."

"Well I don't know everything. Just random things here and there pop into my head. And sometimes I can hear what you're thinking. But I think that's your fault."

"My fault?"

"Yeah, I think you send your thoughts to me somehow."

She flicked her cigarette. "Huh. I didn't realize I was sending anything."

"Regardless, I feel like I know you already even though the last time I remember being with you was a few thousand years ago. Does that makes sense?"

"It does. It's like we've been... friends... for a very long time. And I'm glad you don't know everything." She sat up a little to face him. "First, because some things are just plain private. And second, because I wouldn't want either of us to miss out on the getting to know you stage... again."

Kyle only grinned and they both looked up to gaze into the night sky and enjoy their smokes. It was hard to believe the world would look so different tomorrow, that everything would change in the course of just twenty-four short hours. In the meantime the two of them would share an effortless evening together full of simple indulgences.

"I'd like to know more about you," he said.

She smiled over the rim of her beer bottle, holding it in the same hand as her cigarette. With the other hand she absently tugged on her earlobe.

"Well I'm the one with the learning curve. I think you should tell me more about you so I can catch up." A soft laugh escaped her lips. "You can find out more about me later. I'm sure I'll be broadcasting transmissions throughout the evening."

"Okay. What do you want to know then?" He took a drag of his cigarette, held the butt between his forefinger and his thumb.

"How long have you had those tattoos?"

Kyle felt his face grow warm, remembering the feeling of her eyes on him earlier in the day. "Ah... those are from my bad boy phase."

He took a sip of beer and looked out into the night, glancing up to the moon as he swallowed. He could feel her eyes on him again, saw her staring at his profile in his peripheral vision. Suddenly he wished he could read her thoughts at will.

She waited patiently, smoking and sipping her beer.

He continued. "I had dropped out of college and was pissed off at just about everything. I stole cars, got into way too many fights." He stole a glance in her direction. "I don't recommend spending the night in lock up."

Abby's eyes registered mild surprise. "You were in jail?"

"Well I wasn't in a real prison or anything. I spent a couple of nights in the county jail before I could make bail." He took a long sip from his bottle. "Looking back I think maybe I was just searching for my purpose, trying to figure out who I was. Something I hate to admit because it sounds ridiculous even to me." He paused briefly. "I was living on the road, reading too much angst. Smoking, drinking, using ah... recreational narcotics... going through different women that I barely knew and didn't really like."

Abby studied him. "Life had no real meaning."

"Yeah it was a time of what you might call building character I guess." His fingers made quotes in the air. "But it was so empty and I wasn't a very nice guy."

"What pulled you out of it?"

He laughed quietly. It sounded a little wounded, even to him. "The girl who bailed me out of jail, but not in a good way."

Abby leaned in, waiting for more and smoking her cigarette like it was something she still did every day.

"She was more messed up than I was and I was sort of implicated by association." He chuckled sarcastically. "To keep the story short I got my ass kicked one too many times and I wanted out. Joining your uncle on the farm was my way of starting over and cleaning up. The land had always called to me and I wanted to... ah commune I guess."

He waited a second for her reaction, but her face never changed. "You think I'm a delinquent now."

Abby shook her head, eyeing him with an expression he couldn't read. "No. I think you're just you."

Kyle was glad she didn't press him further. He flicked his cigarette into the grass. Smoke billowed up around his face as he exhaled the last drag, illuminated by the shining light of his skin. "After that vision the other night," he began again. "I think maybe I got the tattoos because of some subconscious past life memory."

Abby's eyes widened just slightly in agreement. "I was thinking something like that also. They look too much like the ones you... um... used to have."

"Do you have any tattoos?" She blushed from her chin to her forehead and he suddenly heard the answer in his head. If she had a tattoo, she wanted him to find out where it was on his own.

They were quiet for a second before Abby blurted out her next question. "What do you remember? About us, I mean. All that time ago?"

Kyle turned, his eyes sweeping over her body until they reached her face. He watched her cheeks flush again, could almost hear her blood quicken.

"I remember you on a summer night moving around an open fire. There was drumming and dancing and people coming together all around us." His words were soft as he moved closer to her. "I remember how I felt, how strong it was." His gaze fell to her lips.

"I remember that too. I was waiting for you, wanting you." She was breathless, her voice a faint whisper. "And what about now? How do you feel now?"

Their hands brushed against each other on the downy blanket and Kyle grabbed a hold of her thumb to pull her towards him. He leaned in, never taking his eyes from her lips. He stayed there, hesitating, not yet ready to give in. He felt her breath on his mouth and dipped just a little closer. She shut her eyes, moved in. He backed just out of her reach as her lips grazed his with an electric charge.

He moved forward again, took her bottom lip between his teeth gently. She responded, sliding her arms around his neck and pulling him in.

Her breathing was heavy, matching his own rhythm. Their lips connected and Kyle pulling back once more. Never had a kiss held so much power over him. He glanced at her lips, feeling his control slip away. With one deft movement and far more urgency than he intended he pushed her to her back, settled himself over her, and crushed her open mouth under his.

She explored under his shirt to trail fingers over the skin of his back, rocked forward as he brought his mouth down to nuzzle the softness of her neck.

His breathing deepened further, his blood burning as his hands clasped onto her hips. He ran one hand down her thigh, gripped her leg under the knee, and pulled it up tight around his waist. She trembled, let out a soft gasp into his mouth as his body pressed into hers.

Through a haze he heard her say his name.

"Kyle." Her voice was muffled under his lips. He was too preoccupied for the tone of her voice to register but looked up when she gave him a light shove to one shoulder. "Kyle, look. Down by the road."

He halfheartedly pulled away from kissing her and followed her line of sight with squinted eyes to where a group of people walked down the street. It was a much less severe version of the scene he had witnessed the day before. This time there were no children and the people had a faint shine of light outlining their bodies. They were glowing, but it wasn't the subtle white shimmer Abby and Kyle possessed. There were colors; blue, green, and a butter yellow surrounding them.

"Do you see that?" Abby was visibly shaken, struggling to catch her breath. "They're glowing. Like us. Well sort of anyway. What do you think it means?"

"I have no idea." Reluctantly he stood, straightened his shirt and smoothed out his hair. "But I guess we should catch up with them and see what we can find out."

The two of them jogged down to the country road, slowing down to a brisk walk as they approached the group of travelers.

"Excuse me. We were just wondering..." Kyle stopped short when he noticed the look of shock on the faces of the five strangers in front of him. There were three men and two women, all emanating a faint colored light.

The tallest and presumably oldest of the three men stepped up in front, staring at Abby and Kyle like they were ghosts. "What are you?"

"Well, we can explain that in a minute," Kyle answered. "The real question is what are the five of you?" When not one of them spoke up Kyle looked to Abby.

"Did you know you guys are all shiny and glowing?" Apparently she wasn't going to be tactful. "Like you back there, girl with long dark hair. You're a very pretty shade of green. And tough guy here..." She motioned to the tall man in front. "He's like a light yellowish color. Do any of you know why? Have any of you been experiencing weird dreams lately? Visions of any kind?"

The other woman, a big eyed red head stepped out from behind the boys. Her light was pale blue. "Yeah, we all have. And we know about the colors. That's how we found each other in the first place. We're not sure what it means. We just knew that we needed to work together to survive." She heaved a breath. "We think this is the Second Coming or at least something very close to it."

"Yep, that's pretty much right on the money," Kyle said casually, nodding and gesturing to himself and Abby. "We've been through the same thing, had the same dreams. I think maybe you're supposed to be here. With us." Again none of them responded. "We can try to figure out some answers about why you're all walking fireflies and we even have a bomb shelter that can hold up to ten people stocked with lots of food and water to share."

"I think that's a good idea David," the dark haired girl called out without pause.

The tall guy held up his hand. "How do we know they're not crazy people Evie? Or sex maniac cult leaders? The girl looks like she's had his five-o-clock shadow rubbed all over her face and Farmer John here's got some rosy lip gloss on his chin."

"No, Evie's right." One of the other men, shorter and darker, spoke up. "It's not coincidence we were walking down this road at this exact time. None of us even knew where we were going. Our van broke down in Topeka and we just came here where there's nothing but corn and cows. That's not weird to anyone else?"

"I think you're out voted David." The little red head set her mouth into a firm line. "We want to stay here, stay safe."

"Yeah, I'm with them," the third man chimed in. "Where else do we have to go? The odds of out running the apocalypse aren't exactly in our favor."

"These people are willing to help us figure out what's happening to us and let us hide out in their shelter when the time comes." Evie's voice was sharp and determined. "I don't care what they are or what they do. I just want to stay alive."

David took a moment to scowl. "Fine. But when they start asking you to participate in their orgies and pray to comets, don't say I didn't warn you."

"Blondie can invite me to an orgy any day." The third guy gave Abby a suggestive look over. "I'll pray to anything she wants me to."

Kyle felt a hot surge run up his spine. He shot the other man a look of warning and then leaned in towards his face. In an even tone he said, "That's enough."

The other man took a step back, held up his hands with a plea. "Okay dude. I get it. She's your girl."

Abby and Kyle exchanged curious and slightly amused looks before he put his arm around her waist and headed up to the driveway. The five newcomers followed on their heels.

CHAPTER TWELVE

Thursday, December 20th 2012, 12:45am

Abby sat on Kyle's bed, waiting for him to get the new people settled in between his house and Jim's. Anticipation trickled over her skin as she thought back to earlier in the night. Instead of just sitting there feeling antsy, she stood to examine his room.

She noticed colors first; steel grey walls, sheer white curtains, charcoal linens on the unmade bed. Clothes were strewn along the floor in small piles, mostly jeans and tee shirts. More of his black and white photos hung on the walls with a blown up print of the barn doors hanging over his headboard.

His dresser was clear of clutter. Only a plain blue bowl filled with silver and copper change sat in the center. His nightstand held only a lamp, an alarm clock, and another copy of Oscar Wilde. This one was much loved, dog eared and bookmarked to his favorite poems.

She turned to one of the marked pages and read the first line of Madonna Mia. "A lily girl, not made for this world's pain..."

"That's one of my favorites," Kyle said, suddenly behind her.

She jumped, closed the book and set it back in its place. "I was reading your other copy earlier. I hadn't gotten to that one yet."

"I sort of have a thing for Wilde. There's a third copy around here somewhere."

"Everyone settled in alright?" she asked.

"Yeah, all set." He moved to the dresser, slipped the watch off his wrist and set it in the blue bowl followed by the wallet he kept in his back pocket. "The brothers Sam and Jake pushed Alex to the couch in order to share the spare bed at Jimmy's, Hanna and Evie are tucked in the room across the hall from us, and David is downstairs on the couch scowling." His keys followed with a twang as they jangled against the ceramic.

"Well that worked out well then. What's with that guy David, by the way? He makes crazy assumptions in the rudest possible ways."

"I think he's got some kind of god complex. He seems to get off on being judge and jury. A control freak."

Abby made a face and shuddered a little. "He gives me the creeps. I hope he lightens up at some point. I'm not looking forward to being stuck in the bunker with him."

Kyle smiled. "Well maybe he'll hook up with one of the girls and learn to relax."

"We could only hope. Oh, did you figure out anything about the colors? Any visions or insights?"

"No, not yet. I did hear one of the girls talking about being an environmental scientist and a botanist. Maybe that's why she's green."

"Hmm... that's a good thought. I should've paid more attention to my new agey friends. We could look into auras if we can get the internet to come up in the morning. Maybe there will be some clues there. And we should call the five of them something besides the Colors I think."

"Well they do have a nice subtle gleam to them." Kyle cocked his head. "So how about we call them Gleamers then."

Abby mirrored his head tilt. "That does have a better ring to it. Colors wasn't very imaginative of us."

"Yes, but we had other things on our mind at the time." Kyle's eyes were dark and purposeful as he pulled her up to stand on her feet.

"Ah that's right. We were distracted."

Kyle slipped his thumbs through her belt loops and pulled her hips into his. The kiss was gentle at first then quickly picked up where they had left off outside.

It was the piercing sound of female screams coming from the spare room that forced them to surface from each other for the second time that night.

Kyle groaned mid kiss. "What now?"

"Hey guys," one of the girls shouted through the wooden door. "You should probably come see this."

He groaned again more audibly then opened the door to see Hanna standing in the hall. Her face was pale and her doe like eyes had grown larger with fear.

Kyle plowed over the threshold with Abby on his heels. "What is it?"

Hanna said nothing, only pointed into the spare room where Evie stood looking ghost-like in a long white nightshirt staring out the window. Kyle and Abby followed Evie's gaze and simultaneously took in their breath sharply.

Kyle was the first to break the amazed silence. "A new moon." His voice was so low it was barely perceptible, little more than a breath on his lips.

Through the window they could see a bright orange object in the sky, sitting next to the moon almost rivaling it in size. As they stared with a mix of wonder and horror more objects began to appear. They were smaller, looking like stars at first then growing as they moved towards the Earth. Shooting stars whizzed through the night sky, their flaming tails blazing behind them.

"Oh god." Evie's face was contorted in fear. "There's more of them, little ones, and they're coming towards us."

Abby looked at Kyle. "But we were supposed to have more time. This isn't it. Is it?"

Kyle didn't look away from the window. "No, it's not"

"Should we go underground again?" Abby wrapped her hand around his arm, squeezed it lightly.

Kyle shook his head. "No, this isn't right. It's one of the last signs, that's all. Not the end yet."

Hanna looked from Abby to Kyle and back again. "What's he talking about? Is it time to run for our lives or not?"

"No." Kyle shook his head again. "No it's not time yet. We'll sleep one more night above ground."

A second later a mass of rock and fire plummeted to the land in the distance. The impact was miles away but the Earth shook, the sound echoed through the air, and the light from the explosion made them all step back a foot from the window.

"Are you sure you don't want to rethink that?" Evie's voice caught in her throat. "Because that looked like hide in a bunker type stuff to me."

Kyle shrugged, appearing preoccupied with his own thoughts. "It's a big planet. The odds of one of those things hitting in Kansas again is probably pretty slim."

"Probably?" Hanna wasn't convinced.

"Look, if you three want to get the others and spend the night in the shelter that's a smart idea. I want to go investigate whatever just fell out of the sky, see what I can learn."

"Whoa, the three of us?" Abby touched his forearm. "No, I don't think so. If you're going out there so am I."

He looked at her for an instant, an argument waiting on his lips then sighed. "Okay then. Let's go." He turned to walk out the door of the spare room and called over his shoulder to the other women. "If you want to get the guys and head into the bunker go ahead. We won't be gone long."

Abby and Kyle took off in his truck, stopping for only a moment to explain things to the men who had come out of the Yellow House to stare up into the sky. Once out of the driveway they turned down the road in the direction of the impact.

Abby pulled her hair back out of her eyes, wrapped it tight with a rubber band she'd been carrying in her jeans pocket. "What are you hoping to find besides a really big rock inside a really big hole?"

"I'm not sure." He shifted the truck into third gear. He was driving too fast, but he didn't seem to notice "I guess I was thinking I might get some kind of insight or vision. I don't know. It's just a feeling I got when I saw it fall."

"You're more connected to this thing than I am. To the whole doomsday situation. I mean, I didn't feel a thing before or after the meteor, or whatever it is, fell to Earth."

"You know that vision we had the other night? Well, I remember lots of details about that time. I was some sort of leader. A priest or something."

"Yeah I remember that too. I know who you were and what you did."

"Right, but it was my job to prophesize, to be the keeper of time; past, present, and future. I remember being trained by priests, spending years studying the signs of nature."

"Okay, so that might explain why you're more in tune with what's happening?"

"I think so. I'm not completely certain, but that seems to make a lot of sense to me. And the last time this Destroyer thing came around it wasn't the end of the world, but many of our people died." Kyle took a deep breath, turned the truck down an old dirt road. "And I was supposed to have been able to predict it, to save them. They counted on me."

Abby fidgeted, wrung her hands together. "But something went wrong."

"Yes. I wasn't prepared enough. I couldn't figure out the puzzle and they all died. Every single one of them."

Abby sat in thought for a minute. "I've seen the beginning of the destruction, but none of the details after."

"I figured as much." He glared out the windshield, his mouth in a tight line. "Anyway, I feel like I'm on my way to making up for that mistake but..."

"You're scared you'll make it twice." Abby said the words heavily. "That's why you wanted to push me away, avoid distractions?"

Kyle exhaled, leaned back on the headrest of his seat. "Yeah."

Abby gave him a minute and put her hand over his where it rested on the gear shift. Gently, she brushed her fingertips along his knuckles. "We're not those people anymore Kyle. It's been a long time since then. We have to live this life in this time, learn all new lessons." Her voice was gentle. "Just because something happened once doesn't mean it's going to happen again. Things are different this time."

Kyle furrowed his brow and kept his eyes on the road. "And what if I can't save them now? What if I can't save you?"

Abby rotated in her seat to face him. Again her voice was calm as she tried to reassure him. "You might be the one with more visions and gut feelings but you're not the only one with special talents. And you're not the only one who glows with white light or remembers past lives either. I'm in this too. I have as much responsibility as you do. This is not all on your shoulders and it's okay to let someone help you. We're a package deal now. I go where you go."

He didn't respond and the conversation ended as they pulled up to the impact site. Smoke wafted up out of the ground above the high walls of the crater.

The heat hit Abby in the face as she stepped from the truck. "Wow, that's a huge rock. Do you think..." One look from Kyle told her to be quiet. "Sorry." She smiled meekly.

He walked around the crater like he was hoping a magical creature was going to pop out and give him some answers. Fragments from the explosion littered the ground around the site. Kyle bent down and gingerly picked one up, checking to make sure it wouldn't burn him first. He closed his eyes while he held the stone tightly in one hand.

"I've got nothing." He tossed the rock up, caught it again. "Nothing at all. I was expecting something. Anything." He was obviously disappointed.

Abby walked the few steps between them and reached out her hand. Kyle opened his fingers to offer her the stone, but she didn't take it from him. Instead she closed her hand over his with the stone between them.

The reaction was instantaneous. The glow that was naturally always around them became at least ten times brighter as it engulfed them both, becoming one single light. As the two of them awed at the display a sudden and quick flash burst out from the stone sending Kyle and Abby flying in opposite directions.

It took them a moment to recover. Abby was the first to speak. "Ouch. That was unexpected."

She rubbed her sore tail bone with the heel of her hand. Her head ached slightly and her limbs suddenly felt like they weighed a ton.

Kyle let out a pained sound, pinched the bridge of his nose between his finger and thumb. He worked a crick out his neck and raised to his feet gingerly. Once recovered, he went to her quickly, gripping her shoulders with urgency. "What did you see Abby."

She was caught off guard, needed a minute to think. "Um... I don't know. It was dark and there was snow on the ground. No, it wasn't snow. It was something else. Ashes I think."

"I saw that too. What else?" He was urgent, slightly panicked.

"Uh, lots of heat. Like the sun had come down to touch the Earth. What's going on Kyle?"

"I think I know what's next. I think the increase in earthquakes, in seismic activity, is going to cause multiple volcanoes to erupt some time tomorrow."

Abby stood up and brushed off her jeans. "Okay, there are no volcanoes in Kansas."

"No, but there are volcanoes all down the west coast as far in as Colorado. And then there's Yellowstone."

"That's in Washington isn't it?"

Kyle offered his hand and helped her to stand. "Wyoming and it doesn't matter how far away it is. The Yellowstone caldera is gigantic. They call it a super volcano. If that thing goes off it will be like a nuclear explosion followed by a nuclear winter. Ash will be so thick that roofs collapse, no one will be able to breathe as it rains down all over the country maybe all over the globe. It's going to change this planet into something we don't even recognize."

"So does that explain the heat we felt too?"

"I don't think so. I think that's something else. Something worse, if that's possible. Did you see any people?"

Abby shook her head. "No. I just saw the farm under layers of ash and it felt like a seriously hot summer day in the desert."

Kyle grimaced. "I saw people and they looked like horror movie extras lying in ash. Their skin was peeling and bloody and their hair was falling out."

"Like radiation poisoning. Do you think someone's going to drop a bomb on us?"

"No, that's not it. It's something to do with that sun and the black hole thing I think. It's environmental. I'm sure of it and it means there will be solar radiation on top of everything else."

Kyle pocketed the meteor rock before climbing back into the truck. "We've got one more day." He started the engine and put it in drive. "Let's make sure everyone makes the best of it."

"We'll make it."

He nodded. "Though surviving the aftermath in one piece is going to be an entirely different story."

Abby noticed the implications in his voice, like he knew something she could only guess at. A shudder poured over her shoulders and slid down her spine.

He grinned without it touching his eyes. "We'll make it."

Abby tried to return the grin, hoping she looked convincing.

When they returned to the house Abby headed for the stairs, feeling as though her legs were made of stone. She was completely and utterly exhausted.

She heard Kyle call from the kitchen. "Be right up. I just have to jot a few things down before I forget them. If it's okay, I'll sleep in the chair in the bedroom."

Abby stopped mid-step, turned to meet his eyes. "We can share the bed if you want. I... I don't mind."

Kyle nodded and scooted her off. "Get some rest."

She nodded back, smiled warmly at him, and climbed each step like a rusty robot. When she got to his bed she quickly shrugged off her jeans and fell into the plush mattress. She was asleep in an instant.

CHAPTER THIRTEEN

Thursday, December 20th 2012, 9:45am

Abby awoke the next morning feeling as though she had barely slept. The dreams had come as they always did, and the stress of living through them made her body ache and her head throb. Real, restful sleep was something she was beginning to forget. It was dark outside but one look to Kyle's alarm clock showed her it was almost ten in the morning.

The day of darkness had come and Abby felt a little shudder in the pit of her stomach. She wasn't surprised, only anxious. Though she was eased greatly by where she was, wrapped in the warmth of Kyle's bed, enveloped by his scent.

Abby felt his arms wrapped around her, his face close against the back of her neck. She could hear him breathing, feel the rhythmic brush of it on her skin.

They were both wearing clothes, Kyle in a pair of black flannel pajama bottoms and Abby in the tee shirt she had worn the day before. Being there next to him, feeling the way he had pulled her close in his sleep, she felt a sense of innocence she had long forgotten within a sea of unfortunate relationships and too many bad choices.

There was something pure about the two of them together; something real. It felt to Abby like neither of them had ulterior motives. It wasn't about sex. Or at least it wasn't just about sex. She wanted to be near him, be close to him. Anything that came after that was a bonus.

This was what she had always been looking for, Abby thought. This is why she stopped taking her pills. Instead of being a ghost of a girl who went through the motions, she felt solid for the first time in years. She felt normal, real, and all those things she imagined other people experienced daily. But maybe it wasn't just being off her medication that caused the change in her. Maybe the man sleeping beside her had something to do with it too.

Kyle stirred and Abby flipped over slowly to face him. She waited to see if her movement would wake him, but his eyes remained closed. For a short moment she watched his sleeping face, feeling emotion she'd never before experienced. "Good morning," she finally whispered.

At the sound of her voice his eyes fluttered open slowly. "It's still dark." He pulled her close, pressing her cheek to his chest. "We have a few more hours."

"It's almost ten. The day of darkness, remember?"

He turned to check the clock on his nightstand. "Oh. We should get up, check on the others."

Her lips found his neck, nipped at him playfully. She slipped her hands down, trailed her fingers along his side until she hit the waistband of his pants. "I'm sure we can spare another hour or two."

His hand was immediately on hers, bringing it back up between them. "We need to talk."

The tone of his voice made her face fall. "That doesn't sound good."

Suddenly a knock sounded on the door and Evie's voice projected into the room. "Hey you guys awake?"

Kyle pushed Abby away an inch and bellowed over his shoulder. "No we're not!" He spoke again to Abby. "This... thing between us... I should never have let it get so far. It was a mistake."

Abby wasn't sure she had heard him right. "What are you talking about?"

One hand flew up to his hair, his fingers combing through the top. "It's just better if we don't get too close."

Abby's expression was clouded by confusion. Worry began dancing the polka with heartache in her gut. "But dinner and our cheesecake picnic... and we're here in the same bed together. I don't understand."

"You're right. That's my fault. I let this get out of hand. I knew it was wrong to get distracted and I'm sorry. I really am." His mouth tightened. "I'm just glad we didn't round second base."

She clenched her eyes and shook her head. "Wait. After last night I thought..."

"Thought what? That we were going to live happily ever after?"

Abby felts his words like a knife and tried to hide the tears from her voice. "I thought you felt the same way I felt. I thought you remembered what we are to each other."

"We can't afford to get wrapped up in these feelings right now, Abby. I made a mistake and I'm sorry. You should move on, forget last night ever happened. We have jobs to do."

"But everything's done now. All we have to do now is get in the bunker. I can't forget. I won't. Please Callum."

He flinched at the word. "Please don't say that name."

"But it's who you are. You are that man who was my husband so long ago. I remember you Kyle. I remember the flowers you brought me as a boy, the way you never failed to make me smile even on my darkest day. You are that same man. I see him in your eyes and you see your wife in mine. I know you love me Kyle. I feel it."

Evie yelled through the door again. "Sorry to bother you guys. We were just wondering where to find your towels."

Kyle sighed, turned his head to shout towards the door again. "Linen closet. Hallway."

"What?" Evie's voice rang out again. "I can't find them. What did you say?" There was a brief pause as a muffled male voice drifted up the stairs. "And David is yelling up about coffee filters. He says he can't find a thing in your mess of a kitchen. His words not mine."

Kyle rubbed a hand across his face. "Have I fallen down a rabbit hole or something?"

Abby rolled her legs over the edge of the bed and sat while she pulled on her jeans. "We have never been strangers. Please talk to me. Help me understand."

He got out of bed, looking exasperated as he pulled a white tee shirt over his head. "Look, I'm sorry Abby. I can't do this right now. I told you I wasn't a nice guy. Just forget about this whole thing, whatever this is between us. Three days ago you had no idea who I was."

But she had known. Her soul had always know him, always missed him.

"If you're not a nice guy why didn't you just sleep with me and call it another notch on your bedpost?"

His mouth opened, closed again. "Because..." He hesitated for a long moment, appearing to rack his brain for a good enough excuse. "Because Jim is a good friend and I wouldn't want to piss him off."

Abby watched as Kyle went to the door and slung it open wide. He took big barefoot strides straight into the hallway, past Evie and

Hanna to the linen closet. His aggravation was obvious.

Without word or expression he motioned to the closet door like he was a game show spokes model before pulling it open with a yank. "Towels."

Neither of the women spoke and Kyle descended the stairs fast without another word.

Abby came out of the doorway with a shrug of her shoulders. "Guess he needs some coffee or something."

Hanna and Evie nodded in unison. "Oh."

* * *

A few hours later the entire group of nine was sitting on the porch of the Yellow House, finishing up a late lunch of cold cuts and fruit.

Abby looked at Evie, carefully avoiding Kyle's face, as she sank her teeth into an apple. "So you've just finished a degree in environmental science with a minor in botany?"

Evie nodded, her long dark hair blowing around her exquisite features. "Yes, I basically work with plants. Green things are sort of my specialty." She bit into an orange slice and paused to chew. "Ever since I was a little kid I've had a talent for growing things."

Evie reminded Abby of one of the Tahitian women Gauguin loved to paint. She was tall and thin, with curves that were the epitome of hourglass. Abby half expected her to pose seductively, tuck a flower behind her ear, and cradle the bowl of oranges in her arms.

Kyle turned to Hanna. "And you're a med student right?"

Hanna smiled with big perfect teeth. "Yeah, I'm just second year though."

Hanna blushed. A pretty shade of red covered her freckles under Kyle's gaze and Abby frowned. Apparently she wasn't the only one affected by him.

Kyle walked down the porch stairs and lit himself a cigarette before tossing the pack up to Abby without a word. "Still that will probably come in handy one day. I think we can count on hospitals being closed for business in the near future. Any kind of healer will be a precious member of society."

Abby didn't look up but lit herself a dose of nicotine. After the first drag some of the tension in her neck started to fade.

"What's this? You smoke now?" Alex eyed Abby with a hint of amazement mixed with disgust.

Abby looked up at him. "Focus Alex. We have bigger problems. Besides, this is just end of the world smoking. I'm not falling off the wagon."

"Oh, end of the world smoking. Right. I think you two are a bad influence on each other."

This coming from the guy who could suck down a twelve pack in a couple of hours, Abby thought. She purposely resisted looking at Kyle.

David chimed in unexpectedly. "That's an understatement."

Alex glanced over with a derisive snort. "No one asked you Dave. I know her. She's a friend of mine. You just got here so you don't get to have an opinion."

David didn't say another word and Abby looked up at Alex with gratitude. "It's just temporary Alex. Don't worry."

Alex only nodded and the conversation continued with Sam and Jake, the two brothers in the group. Sam was an engineer who had graduated from MIT. He was smart but rough around the edges. This guy wasn't going to wear a pocket protector to save his life. His brother was an electrician. Both of their hands on experience and technical know-how would be valued when the time came to rebuild.

Kyle looked over to David. "What do you do then? You must have some sort of mechanical talent since you're yellow too."

"I'm in construction." He muttered the words with downcast eyes as though he was ashamed to say them. "But I have much bigger plans once I can get the money together for school."

Jim stood up, walked to the porch railing. "I don't know if that's going to work out for you now Dave. There won't be any colleges to go to pretty soon."

David shrugged. "That won't stop me."

The rest of the group seemed to look around at each other, waiting to see if anyone would have a response. Apparently David had a way of sucking the life out of everyone.

Kyle broke the silence with a quick clap of his hands. "Ok then. We have the mystery of the colors all figured out. Blues are Healers, Yellows are Builders, and Greens are... well I guess Greens are Growers." He paused momentarily to make sure everyone was in agreement. "Okay then. Now let's all make sure we're packed up and ready to go into the bunker tonight. Everybody pick a bunk, get settled in. Okay?"

There were nods and grumbles as the new group went about gathering their things. Within twenty minutes all nine of them were in the shelter listening to Kyle talk about their new accommodations like he was a real estate agent trying his hardest to sell them on a unique fixer upper.

"This is a modern, state of the art fallout shelter complete with a living area here in the front with tables and bench seating, plus a bathroom with a flush toilet and a grey water shower. The sleeping area is in the back through that there." He pointed towards the curtain that served as a door. "You'll find twelve bunks, stacked two by two down the narrow hall. A few of them are being used for storage so we might have to move some things around. It's going to feel a little bit like a submarine, but at least the curtains on each bed provide some privacy."

Everyone went to claim a bunk while Kyle, Jim, and Abby stayed in the living space. Kyle moved to the sink where he pulled down a heavy metal door from underneath the counter. "There's a freezer here full of... well frozen things that can be heated on the stove. I think there's even a steak somewhere in there." His smile was small. "The whole place is running on the turbines and solar panels, as you know, but there's a backup generator too."

Jim examined a row of small digital screens and buttons. "What's this here? Radiation meters, environmental controls." He read the labels blankly.

Kyle flipped a panel down to reveal more buttons. "This stuff controls the heat in here, the air quality, etcetera. And this screen gives a reading for the temperature and radiation above ground. You're familiar with safe levels?"

Jim nodded. "Yeah, had to learn that in the army. Hazmat training is not an easy experience to forget. I remember what's good and what's bad. I'll be in charge of that if it's something we need."

"Okay, good. So that's about it. You guys know everything else by now." Kyle glanced at Abby for a millisecond. "We're as ready as we're going to be I guess. It's just a matter of time. Now we sit back and wait for the apocalypse to come."

CHAPTER FOURTEEN

Thursday, December 20th 2012, 5:27pm

By late afternoon the temperature on the farm had hit somewhere in the high 90s. It was just around the time the sun would normally set when the ash started falling. By six-o-clock the farm looked like a scene stuck inside a poorly designed snow globe.

Any other year there would've been holiday cheer blanketing the land instead of a layer of thick, acidic ash. People would be bundled up against the cold and happily caroling through the town. Christmas trees would be lit up inside every home with lights outside, wrapped around porch railings and stapled along rooftops, illuminating each quaint street with electric happiness. But that was not the case this year. This year was a holiday in hell.

Abby wiped the sweat from her brow as the group of nine people and two dogs made their way to the bunker. Like the rest of them, the lower half of her face was covered with a strip of fabric to keep the ash from entering her lungs. Even the dogs had pillow cases lightly placed over their heads as they were carried to the shelter by Jim and Kyle.

After being shown the accommodations of the underground bunker, the group had gone above for a few more quiet pleasures like hot showers and indulgently huge chocolate sundaes with all the fixings provided by Kyle.

Daisy let out a soft whine prompting Kyle to pat her head through the cloth. "It's okay girl. Almost there now."

His voice was muffled through the steel grey strip of tee shirt wrapped around his face, leaving only the top half exposed to the early night air. Sweat dripped down his forehead and into his eyes, making him squint as he struggled with the light weight yet cumbersome animal in his arms.

Evie and Hanna were the first to get down into the bunker. The men turned to Abby next, as if to say women and children first, but one look from her and an emphatic shake of her head had them lowering the two hounds down next.

It was then that Abby saw the flashlights. Elevated voices followed, screaming above each other like a deranged choir.

"Connelly! We know you have that old bomb shelter on this farm and you're gonna let us in it."

"Shit. Here they come." Kyle's head popped up quickly, his eyes wide. "Everyone in the bunker now!"

Kyle grabbed Abby's arm but she shrugged him off. He latched on again, this time with more strength. "Get in the god damn bunker Abby."

Abby heard the fear in his voice but resisted anyway. She couldn't shake off his grip this time, but fixed her eyes to his with a determined stare. "Let go Kyle. I'll go when you go."

He shook his head, looked up at the mob that was closing in on them fast. "Don't do this Abby. I can't protect you up here. I won't risk your life again."

"What about you?"

Kyle met her gaze with sadness buried behind his eyes. He pulled the cloth from both of their faces and kissed her hard, lingering for only a moment with his hands gripping her cheeks. Then all at once he shoved her towards Alex and Jim.

He pulled his mask up again. "Get her in and keep her there. And lock up the hatch tight."

Suddenly he was gone, crossing the distance to the big red barn without looking back.

Abby couldn't fight the two men holding her, though she tried like hell. "Kyle!"

She turned desperate eyes on her uncle. "Where is he going? No. Don't. Let go of me. We have to help him. How will he get in with us if it's locked? How will we know when to open it for him?" Neither of the men spoke, just worked together to pull her down into to the bunker like she was a ragdoll. "Jimmy, please. We have to help him."

Abby turned her body and flailed wildly, striking Alex in the face before she brought her heel down on her uncle's toes. Their grips loosened just enough for her to squeeze away.

Once free she began to run towards the barn. Looking up she saw Kyle, glowing in the ash like a flaming beacon on a dark, desolate shore. She stopped in the layer of soot, watching as the mob broke windows out of her uncle's house. The beams from their flashlights shot out into the night and Abby was certain she noticed the glint of a gun barrel.

One of the pillagers caught sight of her and yelled towards the others. "Hey, over there! There's one of them."

Abby looked again to Kyle. His eyes bore straight through her as he held a shotgun in one hand and a lantern in the other. For an instant he was Callum, standing on the hill, her priest and her husband. He held the stare for a long moment and Abby sensed he was trying to tell her something, could almost hear him whispering to her. But his voice stayed out of range; too faint for her mind to grab onto.

He removed the cloth from his face again to reveal a faint smile. It was a smile for her benefit, meant to reassure her, but it didn't touch his eyes.

With a final look he held the lantern high in the air. "This way everyone! Follow me. The shelter is over here!"

"Oh my god." She took a step to start running only to be stopped by Alex's body falling over top of her in a messy tackle. His stocky frame pressed down on her hard making it difficult to raise her head to see Kyle. The mob was moving towards him now, running for their very lives to seek the safety of the imaginary shelter he promised them.

Before she could see anything else Alex dragged her off the ground and slung her over his shoulder. Her arms and legs flailed wildly, kicking into his stomach and beating his back with balled up fists.

"Stop it Abby." Alex spoke between his teeth, holding her feet down with his arms.

"Why are you doing this Alex? Put me down and go help him."

Abby was half way down the hatch of the bunker when she heard the first shot. More shots followed, one on top of the other. The echoes invaded her ears with a painful sharpness, stabbing into her like the tips of burning hot blades. She flung her limbs around again, screaming and beating into Alex's back with renewed force.

He threw her down hard as they reached the floor of the bunker, leaving the beginnings of a fresh bruise on her tailbone. She stood up quickly despite the pain in her backside and made a move towards the door. Her uncle quickly blocked her path with Alex stepping in beside him to create a firm wall between her and the way to the surface.

She felt the sting of panic in her chest, the first welling of tears behind her eyes. "Why is he doing this? How will he get in the shelter? How could you leave him out there to fend for himself?"

Alex spoke first. His eyes were stern while he rubbed his gut where she had kicked him. "Because he told us to."

"What?" Abby looked up confused, salty tears running down her cheeks. "I don't understand. What do you mean he told you to? Why would he do that?"

Jim looked to the other five people, gestured for them to go into the sleeping area. When they were gone he gripped his niece's shoulders to look her in the eye, took a breath to gather the right words.

"He knew something was going to happen, knew we'd never be able to support all of those people in here. There's not enough food, especially after we took on the others." When she continued to stare blankly he continued. "Those people were fighting for their lives. They would've killed us to get in here. Kyle sacrificed himself to save us."

Abby allowed herself to be led to a bench behind one of the tables, sunk down into the seat with a sob on her lips. She was in shock but definitely not numb. The weight of a two ton brick pressed in on her chest. She swallowed the ball of panic in her throat, bit her lip to keep from screaming.

Jim continued. His voice was strained with grief. "He warned us ahead of time that you were going to fight, that you wouldn't go quietly into the shelter without him. He told us you went where he went." Jim smiled, rubbed the back of Abby's hand softly. "And that we would have to restrain you, force you underground to protect you."

"But he can't make it up there alone, not against what's coming." She made a move to stand up again but her uncle held her in her seat. She looked at him with complete desperation. "Please. We have to help him. Damn it. He won't survive."

Alex shook his head, looked down at Abby with something like tenderness. "He made us swear not to let you leave and he made us swear not to come out of the shelter to help him. Not under any circumstances."

"And you're just going to listen to him? Why? He might glow and have visions of the future but he's not super human. He needs saving sometimes too."

"He made us swear Abby," Alex repeated. "He made us swear on our lives. He's the one who knew what was coming. He's the one who knew about all of this before any of us did. There is no reason not to trust him."

Jim rotated in the bench. "We did trust him Abby. We believed in him and the things he knew. And now we have to believe in you. It's your gifts that are going to get us through the days to come."

"No." Abby set her jaw, looked at the both of them defiantly. "He's coming back. Kyle will find a way."

Jim and Alex looked at each other in silent communication. It was Alex who drew the short straw and bent down to take on the task of telling Abby the last of the brutal truth. "No he's not honey." He took a deep breath and continued softly. "He's never coming back and he knew it."

"I don't believe that. He would've made more time for us. He would've..." Her sobs came then, choking her words.

After a sea of tears and lots of arguing Abby finally allowed herself to be led to her bunk. She cuddled up her tired body within freshly washed blankets and closed her eyes. As she drifted off she heard Alex say something about keeping an eye on her, and making sure sharp objects were out of her reach.

"I don't trust that she won't do something stupid." Alex stood by the sink, staring up at one of the control panels on the opposite wall.

"You really think so?" Jim joined him by the sink, keeping his voice low. "They didn't really know each other that long, barely had time to get cozy or anything."

Alex sent the older man a look that said he was completely oblivious. "Didn't she tell you about the visions, about the connection they shared, the past life thing?" Jim shook his head and Alex went on. "She's completely in love with him. Believe me, I know. She never looked at me the way she looked at him. He was her one and he's gone now. Who knows how she's going to react to something like that?"

Jim exhaled heavily. "Where have I been the last few days? I thought they were just falling victim to unusual and dramatic circumstances, letting their hormones get the best of them."

Alex huffed a laugh. "No, that's something I'm familiar with, especially when it comes to your niece."

Jim shot the younger man a look of warning.

"Sorry, but it's a fact. With me it was hormones and a certain kind of desperate need for connection. Everything about her was different. There were no real emotions, nothing you could really call love. At least not on her end."

"You loved her." It was a statement instead of a question.

Alex nodded with a touch of sadness and dropped his head. "Still do I guess. But I was okay with Kyle. Not at first, of course. I thought maybe she'd come around to me again, realize that we could be good together, especially since she'd stopped taking her pills."

Jim tilted his head in question. "Pills? Is she sick or something?"

"Not really sick, just diagnosed seriously depressed. She's been taking them for years, since right about the time she left your house and came to live in New York." Alex crossed his arms over his chest. "I knew about her taking them, but she has never given me the details as to why she took them or told me what led her to being medicated." Alex glanced toward the curtained door of the sleeping area and lowered his voice to a whisper. "Though I've seen her naked, and not that you want the details, but she has a nasty scar along the inside of her right thigh, right were that big artery would be."

Jim's eyes widened. "You think she tried to kill herself? No, that's not possible. Not Abby."

Alex held up his hand with a hush, glanced again towards the curtain. "Well, what would your guess be? It's either that or she was in a really bad accident no one knows about and she sustained no other injury."

"I can't believe that. Why wouldn't she talk to me, come home or something? I would've been there for her. She knows that."

"I don't know. She never talks about it, but I'm pretty sure her mother's death affected her more than she lets on. That and she didn't seem to function well before she took the pills. From what I've heard from some older acquaintances, she did little more than sit around her apartment watching television and waiting for work to come to her. She barely painted, barely did anything besides go out and drink every weekend."

Jim pursed his lips, let out a heavy sigh. "She was born a melancholy child. Since the day she came into the world it seemed like some part of her was missing and she was constantly searching for it. She was always more emotional, always quietly discontented with life. Losing her mother too soon didn't help." He crossed to the table and sat. "We'll take turns watching her, work as a team. The next few days are probably going to tell us whether or not we really have to worry."

Alex nodded. "Well we promised Kyle we'd keep her safe anyway, so it's not like we have a choice. He might've stolen the heart of the woman I love in about five minutes flat, but he also saved all of our lives without thinking twice about himself. I don't blame her for loving him."

Jim smiled sadly. "He was my best friend and I would've died for him. But he wanted me to watch after Abby instead, so that's what I'm going to do."

Alex nodded and pulled two beers from the backpack he had brought with him into the bunker. "To Kyle." He handed Jim a bottle and raised it high before taking a long swig."

Jim took his beer, poured a sip into the sink then took one himself. "To Windstone. The best damn farmer and friend I ever had the pleasure of knowing. May his name live on in the legends of generations to come."

CHAPTER FIFTEEN

Friday, December 21st 2012, 12:01am

Abby was on fire. Not the metaphorical, sweating buckets in the summer sun kind of on fire. No, she was literally burning.

Her body screamed out like a trapped animal, flames licking her flesh ruthlessly. She felt herself melting from the outside in, her organs cooking like a goulash on a stove burner turned to the highest setting. Her limbs seized up, her lungs fought for breath, and her heart pumped one last ounce of life's blood through her veins. Blackness was all that remained and Kyle was the one word she still remembered in the still emptiness of death.

Abby sat up with a start, smacking her head on the underside of the bunk above her. "Ow... shit!"

For a moment she wasn't sure where she was, but with the faint light dripping in through the curtain hanging between the bunk area and the main room she could see the others spread out along their beds. Some of them snored gently in sleep, others appeared to be quietly dreaming. She remembered all too well where she was and why. And worse, she remembered who was missing – who wasn't sleeping in the stacked rows of bunks along the concrete walls of the bomb shelter.

The dream was not part of her usual nightmare. It was all together different and far too real for Abby's taste. She could still feel the pain, the sensation of dying while engulfed in invisible flame. She recalled the exact moment her heart had stopped leaving a residual ache in her chest like she had been stabbed with something dull. She shuddered, wishing she could shove the memory away, toss it into the abyss of her mind behind metaphorical locks and keys.

She made her way to the living area to see her uncle sitting at the table with a steaming cup of coffee in front of him. His head hung low like a cement block had been glued to his shoulders.

He looked up with tired bags under his eyes. "Hey Kiddo. Feeling any better?"

He looks so old, Abby thought. When did those wrinkles appear around his eyes? The creases on his forehead? His voice was a mere croak, sounding as though he had been smoking a dozen Cuban cigars a day for a decade. Without words she sat down beside him, put her arm around his back and let her cheek fall against his shoulder.

One of the gauges on the wall blinked madly, drawing Abby's attention. "What's that mean?" she asked without lifting her head.

Jim glanced up, took a tiny sip of coffee. "It's the radiation meter. I'm not sure exactly what's going on up there, but nothing could survive it."

He stood, careful to slip from under her head gently, and walked to the wall where the gauges blipped and pulsed. He pointed to a meter, the needle flipped to the extreme right. "And it's hot. Crazy hot. I can't let myself imagine what we'll find when we surface. Not yet."

Abby felt faint. Her heart raced, beat like the feet of a thousand stampeding cattle inside her rib cage. Had she experienced Kyle's death in her dream? Was it him up there dead and disintegrating in waves of hot radiation? Her body lurched, stomach acid shooting up into her throat giving her just enough warning to make it into the bathroom before retching.

After rinsing out her mouth Abby returned to her uncle who was staring at the bathroom door in worried anticipation.

"You okay Kiddo?"

"Yeah." She wiped her mouth, steadied herself. Her body felt so heavy. "I had a terrible dream about fire, about burning alive."

Jim clenched his eyes shut. "That's awful." He stood up, crossed the short distance between them. "Look Kiddo, I think you should try tapping into these extra sensory gifts of yours. It might be helpful to see what's happening on the surface." His eyes examined her face carefully. "I know there's a lot going on right now, and maybe you don't want to see everything that's happening up there, but Kyle seemed to believe you were just as strong as he was, just as gifted."

"He was wrong." Sorrow embraced her like an old friend she remembered all too well. "I don't have half of the power he did."

"Well, maybe you could just try a little, dig down deep or whatever it takes. Reach inside somehow and find the strength."

Abby's sigh spelled defeat. "I'm not a hero Jimmy. I wouldn't even know where to begin."

"But couldn't you..."

Abby hit the table with her fist, stepped back and let her shoulders drop. "He was the holy man, the great profit of the people. I had no purpose other than to be with him."

Jim furrowed his brow, shook his head lightly. "I don't know about those things, past things. But I know who you are now. You're far more important than you've ever imagined and Kyle believed our hopes belonged with you."

"Well he was..." She lost her breath for a second, realizing she had been using the past tense. "...flawed just like everyone else, and not always right about everything."

Jim turned on her with furious eyes. "Damn it Abby. Just try. Somewhere inside you must know what to do." He relaxed again, softened just a little.

His eyes echoed her own grief. She realized then that her own pain had shadowed the fact that Jimmy was hurting too.

He gathered himself, took a sip of coffee. "Just try Kiddo."

She glared for a brief moment. What was she supposed to do? Say the magic words and become the Amazing Abby? How was she supposed to dig deep? What did that even mean?

Realizing her uncle was not going to give up she let out a heavy sigh. She resigned a nod, leaned against the counter to search her mind for something, anything at all that might point her in the right direction. Help me Kyle, she thought. I don't know what to do.

Abby didn't know if it was her imagination or some lingering effect of their connection, but she heard Kyle's voice clearly in her head.

There was strain in his voice. "You're trying too hard." His voice was dropped to a whisper. "It's like a reflex. Just clear your mind."

Abby closed her eyes, fought back a fresh wave of tears and let her limbs relax. She pushed thoughts of Kyle, the end of humanity, all the sadness in her heart aside; shoved them in some imaginary foot locker and slammed the lid closed.

All at once she began to see it. She saw the Earth above them, hot and toxic. Even through the haze of ash she could see the sun. It was monstrous, appearing to shoot long waves of fire from its surface. The Destroyer, the Second Moon hung beside it, also flaming in the sky.

Shingles melted on rooftops, horses lie dead in the barn. She saw the chicken coop, watched as eggs popped and began boiling in the extreme heat. As her focus changed a foot came into view, wearing a familiar style of work boot.

Abby's eyes flew open. "No. I don't want to see any more." Tears flooded her throat. "I can't. I won't." She stumbled on her feet, feeling dizzy.

Jim went to her, wrapped strong arms around her shoulders for support. "What did you see? What's going on up there?"

A tear fell down Abby's cheek, slid silently past her chin. "The end of everything."

She thought of Kyle's face, the boyish grin that made his face light up with goodness. She heard his laugh and let a faint smile touch her eyes as she silently said goodbye.

Any hope she had that he might've made it to somewhere safe was quickly disappearing. She let all but the tiniest ember of a wish smolder away into the dark void that was slowly becoming her heart.

Abby explained what she had seen to her uncle, her voice a monotone thrum. She left out the part about seeing the human foot she feared belonged to Kyle. Between her insights and what Kyle had told him, Jim managed to put things together.

"Okay, I have no idea about the science of the situation, and frankly I don't really care," Jim began. "It doesn't matter why, only how we can make it out of this thing alive."

He sipped his coffee casually, appearing to be holding himself together far too well for the circumstances. It infuriated Abby that he could be so calm when every part of her was screaming out in agony.

Jim continued, his light eyebrows raised. "But I guess that explains the radiation and the sudden heat wave. I thought the volcanoes were the end, but it seems like we're talking serious extinction. No vegetation, no animals."

"No people," Abby added. "It's all gone. Everything. What's the point of all this? What's the point of going on? It would've been a whole lot easier to accept our fate. To rot up there with Kyle... with Mom... with everyone else."

Jim let his disapproval wear on his face. "Why don't you go back to bed Abigail? When you're done feeling sorry for yourself come find me and we can start working to figure out how to get through this mess together." He waved his hand dismissively. "I plan to live and I would prefer if we were on the same page. If you can't do that, the others and I will figure this out without your help."

With a shrug and a small huff Abby went back to her bunk. What did it matter? They might've made it through the initial onslaught but they would soon be facing starvation and a harsh, unfamiliar planet where their odds of survival were less than slim. Abby would rather die in her sleep. Silently she wished for an early heart attack or a sudden brain aneurism – anything to stop the constant ache.

She lay down, closed her eyes, and prayed that she might be able to dream of beautiful things, of different times when she remembered what it was to have hope; to believe in something other than death and destruction.

She tossed about in the bunk restlessly, angrily. Frustration and despair seeped from her every pore. For an instant she contemplated banging her head on the wall or at the very least pounding her fists against the thick layers of concrete. The physical pain would surely dull the ache in her chest. Tears came again instead, hard shallow sobs that seemed to shake the bunk beneath her.

A weight settled into her bed and warm arms wrapped around her, pulling her in tight. Somewhere in the back of her mind she knew it was Alex who came to comfort her. But for the moment she allowed herself the delusion of believing it was Kyle. She imagined his scent, the sound of his voice, the way his eyes grew dark when he touched her.

Alex's voice shattered her fantasy. "It's alright. Everything will be okay."

They both knew his words were empty. Nothing would ever be okay again. The world as they knew it was gone, completely wiped from existence as easily as a swatted fly.

They lay together, ex-lovers turned friends, and Abby cried until there were no more tears; until she was safe in the darkness of a dreamless, death-like sleep.

CHAPTER SIXTEEN

Monday, December 24th 2012, 8:19pm

Three days in a bomb shelter had a way of feeling more like three long months. Abby had spent the last of her tears and was now content hiding in her bunk, curtain drawn to keep out the sorrowful eyes around her. She couldn't take one more look of pity from any of them.

Within the confines of her bunk she did little more than daydream, thinking back on her few moments with Kyle. She remembered the sound of his laugh, the way he looked squinting in the sunlight, how he drank coffee in the morning; anything that would help her hold on to the memory of him. She couldn't stand to think that she'd forget those details one day.

She shook her head hard to clear the cobwebs of sorrow that had gathered there. She would remember more than insignificant facts. She would remember who he was. He was the man who rescued terrified dogs and found pleasure in sneaking carrots to horses. He was the unassuming yet unrepentant romantic with a love for poetry who fed her cheesecake under the stars. He was the man she had shared a life with once upon a time in a land full of wildflowers and mist from the sea.

Abby smiled to herself. She knew him, knew his heart the way she knew how to mix colors on a palette. He was part of her. She understood him better than she understood anything else regardless of whether or not she could put that knowledge into words that made sense to anyone else. No, it was something too complicated for words, she told herself.

It was then that she heard his voice. She hadn't heard it since that first night in the shelter when her uncle had probed her to delve deep within herself and pull out visions of the world on the surface.

"My lily girl, not made for this world's pain."

She heard him like an echo in her head, flinched at the poetry on his tongue and the way it stabbed into her heart.

His voice came again, full of reproach. "Stop sulking Abby. There is work to be done."

"What am I supposed to do?" She whispered between her teeth into the bunk above her. "I'm stuck in a freaking bomb shelter and you're not here." She held back a sob. "You're not here."

The voice continued. "You knew me for three days out of your life. You'll be fine for the rest of it without me."

"Oh really? Well I remember a lot more than just those three days. And that's easy for you to say. You're dead. Dying is easy."

She heard his laughter reverberate through her mind. "Yes, that's right. I'm a dead man. I almost forgot."

Abby was trying to deal with her insane delusions when suddenly Alex was pulling her curtain open and peering at her. He kept the fabric tight around his face so she could see only the center of his features between the panels of cloth. "You okay?"

Abby cursed herself for not being more quiet. Now she'd get even more pathetic stares. Plus Alex and her uncle would never let her off suicide watch if she kept acting like a head case.

"Yes. I'm fine Alex." She didn't sound very convincing, even to herself. "Go back to playing Santa."

He ignored her dismissal. "Who you talkin' to?"

He was being a bit silly, continuing to keep the curtain tight to his face with his questions coming in playful one sentence bursts.

"No one."

"Okay then." He kept staring at her, looking like a deranged baby being born through the folds of the slate grey curtain.

Abby let out a reluctant laugh. "You're being really weird Alex. Are you drunk?"

"Maybe, but guess what?"

She rolled her eyes. "What?"

"It's Christmas and there are presents out here."

"That's great Alex. Why don't you go open them? Maybe someone gave you some new hair products."

He shook his head lightly. "There are presents for you." With eyebrows raised he continued. "You should come out and open them up before I trade them for the last chicken stew MRE. It's the end of the world, in case you missed the news flash. Christmas presents have become a very serious luxury which in turn makes them very precious commodities."

Abby was intrigued but not quite ready to leave the confines of her self-imposed prison. She could think of a million other things to do besides mingle with seven people who were waiting for her to snap in a fit of grief.

"You can have them. Or give them to Evie. I know you've been trying to get her attention lately."

Alex shook his head, again looking silly and child like. "They're not from me, or Jim, or anyone else who lives in this bunker." With that he left, the curtain closing again behind him with a flutter.

That had Abby's interest peaked. If they weren't from anyone in the bunker that only left one option.

She bolted from the bunk and ran out into the living area. Seven pairs of eyes turned to her immediately. Well nine if she counted the dogs.

Abby wasn't exactly expecting the scene before her. The two tables that usually sat against the walls had been pulled out into the middle of the room and pushed together. In the center, above a runner of pale blue fabric sat a small plastic Christmas tree with presents wrapped in bright silver paper pushed under its low branches.

"Wanna put the star on top?" Alex asked with a smile. "Or there's some hot chocolate on the stove. It's instant but still pretty good."

"Don't believe him Abby." Evie turned in her seat, flashing a smile towards Abby. "He just got me to eat the MRE hot dog." Evie made a face. "I don't recommend it. Not unless you're into eating foamy meat product."

Abby didn't want to laugh, but a rogue giggle tumbled out of her anyway. All eyes turned in her direction. Her stomach did back flips and she tried to breathe. She forced herself to walk further into the room instead of fleeing to the safety of her bunk.

When she didn't speak, her uncle chimed in. "There are some things here for you Kiddo." He paused, words sticking on his tongue. "They're from Kyle."

Abby shook her head a little, confusion sweeping over her. "How?" Her voice was less than a whisper.

"He stashed them away in here along with the tree and the little ornaments on the day the tornadoes hit. After he got back from town." Jim handed her a cup of hot chocolate, gestured to Alex. "He told us where to find them."

Abby almost laughed. Even in... her mind tripped over the word... death he was still surprising her. Choking back sudden tears she took a sip of the watered down hot chocolate.

She stayed with her companions, listening as they told stories of Christmases past, trying to enjoy herself. More than once she held back tears, choosing instead to smile as Alex rattled on about his family and the time he climbed onto the roof in his pajamas at the age of eight to prove to everyone that Santa was real.

Abby thought of her own childhood memories and how she had held on to the idea of Christmas magic for as long as she could, never giving up hope that a fat man in a red suit would show up through the fireplace and grant her little girl requests.

She closed her eyes tight, made a silent wish with such desperation that it made her heart ache. Give me hope, she said over and over again in her head. Give me just a little bit to hold on to. Please.

After a short time she politely excused herself and took her handful of presents back to her bunk. She wanted to open them alone so she could break down in private if she needed to. She didn't want to make a spectacle of herself and ruin the night for everyone else.

There were three boxes; one fairly large deep shirt box and two medium sized shoe boxes. Abby had no idea what could be inside of them but she was eager to find out. With shaky hands she glanced at the tags where Kyle had scrawled her name in black marker. With a touch of trepidation, she tore the paper from the biggest box.

Her breath became trapped in her throat as she pulled the item from the box. She immediately recognized it as a table top easel, obviously made by Kyle's own hand. It was primitive, crafted from sanded and polished scraps of different thicknesses, yet somehow it was also extremely ingenious. Examining it further she realized the legs were hinged and folded up under the main frame of the easel. It would stand on its own, a freestanding easel and not a table top version.

"So that's what he was building in the barn," she mumbled quietly, thinking back to the day. A tiny smile turned up the side of her mouth, more full of sadness than anything resembling joy.

Taking a deep breath, Abby turned to the other boxes. In the second one there were at least two dozen small tubes of paint, brushes, and thin pieces of plywood cut to fit the easel. He had thought of everything. Too bad the last thing Abby wanted to do now was paint. She couldn't find the inspiration if she wanted to. A small note sat at the bottom of the box.

Paint Abby. Paint for you.

K.W.

In the third and smallest box she found two journals, both bound in black leather, and the copy of Oscar Wilde's poetry she'd been reading just days before on Kyle's couch. An inscription was scrawled on the inside cover.

To my lily girl.

She fought to keep her hands from shaking and turned to the journals. The first one she opened was blank, without a single word written on the pages. When she opened the second journal she could see that it was nearly full of scratchy handwriting.

January 4th 2012

Had the dream again last night. I'm still not sure what it means. I know it's important - something I need to figure out - but I need some more clues. Or maybe I'm just losing it.

Abby flipped through the pages, breezing over Kyle's detailed description of the past year of his life and his struggles with the visions that plagued his mind. There were lists of items he needed to buy: water, dry goods, dehydrated fruits, toilet paper – all survival materials.

Eager to see what he had written over the past few days, Abby turned quickly to the back of the journal. Her hands shook and her breathing quickening as she stopped on the pages she was looking for. She recognized her name among the words and edged closer to the light that hung on the wall beside her bunk. Though she didn't need it. Not with the glow that continually flowed from her skin.

December 17th 2012

Met Jim's niece tonight – Abby. She glows like something out of a sci-fi movie. Apparently so do I. I feel like I know her already somehow – and not in a vague, shallow sort of way. When I'm near her flashes from her mind pop into mine like rain drops dripping into a puddle - complete with little ripples of emotion.

I get a sense that she's in this for a reason – a big one that I don't understand yet. It's coming soon. That's why she's here. She knows what I know – has had the dreams too. There's a strong attraction, a pull towards her I can't explain. For the first time in a long time I feel like writing poetry – poetry about the glowing girl I met on the porch of the Yellow House tonight.

There were no other entries. Abby flipped page after page furiously seeing nothing but blank white paper. Finally she reached the last page of the book and sucked in her breath. Her name jumped off of the paper, hitting her in the heart like a massive sledgehammer. She held her hand over the page to see it more clearly, letting her light drip over the words. She should've been wearing her glasses, but she didn't feel like trying to find them.

Abby,

I don't know how things are going to work out yet. I have a plan but I'm preparing for the worst. I guess if you're reading this then the worst is exactly what's happened.

I'm sorry. I know I acted weird, but I wasn't prepared for you to come into my life the way you did. Especially not now. I wanted to be with you – had finally begun to believe we had some kind of shot. I should've made more time.

But now you have to step up. No feeling sorry for yourself. No wasting time away in the bunker. You are just as powerful as I am. Use the time below to harness that power. Prepare yourself and the others for the hard tasks ahead. The weight is on you now. You're the only one who can save them.

I want you to continue the story. Use the blank journal to finish our saga of survival. Press on and don't give up. You have such a greater purpose and I believe you have it in you to get through anything. I know you well. Remember?

There is nothing I can say now to make you realize what you mean to me and what I know in my heart we could be. I know that you were my one real chance in this life or any other, and I desperately wanted to take that chance with you.

In another time I will be waiting – searching for you to wander into my sights again, revealing to me secrets only the light of your soul can expose.

Fight to live Abby. Fight so that the human race can go on and we can come back to each other someday. One way or another we will get our chance.

Kyle

Abby felt the tears streaming down her cheeks and let them fall. She kept her eyes on the page, memorizing every word and every haphazardly scribbled letter until her eyes were stone dry.

How could he expect her to just move on? How could he think she wouldn't grieve for him – for what could've been? No. For what should've been.

"How could he expect me to just forget him? To pretend like none of it every happened?" she whispered.

"Because there is no other choice. There are others to think about. They are counting on you now."

Abby heard Kyle's voice as though he were sitting right beside her. She listened but heard nothing more. She knew it was her own imagination. Her therapist would say she was filling the void created by her grief as a way to cope. Part of her didn't care. If she was raving mad for hearing Kyle's voice then she was content to be committed.

Abby sat back on her bunk, exhausted from tears and days of emotional stress. She left the book open to Kyle's letter and closed her eyes. Before drifting off she willed herself to recover from her pain or at the very least learn to go numb again without medication; to shut down and refuse any further tears to fall from her eyes.

With a sigh she rolled over to her side and pretended Kyle was lying beside her. She let her mind drift to the one night when he had held her close, tried to remember what his breathing sounding like in her ear, what it felt like against the back of her neck.

Tomorrow she would try to live up to her potential, but not for herself. And not even for the seven people that wanted to look to her for guidance. She would fight to live only because he had asked her to. Only for the hope that in another life they might meet again.

CHAPTER SEVENTEEN

Friday, December 28th 2012, 11:38am

Abby spent the next few days becoming filled with purpose and a significant amount of crazy. But she was quickly becoming accustomed to being a member of the insane.

Kyle's voice had become a more prominent force in her mind and subsequently she felt herself drifting into a realm where she was sure only poor homeless schizophrenics had gone before.

She didn't have the guts to tell anyone what was going on in her troubled head but she had come dangerously close to confessing to Alex.

He had become a good friend lately, someone she knew she could depend on. It still amazed her that ever since their physical relationship had ended they could spend time together as adults, talking about serious things and confiding in each other eagerly. But she still couldn't tell him that she'd been having conversations with her dead would-be soul mate for nearly a week.

Abby couldn't tell Alex that she had been staying awake into the early hours talking about life, love, and reality television with someone who was supposed to be a corpse. She couldn't stand to imagine the look on his face. Then again, he'd believed her crazy ravings once and it had paid off for him. But Abby didn't even believe Kyle was alive. She was positive he was gone and she just wasn't ready to let go of him.

Alex had recently developed an attraction for Evie, not as though that were a shock to anyone. The tall and curvy Evie was arguably a serenely beautiful creature.

Abby watched the other woman from the confines of her bunk, noting how Alex examined her long legs and glossy black hair hanging down her back and to her waist in a tight braid. But Evie didn't pay Alex the same kind of attention. Of course that didn't dissuade him one bit. He liked a good challenge.

Abby looked on as they flirted by Evie's bunk, talking in hushed whispers with Evie trying desperately not to let Alex make her laugh. Abby felt a tug on her heart, remembering Kyle's smile with sudden sadness. She pressed a palm against the center of her chest and tried to breathe.

"Looks like Alex is making some progress." Kyle's voice echoed in her head a little too loudly startling Abby out of her thoughts.

Abby sunk back into her bunk and closed the curtain swiftly. "Jesus," she muttered. "You scared the crap out of me."

She heard his laughter bounce between her ears. "Sorry."

"I'm such a freak." She said the words more to herself than to her imaginary Kyle. "I've completely lost my damn mind. Not that I had much sanity to begin with."

"Nah," Kyle huffed. "You're completely sane actually."

"Right." She pushed her hair back out of her face and crinkled her nose. "You know my shrink would most likely say I had developed a split personality to cope with my grief. I've been through too much therapy to believe I'm sane anymore. This is not my first neurosis rodeo Kyle."

Again she heard him chuckle softly. "Well, maybe it's not a bad disorder to have then. I for one am glad you're certifiable."

"Thanks," she mumbled. "At least someone is happy about it."

The curtain surrounding her bunk flew open making her jump. "Talking to yourself again Abbs?" Alex's knelt by her bunk grinning. His thin lips turned up a bit more when he saw the look of shock on her face. He gave her a knowing look then gestured for her to go out into the living area. "Everyone's waiting for today's uh…

meeting? Exercise? Whatever. They're all sitting in the front room waiting for you."

Abby shoved herself up from the bunk and followed him into the other room. She appraised the Gleamers, each of them glowing in faint pastels. The colors blended in pretty ways between the few who were close enough as to be touching. Hanna sat sandwiched on the bench between the yellow hues of Sam and Jake creating a pretty green where their individual lights mingled.

David grimaced at the far edge of the bench, his jaw tight making the cleft of his chin seem more pronounced. He rarely looked happy and everyone else was beyond trying to coax him out of his self imposed shell.

Evie leaned against the wall, Alex lingering just to her right. His eyes never left her face. Her soft green shimmer touched his arm, tumbled onto the wall behind her, outlining her body like a layer of sheer jade fabric.

Abby took a spot along the sink wall, smiling at her uncle as she scooted up on the counter beside him. "Okay, what we've tried so far has yielded very little result. So I came up with another idea."

"You finally figured out that holding hands in a circle for an hour was getting us nowhere?" David's voice held his usual bitter note.

Abby glanced in his direction then dismissed him without a word. He was just a pain in the ass. They had two other Builders anyway. It didn't matter if he participated or not.

"I don't like the way he looks at you." Kyle popped into Abby's head as she thought of David.

"Hush," Abby hissed to Kyle. She went on with her makeshift lesson, allowing the group to think she was talking to David. "Anyway, I was thinking about Evie and what sort of power someone with a connection to plants might have." Abby picked up a piece of dried apple from a bowl on the counter. "And I came up with this." She tossed the apple chunk to Evie.

Evie caught the fruit and proceeded to stare at it like it was an alien species she'd never seen before. "What would you like me to do with it?"

Abby sucked in a breath, hoping her crazy wasn't about to start showing. "I want you to focus on bringing it back to life."

"Bringing it back to life?" Evie echoed. Her confusion was obvious on her face. "How exactly would you like me to do that?"

"Focus your mind. Believe that you can rehydrate the apple, bring the molecules back into a state of movement so that life returns into the flesh."

David twirled a finger near his temple. "And I thought the group meditations were ridiculous. This is beyond pointless."

Abby did her best to keep her cool. "Do you have a better idea David?"

He smiled without kindness and shook his head slightly. "Not really."

"Then why don't you just sit there and be quiet. I think there's a reason why I'm the only one in the room who's glowing all white while you're a sick shade of piss yellow." She glanced to Sam and Jake. "No offense."

The brothers shrugged their shoulders and glared down the bench to David. If there was a black sheep in the group David would be it. He had never uttered a positive word to any of them. Most of the time he kept quiet and looked on with his constant judgmental gaze.

Abby turned back to Evie. "Just try to imagine the apple is fresh and juicy and see where that leads. Believe it's possible to bring life back into it."

Evie nodded and, though her face looked reluctant, she closed her eyes to give it a shot.

It seemed like a long while passed with nothing happening. Everyone in the room looked on, holding their breath and waiting for something – anything – out of the ordinary to occur.

Each of them had been racking their brains for days trying to come up with some way to make their gifts materialize. It had to be more than just nightmares and shiny auras. Neither were going to help them survive in a harsh new environment without food or fresh water. There had to be some other reason for the spontaneous mass migration to Kansas. At least that what's Abby's gut feelings had made them believe.

All at once the light from Evie's hands began to grow outwardly. It peaked and popped into a bright flash before receding back into her skin.

"Oh." Evie's mouth gaped open in shock. "I did it. I really did it." Her face beamed as she held her hand out for everyone to see.

In her sun-kissed hand was the slice of apple, no longer shriveled and sapped of its water. It was alive and fresh as through it had been picked from a branch and sliced only minutes earlier.

"That was awesome," Sam said with a boyish laugh. "Do it again Evie."

Abby smiled from ear to ear – perhaps the first genuine smile she'd been able to express since Kyle had shoved her away and ran straight into the face of shotgun wielding, panic stricken townsfolk.

The timbre of Kyle's voice interrupted the moment. "Great job Teach. Now we just have to figure out what the rest of them are good for."

"Not to mention figuring out what the two of us can really do." She mumbled the words low enough but a few of the others turned to look at her in question anyway. She could feel Alex's eyes on her and even noticed David giving her his sulky glare. Abby simply shook her head and smiled. "Wonderful job Evie. Now let's see if the rest of you have some sort of active power as well."

Abby walked to the drawer under the sink and pulled out a red handled utility knife.

Alex straightened from his leaning posture on the wall. "Um... what are you doing Abby?"

She pulled the knife open, slid up her sleeve, and sliced the soft flesh of her forearm in one quick motion.

"Abigail!" Jim's voice bounced off the concrete walls of the shelter. He grabbed her arm, examined the fresh wound with a scowl.

It was Kyle's disapproving voice she heard next. "That was stupid Abby. I think you're going to need stitches. Let's hope your vaccinations are up to date too. Tetanus is no joke."

Abby ignored Kyle's rant and glanced around the room at the stunned faces that surrounded her. "Don't worry. I have a plan. Besides, it's not that bad." Her words were directed at her uncle and Alex, plus the image of Kyle that lived only in her mind.

She felt the pain throb up into her shoulder and down into her fingers. She welcomed it openly. It was a comforting change from the endless dull ache of emptiness that consumed her every waking moment. She clenched her fist, watched as the blood ooze forth.

Abby motioned for Hanna to come stand by her, winced once at the pain. "It's your turn to shine now Hanna."

The little red head gawked at Abby as she stepped forward. "I... I don't know if I can fix that like Evie did the apple. I don't even know where to begin."

Abby tried to send the girl encouragement with her smile. "It's in you somewhere. I know it is. I can feel it. You can do this Hanna. Just concentrate. Imagine the wound healing up, the skin fusing back together like two sides of a zipper."

"Gross," Jake groaned. "What an image."

Abby ignored him and nodded to Hanna. "Go ahead Hanna. You're our Healer."

Hanna visibly gulped and placed her hands over Abby's wound. Blood dripped down Abby's arm along the ground, spotting the grey linoleum tile with stains of deep red.

They didn't have to wait as long this time. In less than a few moments the room lit up with Hanna's blue glow and a small flash sent Abby rocking back on her heels. When she looked down the wound was nearly gone. All that remained was a fresh pink scar that felt tender but not quite painful.

"Did it work?" Hanna's eyes were still clenched shut.

"Open up and have a look." Abby laughed as Hanna opened one eye and then the other.

Abby held out her arm and allowed the younger woman a moment to examine her handiwork. She then moved to show the other members of the group, displaying her freshly healed skin like it was a trophy.

Abby stopped at David, narrowed her eyes and bent down to his face. "Keep your doubts to yourself from now on." It was a warning but he only glared, turning the corners of his mouth up in a cocky grin.

"Okay. I didn't see that coming," Kyle said from within the depths of her skull. "That will be an extremely useful talent to have around."

"Told you I knew what I was doing." Abby grinned, realizing then that she had gained quite a bit of respect from the rest of the group. Well, with the exception of David anyway.

She caught the eye of Alex and Jim, receiving nods of approval from each of them.

"What about us then?" Jake straightened in his seat. "What do you think us yellow guys can do?"

Abby hadn't had the opportunity to think about that question as much as she would've liked. The other two gifts seemed easier to pin-point. They made sense. She knew the three men were all supposed to be builders of some kind; people who constructed and engineered. But she had no idea what kind of active talent the three of them should possess.

"I don't know yet Jake." Abby pulled her sleeve down to cover the scar on her arm. "I need to think a little more on that one. I suggest the rest of you do the same. Let's not forget we're supposed to be a team."

"Oh really? Isn't that convenient? We do all the work and you take all the glory." David leaned his elbows on the table, sitting his weight forward in a challenging gesture. "What can you do then? You had dreams. So did the rest of us.

You had the sense to run to Kansas and hide in your uncle's bomb shelter, which let's face it, is a no brainer. How can you contribute actively besides sitting around here giving orders and watching everyone else create little miracles?"

Abby opened her mouth to respond when Kyle's voice invaded her thoughts again. "You don't have to answer that. There's no getting through to that guy. He just wants to get a rise out of you. Don't let him have the pleasure."

Abby nodded to her phantom Kyle and glared towards David with disdain. "I guess you'll have to wait and see. You should think more before you speak David. And try to have a little faith."

David exhaled a derisive snort. "Right. Whatever you say Queen Abby of the White Light." His hands popped up to taunt her with a fake bow.

Abby felt her temper flaring up and had the sudden urge to throw something at David's smug face.

Alex caught the look, obviously sensed the anger brewing under the surface and came to her rescue immediately. "Why don't we all relax a little? I think that's enough work for one day."

Abby sent David one last threatening look then headed back to her bunk in silence. She had done her job for the day and was suddenly tired. That might also have been due to the stress of being wounded and healed in less than ten minutes time.

"Thanks Alex. I really can't stand that guy." Abby kept her voice hushed as he walked with her to her bunk.

"I know. He's a dick. I don't think he likes not being the one in control of everything. He acts like a cult leader with the others when you're hibernating in your bunk. Constantly telling them what they're doing wrong, spouting off nonsense like he's propagandizing for their loyalty. He's like a dictator."

Abby snorted. "That son of a bitch. I'll set him straight."

Kyle's voice was a booming yell in her head. "You will not. He's not stable and I don't trust him. Let someone else do it."

She brought her hand to her temple and pressed. "Ah… not so loud."

Alex grabbed her upper arm, concern written on his furrowed brow. "Abby? What is it?"

Abby shook her head and groaned inwardly. "It's nothing. I'm fine. Just a tiny headache."

"You should rest then. Get some peace and quiet and take a little nap."

"Yeah." She leaned back onto her bed and sighed. "That's a good idea. Don't let that guy get out of hand though okay?"

"Don't worry about it. I'll say something to him. You relax now." Alex pulled her blankets up over her shoulders and closed her curtain

Abby drifted out of consciousness quickly, sinking into a world of dreams where Kyle was more than just her personal phantom; more than just a delusion of her tattered, grieving mind.

CHAPTER EIGHTTEEN

Monday, December 31st 2012, 11:19pm

It was New Year's Eve and Abby wasn't feeling at all like celebrating. She was more content to hide in her bunk and listen to her figment of Kyle then to drink and play cards as the clock ticked down to 2013. Besides, there was no one she wanted to kiss at midnight. No one alive anyway.

He spoke to her softly. Or at least she imagined his voice sounded soft. The tone of his words made him seem tired and maybe even a little miserable. "Why don't you go out and have some fun with everyone else? There's beer to drink and knowing Jim, at least one shot of tequila for everybody."

"I'm not feeling much like a party at the moment." She methodically recorded the things she had learned about the Gleamers over the past few days, jotting down experiences in detail on the pages of the leather journal Kyle had given her for Christmas. They had been able to feast on fresh fruit salad for the past two days thanks to Evie and Abby had a half a dozen new scars to show for Hanna's newfound confidence.

"Why not?" He yawned at length before going on. "I think it sounds like fun. I could use a shot of tequila."

"Ghosts can't drink. Or more accurately, figments of my imagination can't drink." Abby continued her work, fixing her attention to the black ink marks she made on the page. "Do you seriously need to ask me why I don't feel like celebrating New Year's right now? Isn't it rather self explanatory?"

"Come on Abby." He was annoyed but he didn't yell. "You were picked to live. Yes, the world ended, but you didn't. Stop punishing yourself."

Her face remained expressionless, her voice calm as she kept writing. "I think I've gone through enough traumas lately. Why would I want to punish myself?"

"For surviving."

Abby stopped writing and stared at the wall without actually seeing it.

Kyle continued. "Look, I'm just saying you can't pretend to live. You walk around here like everything is okay and everyone knows it's not. Every single person in this bunker has lost someone now."

She continued her thousand yard stare at the wall and thought of Alex's parents lying dead amid the rubble of their home. She had met them only once but they were nice people with a charming house in Cape Cod and a little black poodle they called Petunia. Abby had overheard Alex talking with Evie about his family earlier, relaying a light hearted story to cheer Evie up while the dark haired girl shed tears over the people she had lost.

Abby wasn't the only one suffering. She knew that. Which made it a million times harder for her to spend time with any of them. They gave her sympathetic glances while she could barely look them in the eye.

"You're not responsible for their pain," Kyle said. "It's not as though you could've stopped the end from coming and there was no way to save everyone we loved."

"We could've given the rest of the world some warning."

"They had warning." He sighed. "And a few of them did make it. What would our warnings have accomplished anyway? Should we have unleashed our burden on them so they could spend their last moments in panic, killing each other out of fear? Is that how you would've wanted to spend those last days?"

"That's different though. I believed we'd survive. All of us. I was afraid, but I knew I was safe too. Because of you... and all the work you'd done. I knew my life wasn't going to end."

"Well it looks like it's over now. Isn't it?" He was goading her.

"No, it's not." Her words were forced, laced with regret.

"Glad to hear it. And that is a good thing. Sweet Abby, you didn't want to die up there. You weren't meant to."

"But you were? I would've rather joined you instead of facing all of this alone. Do you have any idea how terrified I am of going back to the surface? I'd rather suffocate down here than see what's up there. I'm not strong enough to lead these people to anything but their deaths."

"Yes you are Abby. You have all the power I have, all the gifts and strengths you need. The others would most likely have never figured out their abilities if it wasn't for you."

She shook her head, clenched her jaw to keep from crying for the millionth time. "You're wrong. They don't need me." She sniffed, collected herself. "Not to mention all of this is all very easy for you to say since, again, you're dead. You left me to do it all on my own."

"I haven't left you. I'm right here."

"No Kyle." Her voice cracked. "You're just in my head."

There was a long silence before he spoke again. "If that's true – if you're sitting there talking to yourself – then somewhere inside your mind you believe you have the strength. You believe you are powerful and that you can do what you must. You're giving yourself this pep talk then."

Abby rolled her eyes. "Delusions can be a real pain in the ass sometimes."

"Yeah, well the truth isn't always easy to accept. Believe me, I should know."

She closed the journal, tilted an ear to listen. "What do you mean by that?"

He sighed. "Nothing." She heard the smack of his lips as his words sat on his tongue. "It's nothing."

Abby wanted to push for more information but she knew there was no point. She would only be talking to herself anyway. And suddenly she felt the strong urge to talk to someone with a pulse. She'd had enough of this weird, one sided conversation.

"Alex!"

Maybe a minute went by before he showed up at her bunk and pushed aside her curtain.

"What's up? You want a beer or something?" His cheeks were flushed from drinking and he held three beer bottles in his hands. Two of them were unopened. "Sam and Jake can really suck down some booze so I've got my own stash."

"No. Thanks anyway. Listen, can I talk to you about something?"

"Yeah, of course. What's going on?"

Alex plopped down next to her on the bunk, flipped the switch to turn her light on. Abby squinted against the light and waited for her eyes to adjust. She never used the strip light. She didn't need to. Complete darkness was something she never saw anymore.

With her hands folded in her lap, Abby began. "There's really no other way to put this. So uh... I've been hearing Kyle's voice."

Alex didn't skip a beat. "I know. I hear you talking to him. So does everyone else."

"Shit. So I'm the resident crazy person then?"

"Well I wouldn't go that far." He took a swig from his open bottle. "Since you figured out the girl's powers there seems to be a quiet understanding that you have unique methods that just happen to pay off in the long run."

Abby frowned. "I'm not sure that's any better Alex."

He shrugged. "Well, at least they're not calling you Circus Freak anymore."

"What? They called me a circus freak?"

"Not a circus freak. The Circus Freak."

She threw up her hands. "Well that's just great."

Alex chuckled. "Calm down Abbs. It's not that bad. They listen to you and believe you can help them with their special talents... or whatever they are. Don't worry about it."

Abby wasn't convinced but let the subject drop. "Why didn't you say anything to me about talking to Kyle?"

"I figured it would pass and I thought maybe it was kind of normal considering the circumstances."

"The circumstances that he was a guy I knew for three days who sacrificed himself right after he found out we shared a past life together?"

Alex sent her a look. "There was more to it than that and you know it. You cared about him and he cared about you. It was obvious."

"It was?" She was usually the observant one, but sometimes people outside a situation saw things better.

He nodded as he drained the last of his beer and opened another one. "After what you told me, about the connection between the two of you, I was worried you were going to do something stupid when he died."

"Like what?"

He gave her a look, ran a hand along the inside of her thigh.

She smacked his hand and jumped back an inch. "What are doing?"

"Where'd that scar come from Abbs?"

Abby looked down, fidgeted with her hands. "It was a sad time for me. I wasn't thinking straight then."

Alex nodded knowingly. "As long as you're thinking straight now."

"I was just sad. I don't think I really wanted to succeed at... ending it all. Maybe I just wanted to stop for a while. Stop all the hurting."

"And now you're hurting again. And so you hear his voice sometimes. I don't think it makes you crazy and it's better than coping by hurting yourself. You're just sad right now."

She shrugged off her past with a shake of her head. "Maybe. But it's not like I hear him every once in a while when I'm thinking about him or sitting alone killing time. I don't hear him calling my name in the bunker or anything nondescript like that. I literally have conversations with a dead man."

Abby grabbed one of the unopened bottles from his hand and twisted the cap off. "Thing is, I don't want it to go away. Not really. I mean I argue with him about it... well I guess I argue with myself. But I don't really want to stop hearing him."

"How often do you hear him?"

"It's sporadic. Some days it's constant and other times a day or two will go by without a word. It sounds so real Alex, like it's really him."

He leaned in and lowered his voice. "Did you really love him Abbs?"

"I don't think I had a choice in that matter. But I don't know if love is the right term. It seems too small of a word somehow. But who knows? We only had a few days to get to know each other. We might've learned to hate each other eventually if given the chance." Her smile was sad.

Alex wrapped an arm around her shoulders, pulled her head into his chest. "Maybe, but I'm sure it would've been fun getting there. You were connected with each other and he was a part of you. I don't think you're crazy."

Abby swallowed the lump in her throat. "I guess I'm just destined to be haunted then."

He gave her a squeeze. "I'll make sure no one thinks you've lost it. Okay?"

"Okay, but do me a favor? I know you and Jimmy have been doing some bonding since we went under. Don't mention this to him okay? He probably won't notice anything weird anyway. If it's not classic cars or old TV shows he doesn't really pay attention."

"Okay. I won't say anything to him." He paused, pushed a strand of her hair from his chin. "I promise."

CHAPTER NINETEEN

Wednesday, January 9th 2013, 11:27pm

"So what do you think?" Alex leaned against the wall of the bunker, his body propped up next to the bathroom door.

Jim rubbed his sunken eyes with the back of his hand. "Honestly? I think she's having some sort of meltdown. She doesn't want to deal with him being gone and her mind is creating an escape from reality. What else could it be?"

Alex nodded his head heavily. "Yeah, I think you're probably right."

Alex had given Abby over a week to come to grips with her delusions, but even as he broke his promise to her, she was in her bunk carrying on a conversation with a ghost.

"Maybe it has something to do with her visions," Alex pondered. "Maybe they have negative effects."

"Like schizophrenia? I don't know, but nothing would surprise me at this point."

Jim didn't understand. Nothing was logical anymore. He was living in a bomb shelter with one person who could make dried apricots juicy and full of life again and another who could wave one freckled hand and heal deep wounds that would otherwise need sutures. Now his niece was losing her mind. That or she had a direct line to the afterlife. He was suddenly glad he couldn't see any of the glowing. That would likely send him over the edge.

"What should we do about it?" Alex asked. "We can't just hold her down and shake some sense into her."

Jim shook his head, exhausted. "If her mind doesn't want to believe it there's not much we can do."

Alex's let out a heavy sigh, shoved his hands into his pockets. "I promised her I wouldn't say anything to you about it, but I don't want to lose her completely because of all this? There must be some way to shock her back to reality."

"I don't think so. Not until we get up top and show her the...." Jim squeezed his eyes shut against the image in his head. "...body."

Alex nodded then stood up straighter. "I think you should talk to her. You're the closest thing she's ever had to a father. She might listen to you and start letting go."

"I'm not old enough to be her father." Jim shrugged. "But I guess it's worth a try."

The two of them walked the short distance to Abby's bunk in silence. They listened for a second before disturbing her.

"You think so? That actually makes some sense. They're Movers not Builders. Huh? Yeah, I'll try that then."

Alex tapped his fist lightly on the frame of her bunk. "Abby? Can we talk to you?"

She was quiet for a second, not bothering to open the curtain. "Who's we?"

"Uh it's me... Alex. And Jim."

Abby flipped the curtain open with a swoosh. "You told him didn't you?"

Alex looked down at his shoes. "I didn't know what else to do Abbs. We just want to help you get over it."

She sighed heavily and stepped out of her bunk. Her eyes scanned the bunks seeing only closed curtains with no lights shining through. With her head she gestured for the three of them to go into the main room.

Abby turned hot eyes on Alex. "Couldn't keep your mouth shut, could you Alex?"

Jim spoke up in defense. "It's not his fault Abby. I asked him if he knew how you were doing and I pulled it out of him." Jim gave Alex a sideways glance which told him to play along. "We just want to help."

"How? Did you guys recently get degrees in psychology that I don't know about? And what's the point anyway? I'm not hurting anyone. In fact, Kyle is helping me figure out what ability the guys might have."

She stopped and looked passed them, obviously listening to something they couldn't hear.

"What's the voice saying now Abby?" Jim leaned towards her, put his face in her line of sight.

"He's telling me I shouldn't be mad at Alex. That he's grateful I have people around me who care."

Jim raised his eyebrows. "Well you should listen to him. Ghost, delusion, or whatever that's good advice."

Abby plopped down at one of the tables and rested her head in her hand. "Yeah. I've been realizing lately that insane people are full of great advice." She sighed. "Look, I'm okay. Stop worrying. I know that's going to be hard considering I've turned into someone you would avoid on the street, but I'm also someone who has had visions of the future, who glows from the inside out. Whatever I am doesn't come with an instruction manual. I'm sure there's some reason that I can now communicate with the dead or at the very least my own seriously insightful subconscious."

Jim nodded but Alex didn't look convinced. "Just don't go catatonic on me okay?"

Abby managed a chuckle. "I'll do my best Alex."

* * *

The next morning Abby was ready to continue cracking the code of the Yellow Gleamers. After her discussion with herself/Kyle the night before, she had some theories and was eager to try them out.

She finished up a small breakfast of Evie's resurrected fruit before stepping to the doorway of the sleeping area. "Hey guys, meeting in the main room. I'd like everyone, but I especially need to see the Yellow guys."

Everyone gathered around in the living area, looking tired. Even the two hounds looked annoyed as they plopped down onto the floor to get more rest.

Abby began. "I've been thinking a lot lately about what you guys can do." She gestured to the men shining yellow against the back wall. "I think I've come up with a possibility."

David rolled his eyes with an exaggerated movement of his head. "Been talking to your ghost again?"

Alex popped out from the doorway then, glaring at David to let the other man know he'd heard the comment.

Abby ignored the exchange and turned to Jake. "Why don't you go first?"

Jake walked into the center of the room, turned to wink at Hannah. The red head's cheeks darkened with a blush. He seemed to swagger even in sweatpants and a ragged tee shirt.

"Okay, I'm all yours. What am I supposed to do?" Jake asked.

Abby glanced around the room, her eyes settling on a row of unopened water bottles on the counter. "Try to pick one of those bottles up with your mind."

Jake laughed, uneasy. "Right. Seriously, what do you want me to do?"

Abby's face was straight. "I want you to move the water bottle with your mind."

"How exactly am I supposed to do that though?"

She looked up for a second in thought. "Um... try some visualization. That seemed to work with the girls. And try to think of the ability as an instinct. If you are telekinetic, some part of you already knows how to move the bottle."

Jake puffed out his cheeks, turned towards the bottle. "Well, here goes."

He focused on the bottle with intensity, squinting his eyes and holding his breath. Nothing happened. Jake exhaled, relaxed. "I don't know if I'm telewhatever- you-said. I tried but it didn't budge an inch."

Abby put her hand on his shoulder, very aware of the other eyes on her. "Try again but stay relaxed this time. Pushing like that is just going to pop a blood vessel in your eye."

Jake brought a hand up to one eye, made a face. "Okay. That's disturbing."

"Maybe you're wrong," David said.

Alex popped out again. "Seriously dude, you need to shut up. I've had about enough."

Abby held up her hand for quiet. "David, if you have something better to do please feel free to return to your bunk."

There were no more complaints and Abby turned back to Jake with a nod. "Try again. You can do this. Just breathe normally and imagine your hand is physically lifting the bottle from the counter."

He sucked in a breath, exhaled slowly and focused again on the bottle. It immediately started to shake.

The others looked on, letting out hushed gasps as the bottle began to tremble more noticeably.

Abby stood behind Jake, leaned towards his ear with a whisper. "Good Jake. Now lift it."

His eyes narrowed and he lifted his hand from his side to aim it at the bottle. With a flick of his wrist he lifted it a foot from the counter with ease.

"Hold it as long as you can Jake." Abby motioned towards David and Sam. "Join him. Lift the other bottles."

Sam jumped up eagerly. David muttered an objection under his breath but Abby could see the hunger for power in his expression. She half expected him to lick his lips. David and Sam stood next to Jake and mimicked him. Before Abby could deliver more encouragement three bottles of water were floating around the room.

Sam laughed, waving his hand back and forth as his bottle flipped in circles. "This is so cool."

"See you're Movers," Abby said with satisfaction. Kyle had been right. No she had been right, she corrected.

Even David was smiling as the three of them began to play, testing their new found abilities while the rest of the group watched with interest.

Abby let out a laugh. "Okay boys. Have fun but be careful not to wipe yourselves out."

She turned to Evie where the darker woman sat watching the show. Abby took a handful of dried beans from her pocket and placed them on the table. "Do you think you could make one of these grow?"

Evie cocked her head. "I don't know but I can try."

"Yeah, give it a shot. Try doing it with your power alone first though. No water or anything."

Evie nodded and Abby returned to her bunk. She could hear the sounds of the Movers tossing water bottles around the room as she pulled a blanket over her lap and brought her journal out from under her pillow. She was recording notes about the Movers when Alex pushed her curtain aside.

"Hello Alex. Don't you knock?"

He shrugged. "I've seen everything you got anyway."

She sent him a look, noticing his grim expression. "What is it?"

"I'm not sure you should've given David such a strong power."

She pushed her glasses up on her nose. "I didn't give him anything. I just made him aware of it."

"Well I'm hoping that wasn't a bad idea. That guy's already got issues. He skulks around here like he's royalty or something."

"I'm sure it's fine. He's got a bad attitude but he's not evil. He'll warm up eventually."

"Or he'll smother us all with our own pillows while we sleep."

Abby chuckled quietly. "You're being dramatic again."

He huffed, stole a quick glance towards the doorway. "Yeah, maybe. But if you come up with some way to charge me up with some super juice, preferably with something cool like laser eyes, let me know so we have some way to defend ourselves from suffocation."

CHAPTER TWENTY

Sunday, January 13rd 2013, 7:26pm

Painting wasn't something Abby usually did to relax. At least not since it had become her career. But the moment Evie showed her the bean sprouts she had grown with nothing but her glowing, green will, Abby was instantly inspired.

She was currently filling the last of the stack of wood panels Kyle had included in her painting gift box. The easel he had made for her fit nicely in the space between the bunks, but Abby stayed in the back of the sleeping area where the four beds on either side of her were being used for storage. She had been painting a lot over the last few days and didn't want to get in anyone's way while she worked.

True to Kyle's innate knowledge, he had made sure there were at least half a dozen shades of green among the paint tubes. Abby was grateful not to have to do much mixing. She only had a stray piece of cardboard for a palette. And green was pretty much all she needed to compose Evie's pet sprouts onto the surface of the wood.

Kyle's voice hadn't appeared in Abby's head for days and she was starting to think her hallucinations were over. She frowned as she pulled a tube of white from her pocket, screwed the cap off, and dipped her brush inside. Silently she wished his voice hadn't left her so soon. She missed hearing his now familiar timbre reverberating through her head and she wasn't ready to forget it, to forget him. His disembodied voice was all she had left of him.

Since the day she had solved the mystery of the Movers, Kyle hadn't spoken to her. Maybe there was no need for him to speak, she thought. Maybe there was nothing more to discover about the Gleamers. Though Abby was sure there was more to uncover about her own abilities. There had to be something more besides the occasional vision and gut instinct. If there wasn't, David's insinuation of her being useless might be correct after all.

She was stopping to wipe her brush on her shirt when she suddenly had the urge to add a brown shadow to a bean leaf that was hiding from the light source. She wasn't using a still life reference, but in her mind she knew where the light was. She fished through her pockets to pull out the tube, but it was empty.

"Hmm, all out of umber," she muttered. "Guess I'll have to improvise" A shade of red came out of her pocket next and she squeezed a bead of it onto her makeshift pallet. Her brush picked up a darker shade of green and swirled it into the red. As the two colors mixed a muddy, earth-like color started to appear. Suddenly, Abby was struck with a giant light bulb of an epiphany.

With paint, mixing all the colors of the spectrum together created something close to black. But that was not the case with light.

Abby jogged into the main room to see Alex and Evie chatting at one table and Jake, Sam, and Hanna at the other. She didn't care enough about David to wonder where he was and Jimmy was most likely snoozing with his dogs. Days and nights didn't exist in a bomb shelter so people slept when it suited them.

Alex looked up as she slid across the linoleum in her socks. "What's up Abbs? You goin' somewhere?"

"Alex." She excitedly pointed two fingers in his direction. "Just the man I was looking to see. Do me a favor?"

"Um sure. You okay?"

"Yeah, I'm great." She went to a cupboard and pulled out the knife they used for Hanna's healing practice. "I need you to slice something open for me."

His eyes widened. "What for? Hanna's doing great with the healing thing." Alex looked close to whining as he glanced to Hanna. "Right?"

Hanna had been listening. "Yeah, I've got it down now. No problems."

"It's not for Hanna's benefit," Abby said. "It's for mine."

Alex stood up from his seat. "You're going to heal me? Since when can you do that?"

Abby grinned awkwardly. "Well I'm not exactly sure that I can yet. But I have a gut feeling about it."

Again Alex's face took on a pout. "Can't someone else play guinea pig for you then? I'm already covered in scars."

Abby rolled her eyes towards the ceiling. "Don't be a baby Alex."

Alex held up his finger toward her. "Wait, did your... inner voice tell you to do this?"

"No, that's over. I haven't heard anything in days." She waved a hand to dismiss the subject quickly.

"I'll do it," Hanna spoke up. "Everyone else has cut themselves for me."

Sam and Jake observed quietly from their seats, leaning onto their elbows to get a better look.

Abby shook her head. "No, I'm not sure you can heal yourself yet. If someone else is cut, and I can't heal it, at least you're still there to fix it."

Hanna only nodded while Alex moaned audibly. "Fine. I'll do it then," he said. "But stand by Hanna. Just in case I need you to come to the rescue." Alex took the knife from Abby with a huff then stood in thought for a moment.

Abby poked him. "What are you waiting for?"

"I'm trying to figure out which part of my body to injure this time." He cringed. "My arms are starting to look like I was a troubled teen who went through a secret cutter phase."

"Join the club." Abby held out her arms to show off her own disfigurement. "One more won't make much difference. Now get on with it. This is important."

Alex pulled his sleeve up over his shoulder, heaved a sigh, and sliced the blade across the flesh of his bicep. His face registered the pain immediately. "Damn it! That never stops hurting."

Abby held his elbow with her left hand and hovered over the wound with her right. "Okay, let's see if this works."

Using the visualization techniques she'd taught the others, she watched as her light grew out from her hand. Abby knew everyone but Alex could see it too. She imagined the wound healing, saw the skin fuse back together in her mind.

She struggled, pushing the energy from her hand with all her strength. It was taking too long.

And then she heard Kyle. "Make it blue." His voice sounded faint, raspy as if he was having difficulty breathing.

Abby immediately imagined the white light around her hands changing colors, watched as it flickered and shifted around her before transitioning into a pale sky blue. She heard the hushed whispers behind her and focused on Alex's wound.

In a matter of seconds the blood stopped flowing and Alex's flesh was whole again.

"It worked." Abby let out her breath and smiled. "It really worked."

Alex slid his sleeve down quickly. "Thank god. That hurts like a bitch." He grabbed Abby's hand where it still hovered by his arm. "How did you know you could do that?"

Abby grabbed herself a bottle of water off the counter and leaned against the sink. "I was painting and mixing colors when the idea just came to me."

"More bean sprouts?" Alex asked, gesturing to the row of finished paintings propped along the back of the counter.

"Yeah." She took a sip, ignored the art-snob undertone in Alex's voice. "Anyway, I remembered that white light is a combination of all the other colors in the spectrum."

Sam sat up in his seat. "Oh I get it. You're light... your abilities are a mix of everyone else's."

Hanna sat next to him looking thoughtful. "Huh? That makes sense. I wonder what red, orange, and violet can do though?"

"That's actually a really good question." Abby pointed in Hanna's direction with her water bottle. "I plan to find out the answers eventually. May take some time though." Abby felt almost giddy. She wasn't useless after all. She could do everything the Gleamers could do, plus she had her own unique talents that none of them could touch.

That thought reminded Abby that she had more new abilities to test out. Staring at her water bottle she imagined yellow light all around her, felt the change in energy. With one swift motion she released her fingers from around the plastic and watched it hover in front of her.

She waved her hand and sent the bottle flying towards Alex, stopping it right under his nose. "Thirsty Alex?" Abby laughed out loud and brought the bottle back to herself with a cocky, come-hither flick of her finger.

Abby heard Evie's quiet laughter and sent a smile in the other woman's direction. "Should I do the fruit thing now?"

Evie smiled back. "Definitely. I could use some rehydrated bananas anyway." She gestured towards the opened bag of banana chips on the counter.

Abby snatched up the bag and emptied it onto the table where Hanna and the two brothers sat. She took a breath, shifted her light until she could see the green hue along her fingers. With another deep breath she forced out energy through her hands and into the fruit before her.

The slices of banana filled with moisture, grew from thin chips into thick, juicy chunks before their eyes. The room was full of the freshly peeled scent when Abby stepped back, slipping her energy to its normal white shine with a shake of her head.

"Sweet," Jake said. "I was craving something besides petrified Salisbury steak today."

Kyle's voice entered Abby again, abruptly enough to make her jump. "So." He pushed out a hard sigh, coughed twice. "We've got a Healer, a Grower, and three Movers." Another cough. "If we can do everything they can do, what does that make us?"

Her eyebrows came together in confusion. His question didn't register at first. All Abby wanted to know was why an imaginary person would be coughing.

"I don't know." She answered him in her normal voice, loud enough for everyone in the room to hear. "You're the one who likes naming things."

Abby didn't care if they thought she was nuts anymore. She had proven her worth. She was confident in her methods, regardless of how unconventional they may be.

Alex came up behind Abby, stood close. "The voice is back."

His voice sounded ominous, but she didn't react. "Yes." Her eyes met those of the four glowing individuals in the room. "But I think the time has come to accept it. I may be crazy, but apparently crazy pays off. If it weren't for this voice we might never have discovered these talents. Talents that will keep us alive above ground."

She received nods from the brothers, a wide open grin from Hanna, and a look laced with pity from Evie.

"You'll get no complaints out of me," Jake finally said. "You could see dancing dragons on the ceiling for all I care just so long as you keep getting those gut feelings and I still get to play catch with Sam." He leaned back against the wall, locked his hands behind his head. "No hands of course."

Sam nodded in agreement.

Abby's face softened until the corners of her mouth lifted. "Play all the no hands catch you like Jake. Just stop trying to pull my curtain open while I'm changing."

Jake's eyes grew big and he quickly pointed to his brother. "I swear it wasn't me."

"Yeah, that's gotta stop boys," Hanna said.

"Uh huh. We've noticed our curtains slipping open every now and again too," Evie added.

A laugh slipped from Abby as she shifted on her heels to return to her bunk. "I'll see you all later. Think about the missing colors for me in the meantime." With that she left them to return to her painting.

CHAPTER TWENTY-ONE

Friday, January 18th 2013, 9:42pm

Friday nights had become the designated time to hold ritualized poker parties in the bunker. For the first time Abby felt like participating, even though she was a terrible bluffer.

Sam tossed his wager into the center of the table. "I'll bet one spaghetti and meatballs MRE."

Alex was up next. "I'll see your MRE, but this one's uh..." He stopped to read the label. "...beef stew. And I'll raise you two cups of ramen noodles."

Oohs and ahs echoed through the bunker. Ramen noodles were prized among the rations and sometimes fought over like precious jewels.

"Too rich for me." Jake folded his cards in front of him.

"I'm in," Abby said. "I've got another beef stew and I'll see your ramen raise."

"Okay then," Alex said. "Let's see what everyone's got?" He threw down a pair of tens and waited.

Sam placed his cards down with flair one at a time to reveal a flush. Abby flopped down a pair of kings with a playful huff.

"Winner, winner, ramen noodle dinner," Jake said clasping his brother on the back of the neck. "

"Aw, I thought I had that one," Abby said. "I haven't won a single hand. I officially suck at this game."

"Don't worry. I'll share my beef stew with you," Jake said. "I know it's your favorite."

"Don't listen to him Abbs." Alex shuffled the cards noisily. "He's just trying to get on your good side."

"That and your bunk," Sam added.

Abby huffed a laugh. "Well he might have a shot. Fossilized beef stew is the way to this girl's heart."

She was enjoying watching the boys bicker and barter over their food wagers when Kyle's voice came to her for the first time in five days.

"Abby." She could barely hear him. "I..."

"Hush." She craned her head, listened. "Everybody be quiet."

"What's going on?" Alex asked, pausing in the deal.

"I'm hearing him... it again, but the voice is barely a whisper."

They all sat in quiet as Abby looked off into space anticipating her imaginary version of Kyle to speak to her.

It was the coughing she heard first followed by Kyle's weak words. "I need you to listen to me. I need your help."

"With what? I don't understand."

"Just listen. I need you to come to me."

Her head trembled back and forth. "What are you saying?" Was her delusional mind asking her to kill herself now?

He continued. "I think you can withstand the radiation for a while. The levels are almost normal now."

"Where am I going?" She shifted her eyes between the others in the room, noted the way they gawked at her.

"There's another shelter... under the barn. Please." The coughing started again, this time going on for a bit before he could speak. "Use your vision. I'm here... I'm not dead."

Abby flinched. Her body tightened. Cards and food packages stirred as she fought to hold on to the edge of the table while the wind came back into her lungs.

"Abby!" Alex moved around the table to grab her shoulders. "What's happening?"

It took a moment for her to find her voice. When she finally did her words came out in a burst. "He said he's in another shelter under the barn. He said…" She gulped in air. "He's not dead."

"Jim!" Alex yelled over his shoulder, then back to Abby, "Just hold on. We'll figure this out."

Jim was padding into the main room in seconds. The two hounds followed, nails clicking on the linoleum. "What's all the fuss? Is someone dying?"

Two crevices appeared between Abby's brows. She bit her lip and choked on the knot that had formed in her throat.

Alex spoke for her, raised his eyebrows high. "Kyle's voice just told Abby that he's not dead and we need to come get him out of a second bomb shelter under the barn."

Jim almost laughed, but one look at Abby's face held him back. "That's not possible. He would've mentioned something like that."

Abby swallowed the lump and made her voice box work again. "He said I could use my vision to see for myself."

Jim paced a few times, chewing unconsciously on his thumbnail. "Okay, let's say he is alive and you've been hearing his voice this whole time. Why wouldn't he have suggested using your ability to prove he was alright from the start instead of letting you think you were going crazy?"

"I don't know Jimmy." Her breathing started to calm. "If he is alive, I'm sure he'll be willing to explain. Right now I need to find out the truth."

Abby didn't need to close her eyes to use her abilities anymore. She left them open wide, staring past the faces in front of her until her vision vibrated out of focus.

It only took a short time for something to happen. Abby felt as though an electric current were stretching from her body, up and out into the world above, and straight towards the barn.

She refused to look around the grounds of the farm as it blurred by. The barn was her focal point. She didn't want to catch a glimpse of anything resembling death and destruction; no dead horses, no bloated chickens, and certainly no bodiless work boots lying under rubble.

She entered the barn doors, glancing around in her mind's eye to see nothing with the exception of decaying horses and a mess of debris. So much for trying to get out of seeing the death, she thought trying not to let the bile rise in her throat. Thank goodness she couldn't see their faces. Bucky's gorgeous brown eyes, vacant and sunken into his head, was not something she needed to witness.

Ash was everywhere. The right half of the roof had collapsed onto the barn floor leaving a mess of timbres and shingles. Random tools scattered over the ground; spades, rakes, saddles and other tack. Piles of hay were still miraculously stacked in the back corner, somehow having been missed by the falling roof.

She forced her vision down in to the earth under the barn, through the rich soil and roots until she hit a cement wall.

"Oh god." A mixture of fear and hope punctured her heart. The little ember of a wish she had foolishly held on to was beginning to grow inside of her, sparking up into a weak flame.

"What?" She heard Jimmy's voice like it was far away.

"It's here. There's something here."

Abby focused with renewed force and shoved her sight down further until the darkness of the earth opened up into a dimly lit room.

She didn't have to go far once inside. She heard his labored breathing and swung her head to the left. There, on a single bunk in the back corner of the tiny shelter, lay Kyle's motionless body.

Her vision floated closer until she was right beside him. There was weeks of beard on his chin, his dark hair was slick with sweat, stuck to his forehead in little waves. He was trembling with cold as more sweat beaded up along his brow and dripped down onto the pillow.

"He's alive." She said, trying to restrain the joy in her voice. There was no time for celebration.

With one more look at Kyle she snapped her vision back to the bunker on the other side of the farm. Seven worried faces peered back at her.

"I have to move fast," she said. "I don't know how much time he has left."

Jim was at her side immediately. "What did you see? What's wrong with him?"

"I don't know but he's not conscious." She rubbed her hand along the back of her neck. "It doesn't matter. I have to go now."

"Wait Abby," Jim began. "The levels outside aren't low enough yet."

Abby met his eyes defiantly. "Are they close enough for Hanna to heal me if I'm affected?"

"Probably. The radiation is below deadly, but you could still get seriously sick." He looked back at Hanna. "What do you think?"

"I could try." Hanna tucked her curly red hair behind her ears. "I mean, I'm sure I could do it."

Abby took a step towards the release lever. "That settles it then."

"Wait Abby." Alex pinched the back collar of her shirt. "I'm coming with you."

"So am I," Jim said. "I'm not sending you up there alone."

"Us too," Jake said, his brother beside him.

"Don't look at me," David said as he stepped into the room. "I don't care if he's alive, dead, or somewhere in between."

"We weren't planning on bugging you Dave." Alex sneered.

"We're wasting too much time. We have to go now." Abby raised her hand over the lever again. "Those of you who are staying get in the back and don't move until we return."

She waited for them to move, flipped the lever, and bolted up the stairs with the four men behind her.

Once they reached the surface they all realized quickly that none of them had thought the operation through. It was winter and the ash cloud still hung in the sky, obstructing any heat from the sun. Instantly they were freezing.

Abby clenched her fists at her sides and listened to her teeth chatter. Her breath was visible in front of her. "We have to run."

The five of them sprinted through the ash, slugging along where it was especially thick as though they were running on loose sand. Abby kept up pace with the men, pushing her shorter legs to their limits. As the icy wind bit into her flesh and her legs burned beneath her, she kept her mind centered on Kyle. It was that blinders-on focus that made her the first to enter the barn.

All five of them stopped once under the roof, looked around while they caught their breath.

"Oh no Bucky," Jim said.

"Don't Jimmy," Abby said. "You don't want to see. Just help me find the way in."

Abby tried to discern where the hatch would be, thinking back to her vision. She ran to the third stall and started kicking around the hay. Her toe hit metal right away but her feet were too cold to feel the pain.

"It's here!" she called. "Help me."

Jim moved in beside her to sweep off the layer of hay and horse feed until the hatch was completely exposed.

"How will we get it open?" Alex asked. "It's locked from the inside."

"Give me a second," Abby replied before slipping back into her projected sight.

She was next to Kyle with a thought. "Kyle. Please Kyle you need to get up. We can't get you out unless you open the hatch."

He didn't show any signs of hearing her and Abby was sure his breathing had become slower.

"Kyle!" She screamed into his face, willing him to hear her. "Callum, get up!"

When he didn't move a wave of panic landed on top of Abby. There had to be another way. Just as quickly as she had slipped in, she slipped out of the vision and back to the frozen barn.

"Anything?" Jimmy asked beside her.

"Shush. I need to think."

Abby searching her mind for a solution. She was not going to let him die on her. Not again. In a fit of frustration she smacked the side of the stall and watched wood chips fly to reveal a hole the size of her fist. It wasn't just her hand that had hit the wood. It was the ability to throw off a force with only her mind.

"How'd you do that?" Alex asked. "Were you using the yellow light?"

"No I wasn't." She pointed to Sam and Jake. "You two. Put a hand on my shoulders."

The brothers stared, stunned.

"Do it now!"

They flinched but moved to stand beside her as she faced the shelter entrance. Each of them rested one hand on Abby and waited.

"Now help me move the lever inside the hatch. Lend me some of your abilities. I've never tried to use two at once before. I'm not even sure it's possible."

"We'll try," Jake said.

"Thanks," she said before her vision zipped back into the bunker below.

This time she appeared before the lever. She looked back at Kyle for a moment then channeled her strength into moving the red handle with her mind. She could feel the energy of Jake and Sam, soaking into her like warm water to a sponge.

The lever quivered for an instant then was still again. She took a deep breath, clenched her jaw, and pushed again. With a sudden jerk the lever flipped and Abby dropped to her knees. Once again her consciousness was above ground.

"Go," she gasped. "It's open."

Jake flicked his hand and the hatch popped up easily. "Come on Abby." He smiled down on her. "Let's go do some rescuing."

Abby stood and allowed Jake to help her down the narrow stairwell. The other three men were already at Kyle's bedside.

"What's wrong with him?" She heard the panic in her own voice, felt it like a row of rubber bands around her chest. As she approached she read the look in Alex's eyes and she almost fell to her knees again.

Jim had pulled the blankets back to expose Kyle's lifeless body. His lower half was covered in a pair of flannel sleeping pants, one leg of fabric cut off at the thigh.

Abby covered her mouth, let out a suffocated wail, as her eyes fell on the bandages wrapped around his leg. Dried blood caked the outside, having soaked through the layers of wrappings.

"Infection," Jim said. "I'm not sure there's anything we can do. He's... I don't think he's breathing."

A sound issued forth from deep within her, sorrow bouncing off the walls with a hollow echo.

Jake's arm was still under her for support. He tilted to look at her and spoke in a near whisper. "You can heal him."

"But he's..."

"You have to try."

She lifted her head, straightened her back, shrugged off the arm around her, and stood beside Kyle's bed.

One breath was all she needed to transition to the healing, blue light that always resided within her. She felt weak, already sapped from her previous effort as she watched her hands tremble. Hovering both palms over the wound, she poured everything she had into him.

His eyes flew open immediately, staring but not seeing. In the next instant he was squeezing them shut again while his body convulsed as though being tortured. His face contorted in agony and he reached for his leg. It took all four of the other men to hold him down while Abby continued to work.

She glanced at his face, read the searing pain in his wide, watery eyes and concentrated with all her power. Her vision started to blur. Images began to swim through her mind as she fought to stay on her feet. The past began to mingle with the present and she saw Callum standing on the shore as a boy with a sweet, innocent smiled fixed to his lips. Then time moved forward and he was standing next to the other priests as a young man, calling down the blessings of the gods and lighting the ritual fire.

One knee gave out and she dropped, keeping her hands over Kyle. She barely noticed the blood that dripped from her nose and over her lips.

She heard Kyle as though he were miles away. "Abby stop." His raspy voice grew louder. "Stop."

She ignored him, continued her efforts in desperation. She shoved all her strength into his leg, willing him to heal, to live. Until her body collapsed onto the cold floor.

CHAPTER TWENTY-TWO

Saturday, January 19th 2013, 3:28am

When Abby opened her eyes again there was only darkness surrounding her. The damp smell of concrete reminded her that she was in her bunk, exactly where she had been for nearly the past month. She was freezing. Her skin felt like she had been dunked in ice water and stored in a human sized cooler. A shudder rippled through her body as she leaned up on her elbows.

Instantly she noticed the throbbing pain in her head and the tightness in her limbs. Out of habit she lifted an arm to wave some light in front of her eyes. Sucking in her breath she stared at her fingers, turning her hand over and back again. The white light that usually surrounded her was nearly gone, faded to a weak glow she could only make out around her fingernails.

Memories flooded back; Kyle's bunker, his wounded leg, the terrible pain that distorted his features, how badly she had wanted that pain to stop.

She flung open her curtain, squinted in the pale light floating in from the living area, before rolling out of her bed. And landing right on Alex.

She tripped, fell forward, catching herself on the bunk across the way. Alex grunted under her knees.

"Whoa, watch those little feet." He stood up, gripped his gut. "I need that part."

She tried to steady herself, felt the weakness in her bones. "Why are you sleeping on the floor?"

"We were worried. It's my watch."He gripped her arm, helped her to straighten to her feet.

She regained her balance, pushed the hair from her face. "So..." She glanced down at the floor. "I'm not crazy?"

"No. You were never crazy."

Abby released a breath she hadn't realized she was holding. Her chest heaved with the effort and her knees buckled underneath her weight.

Alex's grip tightened on her arm. He was quiet while she breathed. "He's out there." He gestured towards the main room with a tilt of his head.

She looked up into his face, tears already forming at the edge of her lashes. "Is he..."

Alex didn't need her to finish. "I'll get him." He pushed through the curtain, letting light and hushed voices in as he left her.

Her hands shook. She looked down, pressed them together, leaning into the double fist to alleviate the pressure in her chest. Her numb legs took her to the back of the bunk space and she propped herself on the edge of a bed, waiting. She examined her unfinished painting, studying the lines of color to distract her from the ball of anxiety hanging in her throat.

Light filled the room as he stepped past the curtain. She breathed, willing air into her swollen throat. Her eyes remained downcast, almost afraid to look at him; afraid he might disappear again.

She felt him standing beside her, saw the shimmer of light playing off his bare feet. Finally she turned, drew her gaze up him from his toes, over his body until she reached his face. She continued to avoid his eyes, instead wandering over the rest of his features.

After a moment she stood, finally met his gaze as her lips trembled and a small sob trickled from her throat. She blinked back immanent tears and threw her arms around his neck, burying her face in his chest. There was no anger in her words when she finally spoke. "How could you do that to me? How could you let me think you were dead?"

He spoke softly, gently rubbing her hair. "I'm sorry. I never wanted to hurt you."

She reached up, gingerly brought a hand to his freshly shaven cheek, and felt the spark she remembered from his touch. He caught her hand, brought it between them as he wrapped her in his arms.

A downpour of tears streamed over her cheeks as he cradled her head tightly into his chest. "I'm so sorry," he whispered.

She let her tears fall, losing herself in his arms, listening to his heart beat against her cheek. He was warm and breathing. He was alive. Thank you, Abby thought, not knowing who or what she was indebted to.

When she could breathe again, she pushed away tenderly and looked up at his face. "Tell me what happened."

He nodded as he sat on the edge of the bunk. Abby did the same on the opposite side, watching as he eyed her. He looked tired, weak. Dark circles encompassed his eyes, his cheeks sunken just noticeably. He leaned forward, rubbed his palms up and down the top of his thighs once before speaking.

"The night we went to the meteor, my vision was different than the one you had. I saw the people coming, saw them forcing their way into the bunker. There was shooting. You and a few of the others were hit. The last thing I saw was you lying in the ash. Bleeding. Dying. I couldn't allow that to happen." He paused, watched her face. "So when we got back to the house I wrote you the letter, told Alex and Jim what they needed to know, and went to sleep beside you with a plan forming in my head."

Abby took a second to absorb his story. "I wish you would've told me what you saw. I could've helped you."

His eyes held a plea. "It was my vision, my responsibility. I had to make the vision change, put myself in your place. Not get you involved and risk it all coming true. That last morning..." He clenched his eyes shut, opened them again to look at her. "I was trying to make it easier for you. You don't remember the past the way I do Abby. I lost you once. You and the children. I couldn't face that again."

"The children," she whispered. She closed her eyes, sifted through the pieces of memory in her mind. "We had twin girls."

"Esree and Mayra." His voice was heavy. "They had your eyes and my smile. They were smart, beautiful, and loved to listen to me tell stories."

"I remember them, but not clearly. I think they had blonde hair. Didn't we have a son as well?" She smiled at the vision in her mind. "Yes, he was just a baby, chubby and happy." She suddenly remembered the sensation of nursing her little boy, felt the sharp pain of loss in her heart.

"His name was Callum also." Kyle rubbed his temple. "Be grateful you don't remember them as clearly as I do. Sometimes I feel like I was Callum just yesterday. I remember everything. That's probably why I was in so much pain after that first touch. In a matter of minutes an entire lifetime was shoved into my head." He pressed his temple as if remembering the pain. "And now I think I understand why people don't generally get to recall their earlier incarnations. It's too painful to know what's been lost, what you can never have again." After a moment, he continued with their present conversation. "I would've rather been dead than lose you again."

"I didn't want to lose you either Kyle. What made you think I would be able to do all this on my own while grieving for you?"

"You're stronger than I am Abby. I knew you would be okay. You didn't have the same memories of... us. It wasn't as intense for you.

"Just because I don't have as many details as you do doesn't mean I don't have the same feelings."

"Yes, but I thought since I had distanced myself a little that you would move on." He looked away. "And you did."

She didn't argue with him, didn't want to tell him how she had wished she had died when the end came. And she certainly couldn't tell him how many times she had considered it since that terrible day.

"Don't think that Abby. I wanted you to go on even if I wasn't there to be with you."

"I didn't mean for you to hear that, but it's true nonetheless. I wanted to die with you." She spoke without shame, shrugged as though thinking about her own death had become commonplace. "Anyway, why didn't you tell me you were alive from the start?"

"I didn't know how long I could hold on. I knew I was pretty bad off. I tried cutting the buckshot out a few times, but there was no way. It was too deep."

Abby tightened, imagining him cutting his own skin open and mining for tiny pieces of metal embedded in the layers of flesh. Suddenly she was gripped with the urge to touch him and make sure he was really there.

Kyle continued. "An infection was inevitable, no matter how hard I tried to keep it clean. I wanted to tell you, but if you thought I was dead anyway then it didn't matter. No one would ever know the difference." His voice broke but he regained it quickly. "You started getting better, started moving forward. I didn't want to cause any more pain or give you false hope."

He paused, their eyes meeting for a long moment. "I woke up for a little while yesterday, long enough to tell you where I was. I knew the levels had gone down, were almost normal, and I realized it was my only chance."

She was quiet for a long time before she found the courage to speak. She couldn't look at him when the words finally left her mouth. "Where does all of this leave us then?"

He stood, favoring his leg, fiddled with the brushes she had left along the easel. "We need to stay down here for at least a few more days until the radiation goes down another notch or two. Hopefully the temperature will go up as well.

And you need to recover your strength before we go back up and start rebuilding." He rubbed his bad thigh. "I guess we both do."

She stood, took a step towards him. "I meant where does that leave us?"

"Oh." He looked down, scratched a finger between his brows and let out a nervous laugh. His eyes tipped up, looking at her from beneath his lashes. "I didn't sleep in the chair that night because... because I didn't have the strength to resist having just one night to hold you. In the morning..." He breathed through his mouth deeply, looked away and back again. "...getting shot in the leg was easier than pushing you away."

She forced back more tears, slipped her hand into his and leaned against his chest. She shivered and sunk into him.

He pressed his lips to her forehead, rested his chin in her hair. "You need more sleep."

She shook her head. "No, I... I don't want to close my eyes. I'm afraid this will end up being a dream."

"It's okay." He brushed the back of his fingers along her jaw. "I'm here now and I'm never leaving you again. We're a package deal, remember? I go where you go."

They stepped the small distance to Abby's bunk and she climbed in, moving against the wall to make room for him. She watched him struggle with his leg as he lay down beside her and pulled her close into the crook of his shoulder.

"What happened to the people who tried to take the bunker?" Abby asked.

"I had to fire on them." His body tensed. "The others... they died when the end came."

"Where did the other shelter come from?"

"So many questions." He laughed against her hair. "I had it put in when I upgraded the other one."

She looked up at him. "How did you know what was going to happen then?"

"I didn't. Just a gut instinct. A backup plan."

That satisfied Abby. It wouldn't be the first time his gut had proved useful. She scooted closer, threw one leg over his.

He let out a quiet groan.

"Oh. I'm sorry." She removed her leg quickly but carefully. "Does it hurt much?"

"Nah, not too bad. Hanna is going to work on it again later." One of his hands trailed up her spine while the other traced the shallow scars along her forearm. "How are you?"

She yawned in response.

He huffed out a soft chuckle, kissed the top of her head again. "Sleep then. You have a lot to teach me tomorrow."

Abby closed her eyes, tucked her arms in between them. "Kyle," she murmured.

"Hmm?"

"What if it doesn't come back... the light?"

"It will." He pulled the blanket up over her shoulders. "No more worries. Go to sleep."

CHAPTER TWENTY-THREE

Abby felt the light brush of sable against her cheek as her eyes fluttered open. She felt the paintbrush move of its own accord along her cheek, down the length of her jaw, finally resting in the hollow of her throat.

She lay on her back, the curtain open like it always was lately, enough to see Kyle leaning up on one glowing yellow elbow and looking serious from his own bunk across the lane. His hand was in the air, two fingers twirling as the brush spun pirouettes along her collarbone.

They had cleared the two bottom beds in the back of the sleeping area so they could doze off close by each other every night. They chose the back so they could whisper if they wanted to without bothering the others too much. It was as close as they typically got lately.

They had agreed to take their relationship slow, at least for the duration of their stay in the bunker. Neither of them wanted to be on display in front of the other seven people they lived with. Not to mention getting physical wasn't necessarily a comfortable idea considering their privacy was seriously lacking.

Abby wasn't sure she cared about privacy. What she felt for Kyle was so powerful, it seemed at times like nothing else mattered but being close to him. Kyle had said knowing they were not alone would only be a distraction. More distractions, Abby thought. The man simply couldn't multitask at all.

Both of them were frustrated with their circumstances, but Abby felt her will power quickly waning. Kyle had been the one to stay reasonable, suggesting they sleep in separate beds, and more or less stay out of physical contact. With the exception of the occasional touch or innocent kiss, expressing their feelings for each other in the old fashioned way had been put on hold.

Just knowing he was only feet away from her every night was torture. There had been more than one occasion where she thought she might give in and jump into his bunk. Abby had never possessed the virtue of patience and she just plain hated waiting.

Her shirt lifted just an inch and the soft bristles found their way around her bellybutton. She met his gaze, exhaled slowly, knew her thoughts were written on her face.

The brush suddenly flew away from her. He caught it with a snap before a subtle motion of his hand returned her shirt to its place, covering her skin.

He sent her a knowing grin, shrugged. "I was getting sick of calling your name to wake you."

She took a breath, struggled momentarily to collect her composure. Never in her life had a man been able to stir her the way that Kyle did. It felt at once incredible and torturous. She didn't just want him physically. It was his soul she wanted to touch, to combine with her own until they were one thing.

His grin broadened into a lopsided smirk as he watched her. "It's time to wake up now. Everyone's getting ready."

"Oh, that's right. Big day."

In a short time they would be surfacing for the first time as a group, though not for good. There was a ton of work to be done before they could move their residence from the bunker permanently. But today was the day they began the preparations for their future above ground.

Kyle had been right. Her light had returned within a day and together they were learning how to use their abilities. She taught him how to use the extra powers she'd discovered and he taught her how to control her thoughts better. This, he said, would only allow him to see and hear what she wanted him to as opposed to being the open book of information she'd been before.

Abby sighed, looking over his bare chest with longing. She just wanted to touch him, feel his warmth, take in his scent. "You're going to be the death of me I think."

He chuckled deep in his throat. "You? Believe me, I wish we were above ground, lounging in my bed all day and through the night."

"Hmm… sounds lovely." She got out of her bed and went to sit on the edge of his. Her index finger trailed from his throat to his belly button. "We have some time now."

He took her hand, brought it to his lips. "This is too important, Abby. You're too important. It should be right."

"I'm sure it will be beyond right. Perfect even." When he said no more she blew out a resigned breath. "Maybe I'll just go punch Alex a little."

"I'm sure you can take him. Just mess up his hair a little and he'll be easy to overpower."

Abby watched the smile turn his lips, staring at them and wishing she could kiss them whenever and wherever she wanted to. The desire she had for him could fill the ocean to overflowing and she felt the deep stir of something so much greater than physical excitement. She bent to him, gliding her tongue along his bottom lip, slipping it into his mouth.

"Oh god Abby." He pushed her forward, held her at arm's length by her shoulders. "Soon. Okay? I promise. I just want there to be no…"

"Distractions. I know." She pouted good naturedly, huffed a little before plopping back into her own bed.

He laughed again, held her gaze for a moment. "I'm gonna get dressed. See you in the main room." He smiled, flipped his curtain closed with his hand.

Abby quickly shifted the drape open again with her mind.

He was in the middle of pulling on a fresh shirt, stopped with it just over his lower arms. "What?"

She smiled and let her eyes wander over him, along his spiraling tattoos, and across his chest as she focused her thoughts on everything she felt for him. She thought about how she wanted to show him how she felt and let herself soak in the deliciousness of those images for a moment. She blew him a kiss and sent the pictures from her mind along with it.

He sucked in his breath sharply and closed his eyes with a quiet groan. "That's not playing fair."

She only grinned, closed her curtain and started getting dressed. He did the same, finishing quickly and jumping from his bed. She sensed his presence just outside her bunk.

"This means war," he whispered playfully through the fabric between them.

She laughed out loud, pausing as she pulled on some jeans. "You started it."

His finger pulled back the cloth enough for him to peak in. She lay stretched out, just about to hike her jeans up over her hips.

His eyes wandered briefly, tightened as a pained expression crossed his face. "I plan to finish it too."

Her curtain fell back to place and she heard him padding down the hall in his bare feet.

Abby couldn't keep the smile from raising her cheeks. She finished dressing then joined Kyle and the rest of the group in the front room.

Everyone was pulling on coats and shoving shoes on their feet as she walked in. Abby joined them, listening to the friendly chatter of Evie and Hanna.

"Okay," Kyle began. "We're just going up to take a look around, make a mental list of what needs doing. It's still too cold so we'll take no more than two hours. Make sure your skin is covered as best you can and don't wander off alone." He took a deep breath and blew it out forcefully, puffing his cheeks. "There are some bodies up there. Let's avoid them for now. The ground is too frozen to burry anything and this doesn't need to be any harder than it already is. Hopefully they're too covered in ash to see anyway."

Kyle had quickly resumed his role as leader, taking it upon himself to care for each of their safety as though it was what he was born to do. He even watched out for David, though the other man didn't seem to appreciate it in the least. Abby had come to think that David was resentful of Kyle's resurrection and would've liked nothing more than for Kyle to have stayed dead.

Abby zipped up her last boot and pulled her jacket up on her shoulders. Kyle stepped in front of her, zipped up her coat and pulled the hood up over her hair.

"Gloves too," he said, handing her his pair. "When we get up there, keep yourself open. See if we get anything."

She nodded and tried not to appear as anxious as she felt. She had managed to avoid looking too carefully at the devastation before, but now they were going above ground specifically to examine it. She inhaled through her nose and let air slowly out her mouth.

Kyle wore a sweatshirt under his jacket, the hood up and hanging loosely around his features. He bent slightly, looked into her face. "Ready?"

"As I'll ever be."

All of them walked in single file up the narrow hatch passageway until they surfaced from the stillness of the bunker. The wind whipped, beating into them as snow and ash flew through the air.

"Try not to breath in the ash." Kyle yelled to the group above the wind, pulled a section of his hood across the lower half of his face.

They moved into the center of the farm as a unit. Abby looked up to the Blue House, noting the sections of roof that had fallen in, the siding that had been ripped off or melted out of shape in the heat. The porch was in shambles, the railing broken into three pieces and scattered out into the bushes with the tattered spindles mingling with bricks from the now non-existent chimney.

She stole a glance around, swinging her eyes in a circle around the property. Jim's house was in no better shape than Kyle's. The chicken coop had collapsed to a pile of kindling, the corral now two misshapen posts sticking out of the ground. The crops were scorched to the earth and covered in layers of snowy ash.

Kyle looked up at the eight people encircling him, spoke through the fabric over his face. "We should split up into two groups, cover more ground. David, Hanna, and Evie, come with me. Abby you've got the others."

Abby nodded, pulled the high neck of her coat from her mouth before adding, "Everybody pay special attention to repairs we need to make to housing, the energy systems, etcetera. Those are the priorities."

Kyle brought his bare hands together, rubbed them against each other briskly. "Okay, let's get moving before we freeze." He brushed fingers over Abby's gloved hand and the two groups started off in different directions.

Kyle's group made it to the chicken coop and inspected the hen house to find the birds frozen in the stillness of death. Eggs splattered around the bodies as though they had been dropped from the sky.

He stopped amid the death at his feet, removed the hood from his mouth before turning to the others. "Remind me to grab one of these birds before we go back to the bunker."

Even through the scarf around her face, Hanna's disgusted expression was evident. "Okay. Gross."

"You'll see why. Let's head to my house next. Check out the damage there."

When they reached the door, Kyle had to remind himself to stay calm. He had helped build the house with his own two hands, laid up the drywall, built the porch nail by nail. His heart and soul had gone into every detail. Seeing it nearly destroyed was like being gutted.

He climbed the stairs carefully after instructing the others to cover the ground floor, being sure to remind them to take note of the kitchen appliances and other electrical things. Getting the stove to work would be a major advantage.

He went to the spare room first to find it in good shape. It was almost exactly as he'd left it. He stopped in his room next, frowning as he caught sight of the bed. It was covered in debris where the roof had collapsed then layered in a grey mixture of ash and snow. The mess of wood and shingles continued along the floor to a gash in the interior wall that led to his bathroom.

"Damn it," he muttered and kicked a stray shingle across the room.

He heard the sound of footfalls moving up the stairs, looked over his shoulder as David approached.

"Everything okay downstairs?" Kyle asked.

"Yeah." David hesitated, eyed Kyle. "Um... the stove will probably work again. Maybe even the fridge."

"That's good news."

Kyle stepped through the doorway, pulled his keys off the dresser where he'd left them and shoved them in his jeans pocket. It was then that he heard the crunching sound above him. He glanced up, watching as the last of the roof started to fall.

There was no time to get out of the way, no time to find cover. He transitioned to yellow light instinctually, throwing up his hands to stop the weight of wood, shingles, snow, and ash from coming down on his head. The mass stopped inches from his skull, so close that Kyle could've touched it with his finger tips.

He glanced to the doorway to see that David was no longer there. "Hello?" He struggled with the weight, felt his legs starting to buckle at the knees. "Anyone?"

Though he wasn't sure his strength would hold up, he had no choice but to call out to Abby with his mind. He only hoped it was possible with his light glowing a pure hue of yellow.

"Help. Blue House." He said the words between clenched teeth, willing her to hear him.

* * *

Abby and the four men made their way across the farm to the wind turbines, miraculously still spinning in the frost filled air.

"Do they look like they're turning a little slow?" Jim asked.

"I think some of the blades are bent out of shape," Abby replied. "We won't get as much power from them that way." She turned to Jake and Sam. "You guys think you can straighten them out?"

Jake's eyes lit up like a little kid on his birthday. "No problem."

Abby stood back, watched as the two brothers lifted their hands and worked together to straighten the blades of the windmills.

She heard Kyle's voice over the wind, a touch of panic lacing his tone. "Help. Blue House."

Instantly she shot her sight across the farm and found herself standing next to Kyle as he held the falling roof above his head. She knew right away he wouldn't be able to hold on much longer.

"I'm coming," she said before snapping back to the turbines and turning to the men. "Kyle's in trouble."

That was all she said – all she needed to say – before she ran off with the four of them following behind her.

When the five of them reached Kyle's house, Abby bounded the stairs two by two. Her entourage wasn't far behind.

"What's going on?" Evie asked from the kitchen, looking up from inspecting the freezer.

No one answered. They were already up the stairs.

Abby found Kyle where she'd left him in her vision, still holding the roof up with his yellow light. He was getting weaker by the second. He's not strong enough yet, she thought.

"Kyle, can you get out from under it?" she called.

He struggled to speak, holding his breath with the effort of his task. "No. It'll fall."

She was about to go yellow when the two brothers peered in over her, nudged her out of the way, and stood shoulder to shoulder with each other in the doorway. Within seconds the combined power of Sam and Jake had the remnants of the roof flying up and over the back of the house with a crash.

Abby went to Kyle. "You okay?"

He nodded, looked up to Sam and Jake. "Thanks. I don't know where David went off to."

David was suddenly at the bottom of the stairs. "Everything okay up there?"

Jim looked down from the landing. "Didn't you hear the roof collapse?"

David shrugged. "We were busy down here. Didn't hear a thing."

Jim opened his mouth to speak but Kyle cut him off. "It's okay Jim. Oddly, there were only a few creeks before it started falling."

He looked to Abby, sent a thought into her mind. *As though someone had carefully lifted it and started pushing it down over my head.*

Abby cocked her head to the side, eyes widening in realization. Glancing to the others, she forced a smile. "At least you're okay. That's all that matters now."

As a group they started down the stairs, Kyle and Abby pulling up the rear.

"You're always saving me lately," he said "That's seems backwards, doesn't it?"

Abby was serious, her brows still tight with worry. "Well I can play damsel next time if you want."

"No." His brows came together as well, mirroring her concern. "I like it better this way."

CHAPTER TWENTY-FOUR

Tuesday, January 22nd 2013, 9:32pm

It was only Tuesday, but Alex announced it was poker night anyway. The entire group gathered in the front room, dealing cards and carefully calculating whether or not a can of tomato soup was worth as much as a stack of chocolate chip cookies.

"No way," Jake said. "Tomatoes and cookies are completely different animals. There's no way to even compare the two."

"I like tomatoes," Hanna said.

"Would you give up chocolate for them?" Jake asked.

"Well no. Probably not. Especially now with the whole end of the world chocolate shortage going on. Unless Evie can get her hands on some cocoa plants, or wherever chocolate comes from, those cookies are worth more than a bag of diamonds."

"Yes they are," Abby said. "Which is why I plan to win every cookie in the bunker." She was just about to get dealt in on a hand when Kyle sent her a message only she could hear.

"Come to the back with me." Even in her mind she could hear the urgency in his voice though he was definitely trying to hide it with a forced casual tone.

"Is something wrong," Abby replied with her mind.

"No, everything's fine. Just come here. I want to see you."

"Abby," Alex said. "Earth calling Abby. Come in Abby." He waved a hand in front of her face.

She snapped out of her head, looked up. "Huh?"

Alex held the deck of cards between his fingers, getting ready to deal the next hand. "Ante up if you're in."

"Oh. Sorry Alex. Changed my mind." She threw him a sheepish grin then stood to make her way to the doorframe of the sleeping area.

"Damn telepathy," Alex muttered under his breath before tossing cards. "Okay, make your bets kids. And no more fighting over ramen. There are six more cases in storage. Everyone will get a share."

Abby stepped through the curtain, saw Kyle sitting on the edge of his bunk. He didn't look up. "What is it? Did you miss me or something?" Her voice held an edge of worry but she smiled.

He made a humorous, yet almost broken sound in his throat. "Always." His eyes continued to stay down as he ran a hand through his hair.

Abby knew by now that mussing his hair was his one nervous habit.

"What is it Kyle?" She came up close, let her leg brush against his. The air seemed to change, became hotter and heavier around her. She lifted a hand to brush through his hair, fixed the strands that had fallen out of place. His arms reached out, took in her waist, pulled her to him. He rested his head against her middle and she stroked through his thick waves, trailing her fingertips down the back of his neck, over the top of his ears, along his jaw.

Minutes passed as she held him there, drowning in him. She knew at that moment that they were two pieces of a whole. She didn't know if they were one soul, one heart. Flowery words weren't enough. She only knew she was born wanting him. And she knew what she had somehow felt from the first moment she'd seen his face, what she had always known. They belonged to each other.

He stood, keeping his head close to her body, trailing his cheek over the fabric of her shirt until he reached her face. His mouth nipped at her chin, settled into the hollow spot behind her ear lobe.

"My whole life I've missed you. My Abigail. My Aislynn."

She felt the words enter her, fill her every pore. She knew the name was hers, recognized the sound of it on his tongue. She exhaled a shuttering breath as his lips pressed against the tender skin of her throat.

He swayed with her to a silent melody, his hands resting at the small of her back. Abby felt the heat burning from her center as the passion that hadn't dulled in centuries floated to the surface.

He gripped her hips, pulled her body into his with an almost desperate sound on his lips. His hands drew into fists around the hem of her shirt as he finally found her mouth. Their lips mingled together, his tongue dipping into her mouth, tasting her. The tenderness ebbed away and his lips suddenly crashed into hers, possessing her.

She felt the world drop away. The voices in the other room instantly became lost in the sound of her own breathing, in the sensation of Kyle's hand moving under her shirt and over her breasts. She arched just an inch, leaning into his palm, moaning as his thumb manipulated the tender flesh.

He pulled her arms up slowly, trailing the tips of his fingers along the skin and leaving goose bumps in their wake, and lifted her shirt over her head. She responded, pulled up his shirt in turn, running her hands up his back and grabbing at the last remnants of his restraint.

He slipped away just long enough to rip the tee shirt over his head, returned to press his skin against hers. His heat enveloped her and she melted against him, clutching his face and taking his mouth hungrily.

Her hands flew down, pulled at the buttons of his jeans. She felt his fingers tangle with hers, helping her. She stepped back to strip her lower body as he did the same, expectation rippling through her with a vibrating hum.

She felt his eyes on her as she straightened, heard the groan in his throat followed by an unsatisfied sigh. She had only a second to take in the sight of him before his hands were on her. They seized each other frantically, trying to sink in, to cease being two separate entities.

He pulled her leg up by the knee, locked it over his hip and pushed them back against a bunk frame. Her other leg came up around him, gripping his waist as he bent to nip along her throat before returning to her mouth. She could feel that he was ready, knew that he was fighting to savor the moment for as long as he could.

"Please Kyle." Abby let out a moan under his lips. "Please."

His body changed then, tightened as he maneuvered her into his bunk. The control was gone, lost in the heat of their bodies twining together in desperate need. She felt a fresh tingle of pleasure, eager to give herself to him.

Abby moaned a little too loudly, spread herself beneath him. She wrapped her knees around his waist instinctually, felt him enter in one steady movement.

She threw her head back, pulled her to him with her legs. "Oh god."

He watched her eyes as they moved together, and memories flooded her mind. She saw the man he used to be, remembered now that this was not the first time they had joined together. Both her body and soul remembered him with blinding clarity. And suddenly the part of her that had always felt lost was found again in the depths of his eyes and the flaming light of his touch.

Their pace took on a trance-like rhythm, their eyes never parting. She felt the fire building, heard the heaviness of his breathing, and dropped into a sea of something beyond physical pleasure.

She watched his eyes tighten, felt her satisfaction just around the next swell of sensation. Around them the light grew, popped and crackled through the dim light of the bunker. Finally it burst out, exploding around them until the brightness consumed every ounce of darkness beyond.

She heard his thoughts, felt his emotions and his pleasure mingling with her own, and rode wave after wave of pulsing light. She heard the sounds escaping her lips, greedily took his mouth as he brought it down to quiet them.

She continued to match his rhythm, arched her back and gave herself up to him with every shred of her soul.

"Kyle." She whimpered against his lips, felt him tighten and increase the tempo just slightly in response. "Callum."

When Abby thought she might die there happily in his arms, all at once the light flickered, shattered into millions of tiny pieces. It seemed the stars had come down to bless them as they collapsed together, sated and warm.

For a long while they lay together, wrapped in each other's limbs. Abby listened to his heart, absently tickled the skin of his belly and his hips.

She had never experienced anything like that before in her life. She had searched for it in the touch of other men, wished for it always. Now she had finally found it. One time could never be enough, she thought as a smile crossed her lips.

"A billion times could never be enough," he said with a smirk in his voice.

"You heard that?"

"I was thinking the same thing anyway."

"I guess I don't have the strength to keep my thoughts to myself at the moment. You've had uh… quite the effect on me."

"I think I know the feeling. I hope I didn't think anything too… you know…"

She rolled half onto him to turn and look into his eyes. "I already knew it all anyway. You'll never have to tell me how you feel."

"Love's too small a word."

He echoed her thoughts, which was a normal occurrence between them.

She continued to toy with his skin, rolling her thumb along his collarbone. "There's no word for this. No way to give it a name."

He took her hand, squeezed lightly. "Let me work on that one. I'm sure I could come up with something close eventually, even if I have to invent a completely new word."

"Well it is a new world now. We could probably get away with inventing anything we want."

He tilted his head, stopped in thought. "That's actually a good point. We have a very unique opportunity in front of us. We could create any society we design, install new ideas, values."

Abby was quiet, thinking about his words. "That's a huge undertaking."

"We've got plenty of time to think about it now." He squeezed her hand again. "Together we'll make something beautiful out of all the ugliness up there."

"I'm content to be right here for now. By the way, what happened to waiting until we could get out of the bunker?"

"Uh... yeah, I couldn't take it anymore. A man can only withstand so much. Being near you every day, every night..."

"Well I'm extremely glad you ran out of will power, emphasis on the extremely part. But what about the others and all your talk of distractions?" She was teasing him, a smile in her eyes.

"I wanted the first time to be perfect. Actually, I'd like every time to be perfect." He stroked her hair, held her to his chest. "You've never had anyone show you how special you are, how important you are. I wanted you to know that this was way more than just a romp in the sack, that this is real." He sighed.

"It was beyond perfect Kyle. It always will be. There's no way for it not to be. I don't care if I'm trapped in a sewer as long as you're there with me, rats and all."

He nodded, continued. "You deserve a proper wooing. But I decided I had to give in or go completely mad. And Alex kept trying to make me crack. Though he did come through in a clutch tonight."

"Wait, you and Alex arranged this? Are you serious?"

"Who do you think convinced him to make an exception to the Friday-is-poker-night rule?"

"Oh my god." She bit her bottom lip to suppress the laugh waiting on her tongue. "Alex was your accomplice? How did he take it? I'm not sure he's over me and him yet."

Kyle's eyebrows popped up. "He'd better be. I wouldn't want to embarrass him in a fist fight since I learned how to punch a few thousand years before Caesar ruled Rome."

Abby laughed, played with his chest hair. "You can't possibly be jealous of Alex?"

"No, not at all. He's not your type anyway. Real men don't get mani-pedis." He grinned. "I'm not worried about your end one bit. His end, on the other hand, well let's just say he had better know his place or he'll find those two-hundred dollar jeans he wears up around his head."

Abby couldn't hold back the silly smile that spread over her face. She liked that he was just a little possessive. There was no insecurity in his words. In fact he was maybe even a little cocky. But she liked knowing he was ready to fight for her.

"Alex knows all about us. I told him everything about the past and the present. I don't think we have to worry about him coming on to me again anytime soon. Plus he seems to have taken a liking to Evie."

"Good. He's actually an okay guy, so I'd hate to have to knock him out."

"Yeah, he's got a good heart and he's been a really good friend to me since we broke up."

"Um...speaking of that, I wanted to tell you something." She looked up and he went on. "You know what happened between you and Alex... the cheating bit?"

"Oh, I'm so over that whole thing. Actually, I'm not sure I was ever really under it."

Kyle cupped her chin and looked her in the eye. "He was wrong, no matter what his reasons were and I hope you know you'll never have to worry about that with me."

"Even if we learn to hate each other someday and I become a bitter and fickle old woman who wants to leave you?"

"Never gonna happen. I wouldn't let you go. Not in a stalkerish way of course, but I'd fight for you, woo you, and seduce you all over again if that's what it took. No matter how stubborn you might be." He kissed the top of her head as though it was something he had been doing for years. "And I could never hate you. Maybe you'll hate me at some point. I'm not the easiest man to live with. But this is a forever sort of thing. No refunds, no trade-ins. Just me and you."

"Hmm... I like the sound of that." Abby sighed blissfully and made a mental note to remember the moment down to every last detail.

No one had ever fought to have Abby before. They hadn't cared enough to put forth the effort. Not even Alex. Not really anyway. His idea of fighting for her was trying to get her in to bed at every turn. Maybe no one who came before was supposed to fight for her because she hadn't belonged with them. She belonged right where she was, in the arms of a man who had loved her for centuries. And she loved him back, god did she love him back. He consumed her every breath, her every thought. She needed him. And for the first time in her life the idea of needing someone else didn't scare the crap out of her.

She smiled, brought her hand down to his belly. "So does all that mean I can do things like this now?"

He moaned as her hand took him, caressed him slowly. He rolled her body so that she was straddling him and clutched at her backside. "I'm all yours." Lifting her hips, he closed his eyes, sunk her down until they were joined together again. "I've always been yours."

* * *

Abby left the bathroom, closing the door quietly behind her. It was at least three in the morning and the bunker was eerily still. As she headed back to bed the bathroom door opened again. She turned, pulled it shut and made sure the latch had caught. When she removed her hand it fell open again. She glanced behind her and saw the glowing yellow light of David sitting in the corner. She hadn't seen him sitting there before. Where had he come from?

His light had always been muddier than the brothers. It was dark and cold while Sam and Jake always seemed covered in gold. This was something Abby had assumed, until recently, was just a random variation.

Without saying a word to him she started walking back to her bunk. An unseen force stopped her mid step.

"You two created quite the light show earlier." He walked to her casually, spoke close to her ear. "Was it good for you? The sounds alone had me picturing you for myself. You look like a wild one."

Abby spoke between clenched teeth. "What are you doing David?"

He shrugged. "Just wanted to see if you were giving it up to everyone now. You've slept with at least two men in this bunker. Maybe three." He paused, stretched a crude smile over his lips. "I'm sure you've entertained Jake's fantasies at least once or twice. I just thought, since you were making the rounds, we could create some light of our own."

"Is that your way of calling me a whore?"

He shrugged again, scratched his head. "If it walks like a duck... well you know the rest."

Abby glared at him and said nothing. When he moved closer to touch her hair, she glanced towards the curtain where she knew Kyle was sleeping soundly beyond.

"Why don't you call out to him now?" David asked. "Are you accepting my invitation?"

She narrowed her eyes, met his stare straight on. "No. I am not. But he's killed enough for one lifetime. And the rest of us have had our share of death. I wouldn't want to add yours to the body count."

"You know, you're pretty in your own way. Nice curves." His hand moved down to her waist, ran along her hips.

"I wasn't being dramatic David. He'll kill you if he finds out about this. And I'm sure he'll wait until you're sleeping to do it."

He chuckled. It was an ugly sound that came from a hollow place inside him. His hand moved and he released her from his invisible grip. "Let me know if you change your mind. We could lead them together. Just the two of us."

Abby felt an angry fire stir inside her gut. "I'd rather die."

His face was still close to hers. "That can be arranged too. But I'd prefer it my way. You would be so nice to keep around. Very entertaining I'll bet. Tell me, how many men have you been with? I like experienced women."

She walked away again, trying to keep steady, fighting the urge to run to Kyle.

"I wouldn't mention this to him if I were you," David said from behind her. "That is unless you want him to have another accident."

Abby shuddered and flung the curtain back. She speed walked back to bed and climbed in, pressing her body into Kyle and soaking in his warmth.

He nuzzled her neck in his sleep, pulled her closer. "Everything okay?" he asked.

Abby remembered to keep her thoughts hidden from him and tried to sound normal. "Yes. Everything's fine. Go back to sleep, Love."

CHAPTER TWENTY-FIVE

Wednesday, January 23nd 2013, 2:12pm

Dead chickens were notoriously disgusting things. At least that was the general consensus when Kyle pulled the bird from the freezer.

"Oh good god," Jake said. "That's just beyond gross. I can't believe you carried that thing in here."

Sam, in his usual quiet fashion, choked on a gag and covered his mouth from behind his brother.

Kyle stifled a grin. "We've all had chicken nuggets before guys. It's really not that bad."

"Yes it is," Evie said. "Chicken nuggets don't have eyes and beaks and little feet."

"Or feathers," Hanna added.

Abby stood in the back of the group with Hanna. Both of them had their hands pressed against their mouths. Abby glanced towards David, met his eyes with a venom laced glare.

She hadn't mentioned the incident from the night before to Kyle and she wasn't sure whether or not to take David's threats seriously yet. She only hoped that once they were able to leave the bunker that David would go off on his own and never return to the farm. If not... well she didn't like to think about the trouble he could cause.

"So... you want me to make it cluck again right?" Hanna asked through her fingers.

Kyle nodded. "That's the plan. I think it's how we're going to, not only repopulate the planet with animals, but feed ourselves as well."

"We'll help if you need us to Hanna," Abby said. "Kyle and I haven't used the power as much as you have, but we can certainly lend you something extra."

Hanna removed her hand from her mouth, jiggled her arms at her sides, and stepped up to the lifeless poultry on the countertop. With a deep breath she settled her hands over the bird and began sending her blue light into its body.

Before their eyes the chicken began to change. It's grey, dead skin turned pink and feathers grew back over the bald spots. The eye sockets filled again with big shining pupils.

Hanna gasped, drew her hands away. "It's still dead."

"Yeah, and it still stinks," Jake said.

Again Sam gagged, turned around and clutched his stomach.

"Give it a little more Hanna," Abby said. "Think about jump starting the heart." She placed her hand on Hanna's shoulder and the girl continued.

Abby's light shimmered into blue and she allowed the energy to radiate from her hand and into Hanna. Immediately the red head's glow brightened, deepening into an almost opaque shade of sky.

In a matter of seconds the bird blinked, made a very chicken-like sound, and jumped to its feet.

As a group they laughed and applauded Hanna and her freckled cheeks lit up with red.

"Well done," Kyle said with a laugh. "Whoa, someone grab that bird."

Abby jumped aside, laughed as the chicken ran past her feet and straight into Alex's waiting arms. The dogs jumped below him, trying to get the bird from his grasp.

"I got it. No thanks to this one," Alex said glancing at Abby.

"Sorry. I'm not used to being around attack chickens."

Kyle smiled at her, brushed a hand against hers before leaning in to whisper. "Good job. She wouldn't have found the strength without your help."

"Um... guys. What do you want me to do with this thing?" Alex held the chicken in front of him like it was a bomb about to explode.

Kyle looked up. "Kill it."

The girls gasped, Jake made a face, and Sam looked close to retching again.

Jim was the first to recover. "We're going to eat it?"

Kyle pursed his lips, nodded. "Yup. We all need to get used to killing our dinner from now on."

"I'll do it," David said and stepped up from his sulking corner.

Kyle eyed him. A worried look passed through his olive eyes. "That's okay Dave. I'll do it."

"Really, I don't mind," David replied.

"Yes, I'm sure you don't." Kyle's brows came together. "But I'll take care of it. We'll make a lesson of it."

"Oh god, please no," Evie said. "I can't watch. Can't I just live out my life letting you guys kill my dinner?"

"If you want," Kyle said with a shrug. "Eventually, it's something you'll need to get used to though. Supermarkets are not coming back any time soon and we'll need meat to stay healthy."

He was right. There would be no more vacuum packed chicken breasts, no neatly sealed pounds of ground beef. Their rations wouldn't last forever and, while vegetarianism was a choice in a modern society that manufactured dietary supplements, malnutrition would be the only result in the world they suddenly found themselves in. They either learned to kill or they would starve.

"Yeah," Evie finally said. "I guess you're right."

Kyle took the chicken from Alex and held it upside down by its feet. "Sorry little guy." He positioned his other hand low on the chicken's neck and snapped his wrist until a resounding crack echoed through the bunker.

"Ah Jesus." Alex's groan mingled with little screams from the girls.

Sam ran to the bathroom looking green.

The bird's wings continued to flap, hitting Abby in the face with air. Her eyes were on Kyle. He was looking past her face, his eyes not focused. He was having a vision.

She touched his arm, avoiding the dying bird. "What is it?"

"Give me a second," he said.

He took steady breaths through his mouth, still gazing past her head until the chicken's wings finally stopped flapping.

Kyle blinked, scrunched his brows together at Abby. "There are more Gleamers coming."

"More like them?" Abby asked pointing to the others.

He shook his head once. "No, they're different. The other colors. They are being drawn here the way the others were."

There was a hush among the group. Everyone in the room was now listening to Kyle.

"How are they surviving the cold?" Jim asked.

"The red ones have their own heat source and their protecting the others from the weather, walking in a circle with the woman and her teenage son in the center. The boy is glowing orange and his mother is violet. They're walking from the south. Should be here sometime tomorrow."

Silence permeated the room as they all stared at him in awed silence.

Alex finally spoke up. "That's good though, right. We could use fire starters."

"Yeah, I guess so." Kyle looked at Abby. "Could also be a little dangerous." He thought for a second then shook his head and held up the lifeless body of the chicken. "Who wants to do the plucking?"

* * *

Alex woke up sometime in the middle of the night with an overly dry throat. One shake of his water bottle reminded him that it was empty. He rolled out of his bunk, grabbed a flashlight, and stepped into the main room for a fresh bottle.

He stepped up to the counter, lazily stretched himself to reach the open case on the shelf above the sink then snagged his shirt on the hatch release lever.

As he pulled the fabric from the metal he realized the lever was in the wrong position. The hatch was open. He pulled it closed and went straight to wake Abby and Kyle.

The curtain to their bunk was closed as usual so Alex knocked lightly and spoke in a hushed voice. "You guys decent?"

Kyle pulled the curtain open in an instant. He was alone.

"Hey did we forget to close the hatch?" Alex asked. "Where's Abby? Bathroom?"

Kyle narrowed his eyes, cocked his head, then jumped out of the bed with a lightening quick burst.

Alex was immediately alarmed. "What is it? What's going on?"

Kyle was getting dressed, didn't bother to look up. "She's not in the god damn bunker."

"What? What do you mean?"

"I mean she's not here Alex. I can't see her. She's not in the bunker and she's nowhere on the farm."

"Did you guys have a fight or something?"

"No. Everything was fine. I would know if she was mad at me anyway. She can't keep her thoughts to herself when she's angry." He pulled his boots out from under the bunk and started shoving them on his feet. "Something's wrong. She wouldn't just leave without a word."

Jake climbed out of his bunk then, obviously awakened by the voices of the two other men. He stretched, glanced up at the empty bunk above his. "Guys."

Alex had been watching Jake move into the alleyway. He hit Kyle's arm to get his attention away from the boot he was lacing up.

Jake continued. "David's gone too."

"What?" Kyle said, squinting at Jake.

Everyone was up now, rolling from their bunks and standing in the alley.

"You guys are being really loud," Evie said yawning.

"What's going on?" Jim asked.

"That son of a bitch," Alex seethed. "He's kidnapped her."

"It's almost morning," Jake said. "He could be hours away with her by now."

Kyle's face looked like it had been carved in stone. His fists clenched at his sides and he grit his teeth together with suppressed rage. "Jim, did you get that shotgun out of the other bunker?"

"Uh... yeah."

"Find some ammo for me and pack some rations into a bag."

"Put in enough food for two Jim." Alex turned to Kyle. "Now that she's not my girlfriend, Abby might be the best friend I've ever had. If she's in trouble you're not going anywhere without me."

"Obviously I'm going too." Jim said. "My niece, remember?"

Jake stepped up. "You can count on me and Sam."

"Why don't we all go?" Evie asked. "Abby's like our den mother or something. We all care about her?"

"We'll see," Kyle said. "We have to hurry now. He's already got a huge lead on us. Let's move."

* * *

Kyle found no joy in the idea of taking another life. In fact, until the end of the world had come to Kansas, he hadn't even seriously considered the idea of killing another human being. But now he walked down a country road, cold, scared, and pissed off with a shot gun slung over his back. When it came to Abby, he was prepared to destroy a hundred men.

The women had stayed below ground after much argument. Both of them had wanted desperately to help, but the four men agreed that neither of them had the kind of power that was needed and they were too valuable to risk. And neither of them needed to be involved in what Kyle was sure was going to be a bloody standoff.

The sun was coming up as they stepped outside, though it was hard to tell with the perpetual ash cloud lingering in the sky. The temperature had gone up a touch, but the wind was still icy against Kyle's skin.

Alex looked around, turning his head left then right. "Which way?"

Kyle reached out with his vision, pulling back to the present after a second. "I still can't see her. But I think David is going to meet up with the other group, the red ones and the woman with the boy. He's wanted control since the start and they might be easily coerced into joining him."

"You said they're coming in from the south?" Jim asked.

Kyle nodded. "South it is."

They headed out, moving away from the wind with a steady pace.

After a quarter of a mile, Kyle turned to Alex. "Thanks for coming."

Alex smiled. "Did you think I wouldn't?"

"No, just wanted to make sure you knew I appreciated it. And everything you've done for Abby. You were there for her when I couldn't be."

Alex sent him a sideways glance, nodded. "Just do me a favor?"

"Uh yeah. Of course. Whatever you need."

"Make sure this is really forever before you make any promises. She's... emotionally fragile."

Kyle couldn't help but smile. He was glad Abby had a loyal friend in Alex. She wasn't that close with the other women and Alex obviously understood her. He cared for her in an almost brotherly way. Well, as much as he could considering they had been lovers for over a year but that was a fact Kyle tried not to think about.

"She's stronger than you realize."

"Maybe so, but you didn't see her when she thought you were dead. I was terrified she was going to do something stupid."

Kyle looked at his feet as he walked. "I wasn't sure what to do when I first met her. It was all a little much. Overwhelming." He kicked a rock in the road, watched it skip along the ash. "I was completely distracted by her. Couldn't think straight from the first moment. But now I know I can't be without her. I won't let her go."

"Good. That's all I wanted to know."

Kyle smirked. "What is it about you? That's more than I've revealed to another man since... well ever."

Alex shrugged. "Guess I'm easy to talk to."

"Yeah, well that's going to take some getting used to for me. So, let's make sure we have plenty of talks about fixing stuff, or building things out of wood, and other not so deep topics. Deal?"

"Deal. Though I'm not really a fix-it kind of guy. I'm more of the can't-a-hold-a-hammer type of guy."

Kyle grinned and shrugged as they continued walking.

Alex looked thoughtful. "Or maybe a where's-my-avocado-face-peal kind of guy."

Kyle stopped in the ash. He eyed Alex with a sideways glance and let out a chuckle before continuing down the road.

CHAPTER TWENTY-SIX

Thursday, January 24th 2013, 6:25am

They had been walking over three hours and covered almost eight miles when Kyle stopped dead in the road. "I can see her now." "

Where is she?" Jim asked. "Is she okay?"

Kyle sent his vision further, looking more clearly until everything came into focus. He saw her in a white house, lying on an ash covered kitchen floor with her arms tied behind her back. Her hands were wrapped in layers of fabric and tape and she was blindfolded.

"Abby," Kyle said. "Abby can you hear me?"

"What's she saying?" Alex asked.

"She won't answer me." He raised his voice a notch and tried again. "Abby we're coming to get you. Can you hear me?" When he still didn't get a response, he returned to the other men. "I'm going to kill him. I swear to god he's dead."

"What happened?" Alex asked.

"She's not conscious." Kyle had to resist the urge to slam the shotgun into the pavement. When he spoke again his teeth were mashed so hard together that his mouth barely moved. "That fucking bastard knocked her out. He's got her hands wrapped up and her eyes covered so she can't use her abilities. But she can still use her vision. He doesn't realize it, but she doesn't need to physically use her eyes to see or hear me."

"How much farther do we have to go?" Jim asked.

"Another mile or two. I'm not sure. I don't have a magical measuring tape that I can take along with me."

They began walking again and Jim shouted over the wind. "Windstone, keep an eye on her... or whatever... and try to get the lay of the land before we get there. Figure out where David's positioned. Maybe we can sneak up on him. I wish we had more weapons. Even a knife would be useful."

Sam and Jake simultaneously pulled out blades from their pockets. "Like these?" Sam said.

Jim smiled. "You guys don't mess around. The Mason farm is coming up on the left. Let's ransack it. See what else we can find. And Kyle, maybe you should give me the gun."

Kyle's pace was furious. "This is my fight Jim."

"She's my niece so I'd say it's my fight too. And I've got the training."

Kyle sighed. It was on the tip of his tongue to ask Jim how long he'd grieve if Abby died, if his life would change forever without her. Kyle knew what life was like without Abby. It was lifeless, empty, painful. Even if there came a day when he couldn't have her, just knowing she was breathing would be enough to keep him going.

Finally, Kyle responded. "If Dan Mason's guns are still in his cabinet you can have this one."

Fortunately the Mason farm was heavily armed. By the time they walked out of the dilapidated house each of them had at least one rifle hanging on their backs. Jim had two, including the shot gun Kyle had promised him.

An hour later they were standing a few thousand yards outside of the property where Abby was being held. Kyle had been keeping a watch on Abby, walking while visioning most of the way down the road, but she hadn't stirred once.

He leaned against a tree, clenched his eyes in concentration. "Abby. Abby please, wake up."

He saw her tremble in his vision, heard the small gasp escape her.

"Kyle?" Her voice filled his head, laced with fear.

"I'm coming. We're just outside."

"No!"

"Hush. Keep your voice down. He's close by."

"She really needs to figure the whole telepathy thing out," Alex muttered.

Kyle ignored him, not taking the time to explain that the silent telepathy only worked at close range, and listened to Abby's voice bouncing in his head. She sounded completely terrified.

"Turn around," she said. "Don't come here. He's waiting for you."

"I know. It's okay. We're ready."

"No. Kyle. He wants to kill you. The others are with him. He lied about you. Told them you'd done terrible things. They believed him and they think you deserve what's coming."

"What else did you hear?"

"He wants to take control." Her teeth chattered. "Thinks this is his chance to have power. He's crazy Kyle. Delusional. He says things about ruling what's left of the world. Says it's his turn."

"Are you hurt?"

"I'm so cold and I think my shoulder is out of the socket. Kyle, he wants me to stay with him so he can use my power whenever he needs it."

"Oh for fuck's sake."

"What?" Jim was beside him, eagerly awaiting answers.

Kyle put up his finger. "Okay, try not to talk again. I don't want him to hear you and find out we're coming. I'll be there soon."

She whimpered, held back a sob. "Please be careful. I can't lose you. Not again."

"I'm here. I'll never leave you. Now no more worries my lily girl. We'll be back in our bunk by nightfall."

Kyle snapped back to the other men, again resisting the urge to break something. "She's terrified and hurt. She might even be close to hypothermia." He shut his eyes, breathed deeply through his mouth. "Whoever gets to him first, take him out. I don't care about trying to talk to him. I just want him fucking dead."

* * *

Abby shivered, feeling the pain in her shoulder increase as her body tensed with the cold. She was in pain, she was blind, and she had never been so cold in her life. But none of that compared to the overwhelming fear that ate away at her middle. Kyle was coming and he was running right between the crosshairs of a sadistic, power hungry madman.

She heard movement beside her, flinched. "Who's there?"

No one answered but Abby suddenly felt warmer. Hot air wafted in her direction, thawing her cheeks and slowing the shaking in her muscles.

Abby took advantage of the opportunity. "David's lying about Kyle Windstone. He's saved all of our lives and given us the tools we need to survive. He's a good man with a gentle heart. He would never do the things David said."

"Hey, what are you doing in here?" David's voice echoed through the room startling Abby and sending fresh pain through her shoulder. "I told you to watch the bitch not keep her warm."

Suddenly Abby was being yanked up by her wounded shoulder. An agonizing scream pierced the air. "David please," she whimpered. "My arm."

She received his hollow laugh in response. "Did your boyfriend find you yet? Is he on his way? I know you can hear him. Where is he?"

"I... I don't know. I swear."

She felt a fresh burst of cold wind hit her face as he dragged her to the front porch. She sucked in her breath, the frigid air burning her lungs.

He dropped her down hard in a chair. "I know he's out there. It shouldn't be taking this long for him to catch up. Tell me where he is." He slapped her across the face.

Abby reeled back, felt the sting on her skin, the ache in her jaw bone. "I don't know." She struggled to keep her voice from wavering. "Maybe he doesn't know I'm gone."

"I gave you a chance to be honest with me. You should've taken it." He paused, his boots pounding back and forth on the porch floor. Suddenly his face was next to hers. "I heard you whispering to him."

David ripped the blindfold from her eyes, taking some of her hair with it. Abby squinted, her eyes adjusting to the foggy daylight.

He fisted his hand in her hair, yanked her head back with a jerk. "Windstone!" He pressed a cold knife to the base of her throat. "Come out or I'll slit her throat! Think you can make it to her in time to heal her?"

Abby threw her vision out to Kyle, found him waiting behind a shed with Jake. A rifle was positioned in his hands, aiming out over the land at David.

"Stay away Kyle," she whispered. "He won't hurt me. He needs me."

David scoffed with bitterness. "You think I'm bluffing?" He pressed the knife further into the skin of her neck and a line of blood appeared under it. "I've got friends waiting in the windows of this house with shotguns loaded and ready. If you take a shot at me or try to use your Movers to take me out, they will kill you the moment you step out of the shadows." He yanked her head back hard making her whimper. "And your woman will already be dead."

Abby heard Kyle's voice and relayed his message. "He wants to know what you want."

"Her life for yours!" David yelled. "Those are my terms."

She listened again as Kyle spoke. "Tell him I'm coming out."

"No," she whispered.

David removed his hand from the knife, using his ability to keep it against her throat, and stepped to the porch railing. "What did your boyfriend say?"

"He... he says you should kill me then."

"What are you doing Abby?" Kyle yelled into her head. "Tell him I'm coming out."

"No," she whispered again. Tears formed at her lashes. "You can't."

"Okay, enough of this," David said. "I'll kill you both." His hand came up, swiped through the air.

Hot metal cut through Abby's skin, slicing down until blood sprang up around under her chin and slid down onto her chest. She fought to take air, felt her life slipping away as she fell onto the hard floor.

* * *

"No!" Kyle was running before he saw the blade drop to the floor. "God, no."

He slowed as he approached the yard in front of the porch, his hands raised high. "David! I'm here. I'm alone and unarmed."

Kyle's eyes flew to Abby. She was lying on her side, blood pooling around her cheek. Her eyes gaped wide as she struggled to breathe. Memories flashed through his mind of the last time he watched her die.

"You're late Windstone," David said. "Why is he still breathing? Someone shoot him please."

"Wait! Let me heal her first. Please. Let me heal her and then you can kill me if that's what you really want."

David smiled, obviously enjoying the pain he was causing. "Sure. Why not? I didn't want to kill her anyway. Not really. She could be so much fun to have around."

Kyle's lips came up in a snarl as he slowly approached Abby. Rage gathered in his gut, popped into his throat. He wanted to scream, wanted to grasp David's throat with both hands until he stopped squirming.

"But don't try anything stupid." David swung a palm up, the bloody blade flying into it with speed. "And if they're smart, your friends will stay put."

Kyle's hands came up to his sides, signaling to the others to stay in the hiding spots. He felt the wrath explode as he looked down at Abby and struggled to stay in control. Her lips were blue, her eyes starting to close as she lost consciousness. He pulled her head up into his lap, felt the icy coldness of her skin.

His hand was steady as he brought it up over her throat. "I'm here now. Hold on Abby."

He blinked and blue light shone forth from his fingers, poured over her like warm water from a faucet. Kyle kept his eyes open, watched as the wound healed, sealing together until her blood was no longer flowing.

David quickly pulled Abby up by her arm, yanking her to him. She let out a weak cry, struggled to stay on her feet.

"That's good now," David said. "Out into the yard." He gestured to Kyle with the blade then pressed his lips into Abby's ear. "I want you to watch him die so that every time I touch you you'll remember this moment. You'll remember the look on his face as he took his last breaths."

Kyle walked out into the yard without hesitation, keeping his arms out to his sides. He turned, faced Abby and saw the look of torment in her eyes, the tears flowing down her cheeks for him.

The corners of David's mouth turned up in a sick show of humor. "You can shoot him now!"

Abby struggled against David with what little strength she had left. "No. Don't do this. I'll stay with you. I'll tell them all you're the one who can lead us. You can have anything you want."

"This is what I want," David said. He turned his eyes skyward. "Why don't I hear firing up there?"

Kyle stood in the center of the yard, locked eyes with Abby one last time, and then closed them against the barrage of bullets he knew was coming. His eyes flew open again when he heard an unfamiliar voice.

"No one's getting shot," the voice said and a man with a red glow walked onto the porch with a shotgun in his hand. "This is wrong and I won't have a part in it."

David tossed Abby against the house, stalked towards the other man. "This guy has killed children, raped women. He tried to kill us all and he'll try again. He's a madman who deserves to die."

The man with the red light shook his head. "The only madman I see here is you and I'm not playing judge and jury today. And the rest of them are with me."

David projected the knife into the other man's gut with one deft motion of his hand. "Fine. I'll do it then." He reached down, picked up the gun, and let out a scream. When he pulled his hand away from the metal again it was burned through multiple layers, leaving flesh on the barrel of the shotgun.

Kyle moved fast. He was on the porch in seconds and went straight to Abby's side. He lifted her, pulled her as gently as possible into the house and straight up the stairs. He found three other men in a second story bedroom, met their stares, then moved past them to place Abby on the bed.

"Untie her," he said, breathless. "Keep her warm." He stroked her cheek once. "Please."

With that he ran down the stairs again. David was in the yard now, holding his burnt hand into his chest and running for safety.

Kyle found the knife that had been dropped on the porch and shifted his light to yellow. The blade floated then sliced through the air, landing straight into the flesh of David's back.

A howl echoed through the yard, but David didn't slow down for a second.

"Jim!" Kyle called out. "Stop him!"

Jim appeared then, stepping from behind a row of dense pine trees with the muzzle of his gun aimed at David's head. "I've got him."

The others came out then, all three of them zeroing their sights on David.

David swiped his good hand making Jim's gun slip to the side. Jim righted it quickly, pointed it straight between David's eyes. David tried again, dropping to his knees, groaning with the effort.

"It's no good David," Kyle said as he walked up behind him. "Your recruits turned on you, saw you for what you are."

"Just finish it Windstone," David said. "I don't need you rhetoric now."

"What did you think you were going to accomplish here?" Alex said from beside Kyle. "How did you get so fucked up Dave? Mommy didn't love you enough?"

David snorted an empty laugh. "I was supposed to be the one. This was my time to be something. I deserved the power you have, the woman. All of it. It should've been mine."

Kyle almost pitied him. Almost. "You could never be worthy of her. Did you think busting her arm and letting her freeze would win her over?"

David raised his head, glared at Kyle. "I wasn't going to give her a choice and she would've loved it."

"You son of a bitch." Kyle punched David in the face as hard as he could. He felt the sting in his knuckles, punched him again. "Fucking bastard. I'll never let you touch her. You'll never hurt her again."

With a snap he swiped Alex's gun and aimed. David leaned back and clenched his eyes shut tight.

"Kyle," Jim said. "Put the gun down."

Kyle continued to aim, tightening his jaw with the pure fury that filled him. His finger twitched along the trigger. "He has to die Jim. We'll never be safe unless he's gone. Abby will never be safe."

Jim's hand was suddenly on Kyle's shoulder. "Let someone else do it."

Kyle shook his head. "No, I have to do it. It's my responsibility."

"You're responsibility is in that house," Jim replied. "You belong in there with her. Let me take care of this. You've done enough."

Slowly Kyle lowered the weapon. After a long moment of hesitation he gave it to his friend.

"Go to her," Jim said. "She needs you."

Kyle turned and walked away without another word. He was half way through the yard when he heard the shot. He flinched but he didn't look back.

His legs were numb and heavy as he crossed the threshold of the house. When he got to Abby she was lying on the bed and the color had returned to her cheeks. He nodded to the other people in the room, felt the heat hit him as he stepped in.

"Thank you," he said. "Could you give us a minute?"

The room cleared and Kyle went to Abby. He pulled her into his arms gently, careful of her shoulder.

Her eyes flew open, her good arm wrapping around him. "Oh god Kyle. I heard the shot..."

"I'm here. It's okay now. It's over."

Tears came from her then and Kyle held her, feeling his own eyes begin to well up with water.

"He almost...," Abby said.

"I know. Everything's going to be alright now. He can't hurt anyone anymore."

Her arm tightened on him. "There's something I should show you." With a breath she passed on the memory of David threatening her in the bunker, relaying every minute in exact detail. "I'm sorry. I should've told you then. We might've seen this coming."

Kyle laid her back again gently, moved her arm and positioned himself over her shoulder. "It doesn't matter." Blue light shimmered forth from his hand. "I understand." He smiled. "I guess we're even now."

He helped her to sit up, propped himself behind her. "That better?" he asked.

Abby nodded. "Can we make a promise?" He only nodded and she continued. "No more secrets, no matter how noble we think we're trying to be. We tell each other everything, especially if we think someone's trying to kill us."

A weak smile bent his lips. "Okay. No more secrets." He leaned down, pressed his mouth to hers. Emotion emptied from him, passed between them. "I love you Abby."

She touched his cheek, a sigh passing through her lips. "I thought that word was too small."

"It still is." He wrapped his arms around her, held her tight to him. "You're a part of me. I've always loved you."

Abby pulled his face down to hers, tenderly kissed him for a long moment. "It's always been you I was looking for. I've never loved anyone else."

EPILOGUE

The Journal of Abigail Connelly, August 25th 2013

Life on the farm has slowly starting resembling normalcy since we surfaced for good this spring. The weather has become more reasonable over the past few months with the sun now breaking through the clouds more regularly. Crops are even beginning to spring up in the fields without the constant help of Growers.

It took some time to rebuild the houses and make all the repairs, but a new group of Movers from Iowa sped that process up exponentially. The Yellow House and the Blue House are back in one piece, along with a couple other new additions to the property.

Thanks to Hanna and the rest of the Healers, the livestock are reproducing again. We found cows, pigs, sheep, more chickens, and various other animals on the surrounding farms. The populations are now starting to flourish with *little help from humans. The Healers even managed to bring old Bucky and his mare back to life. Kyle quickly resumed his nightly habit of sneaking them treats.*

While the blue light seems to work on animals, no one has yet been able to figure out how to bring a person back from the dead. Some think it's because the human brain is too complex. Others talk of the balance of nature, and how humanity was nearly destroyed for a reason.

Gleamers are coming in from all over the country to join our little community, beckoned by what they call the light of the Eternals. I guess that means me and Kyle. He thinks it hilarious but fitting and says he couldn't have named us better himself.

Evie finally succumbed to Alex's charms and by last summer they were talking about building their own house on the farm. It's now commonly referred to as the Red House by everyone.

Sam and Hanna are finally getting more serious after a long courtship. Kyle thinks there will be red headed little ones running around the corn by next summer. It's lovely to think the laughter of children will soon fill the air.

Jake has his eyes on a few of the newcomers, though he seems to favor the Thermal girls. (Kyle's name for the red Gleamers.) They like to play hard to get and that satisfies Jake's playful spirit nicely.

And Jimmy... well Jimmy is just Jimmy. I'm not sure he'll ever find someone, but that doesn't stop anyone from trying to play matchmaker. There are several good candidates currently staying in the Yellow House. We all have our fingers crossed.

We still aren't sure what the woman with the violet light can do and her teenage son possesses an orange light that is equally confusing. Kyle is sure their abilities will present themselves when they're needed, though the mystery seems to bother him. Sometimes I catch him shifting his light to orange or violet, trying to work out the ability attached to the colors. Until we come to some conclusions, both of them are already valuable members of our society who work hard and contribute eagerly.

We've talked about creating laws, tried to form committees, and hold regular meetings. So far, we haven't had any need for rules. Everyone who's joined us seems happy here, content to be alive. But it's most likely something we'll have to deal with eventually. Hopefully much later than sooner.

I'm not sure what the future holds for humanity. We have the right tools, the best intentions, and the biggest hearts. Hopefully that's enough. Right now, it's enough for me.

I've never known what it meant to be happy and I've never known what it was like to be in love. I had no idea it would take the end of the world for me to finally learn about hope, love, and the courage it takes to not only try to survive, but to want to survive.

I have faith now and I believe in what humanity can accomplish. We can build a better future by learning from our past. We've been given a second chance to do it right and I can't wait to see what we make of it.

Abby set down her pen and closed her eyes with a smile of satisfaction. She could hear Kyle working upstairs, finishing repairs in the bedroom like he'd done for the past month. He hammered in his usual focused way, the sound competing with Movers making repairs outside. She knew she should leave him to his work undistracted, but climbed the stairs anyway.

She watched him from the doorway, noticed the sweat dripping down his bare arms and over his back and couldn't help but sigh contentedly at the sight. She let herself imagine the two of them in bed, allowed herself to go through every motion, and felt the deep passionate fire swell within her. With one thought she sent all of her feelings and images to his mind in stark detail.

His shoulders tightened mid hammer swing and he straightened to his full height. He turned on his heels, looked her in the eye. His face was serious, his eyes hooded as he glanced up from beneath his lashes. That was Abby's favorite look.

She smiled, walked into the room towards him. "Sorry. I know how you feel about distractions."

A sound that was part growl, part laugh left his throat as he lunged at her, threw them both to the springy mattress below.

His mouth was on her in seconds, owning her under him. "I'm counting on you to distract me for the rest of my life."

"In this life and every one after." She kissed him, clutched him to her. She would never let him go. "No returns, no trade-ins. Just you and me forever."

ABOUT THE AUTHOR

Lilah Boone writes sci-fi/paranormal romance full of quirky characters and lots of fast paced storytelling. She lives in Upstate, New York with her soul mate and their two children. Counting Down is her first novel (published July, 2012). A sequel is already in the works. Find out more about Lilah and the Eternal World Series (including interactive features and lost chapters) at www.lilahboone.com.